VANDAL LOVE

VANDAL

LOVE

A novel by

D.Y. BÉCHARD

DOUBLEDAY CANADA

Doubleday Canada and colophon are trademarks.

Library and Archives Canada Cataloguing in Publication

Béchard, Deni Y. (Deni Yvan), 1974–
Vandal love / D.Y. Béchard.

ISBN-13: 978-0-385-66051-8
ISBN-10: 0-385-66051-0

I. Title.

PS8553.E2947V35 2006   C813'.6   C2005-905783-1

Jacket image: John Sleeman/Getty Images
Jacket and text design: Kelly Hill
Printed and bound in the USA

Published in Canada by
Doubleday Canada, a division of
Random House of Canada Limited

Visit Random House of Canada Limited's website:
www.randomhouse.ca

BVG   10   9   8   7   6   5   4   3   2   1A

VANDAL LOVE

BOOK ONE

part one

Québec
1946–1961

Even when Jude was a boy, his arms and legs bulged, his neck corded, his muscled gut humped beneath his chest. On the steep fields above the road, above the river so wide they called it *la mer*, he worked in clothes the colour of dirt, harder and faster than his uncles, though when he paused from digging, he stood awkwardly, uneasy with inaction. By the age of fifteen, he rarely stopped. He sat and ate in the same motion. He undressed and stretched on his bed and slept. Hardship had given his face the uneven angles of an old apple pressed in among others in a cellar crate. He'd never closed his eyes to wonder at what couldn't be seen.

That autumn ended a dry summer. Foliage was dull, like rusted machinery on the hills. Potato harvest had him carving furrows in chill earth. He could never have imagined that a decade later villagers would still discuss the days that led to his disappearance. Or that some nights, watching TV, they would dream his fierce height and red hair, as if they might see him on a Hollywood street.

Of the nineteen Hervé children, he should have been the most content to stay. His grandfather, Hervé Hervé, had raised him, and together they'd fished paternal waters with the regularity of Mass. The Hervés had owned those first rough mountain farms since before the Seven Years War, and when Capt. George Scott burned the French homes, they didn't flee to France. Nor did they relocate for the convenience of a telegraph line and a doctor when Jersey merchants built company villages. But for all their strength the family had developed an unusual trait. Children were born alternately brutes or runts, as if the womb had been exhausted. It was clockwork, enormous child then changeling. Villagers saw and feared this as if through some faint ancient recollection of stories that predated Christianity. They feared even the little ones, frail, scurrying beneath those hulking siblings.

Though half his children were runts as if by biblical curse, Hervé Hervé remained proud. Strong beyond his years, he brought up even the last of his sons to fish and

work the fields at a time when cod stocks were failing and
farmland returning to forest. He'd grown up during the
worst years of the emigration south and had seen too
much change to trust it, the poverty, the wealth of war
and again the poverty until he'd become as hard as the
country that had been fled by hundreds of thousands so
that it was him his children now fled. In fights, men
broke knuckles on his face, his wide, almost Indian features expressionless, his weather-browned skin ignoring
whatever bruise. He took his sons hunting hours through
the drifts. He never used a compass, and once, when
geologists and surveyors sent inland by the province disappeared, he retrieved them. In 1904, walking a dark
road, he heard a shot from the woods and a bullet grazed
his eye. No one believed it was an accident. If anything,
his remaining eye became more intent, imprinted in
memories and imaginations. Some claimed he measured
the distance to the sea by tasting snow.

In his first marriage he fathered three boys and three
girls. Of those sons, two were keepers—he spoke of his
children, if at all, in the language of a fisherman. He
bred his wife hard, and when she foundered in childbed,
he replaced her with Georgianne, a sturdier woman of
no small religious bent who gave him eleven more. Jude
was the illegitimate son of a brutish Scots-American
tourist and Agnès, Georgianne's fourteen-year-old daughter, who, intent on not giving birth, pummelled her
belly, threw herself down hills and stairs, plunged into
icy water and hurtled against low branches so that to the
villagers she looked like a sideshow tough training for a

bareknuckle fight. The pregnancy held and Jude was born with a flat nose and the glassy gaze of a punch-drunk fighter. But he wasn't born alone. He came into the world with a tiny twin sister, in his arms, it was told, as though he expected further violence.

6

All were surprised to see a keeper and a runt together, as if he should have emerged with a bag of gnawed bones. Villagers who knew the family accounts believed the Hervé curse was the result of some past perversion or sin. When winter or sickness came, the runts were the first to go, abused or disregarded by the giants. Oddly, though, with the years, it became apparent that Jude adored his quivering sister. He grew fast and started walking so young the villagers doubted his age, and whenever Isa-Marie, still in diapers, began to cry, he leaned against her cradle like a greaser on his Chevy. No two children could grow to be more different, Isa-Marie often at church, the pages of her school books crammed with magazine clippings of popes or saints, Jude eager for work, slogging up to the fields each spring just to see the sodden furrows set against the sky, the huge vents of mud.

Of Agnès no memory would remain, only a photo, a handsome girl, eyelashes dark and long, lips pushed out to greet the world's pleasures. She'd fed them bitter milk for three months as outside spring lit winter's crevices, the sky bright as a movie screen, the first tourist cars hanging streamers of dust. That July she disappeared, only the orphaned twins and Jude's name to remember her by. The tourist father had been called Jude, she'd told them. As for Isa-Marie, the grandmother had named her for a long-dead sister, some Isabelle from another life.

Hervé Hervé was sixty-six that year, late to be a father again. On the day of Jude's birth he'd recognized the child as one of his own. He'd taken the silent newborn wrapped in a sheet to the salt-pitted scales, in the full April winds off the St. Lawrence, and reckoned his weight to a penny. By the time Jude was seven, Hervé Hervé was casting bets as to what he could pick up: crates of cod, a rusted foremast in the rocks. At his grandfather's command, Jude stripped to chickenflesh and yellowed briefs. The crates went up, the mast wobbled and rose. Hervé Hervé gathered change, fragrant cigarettes brought by a sailor, a dollar pinned beneath a rock against the wind. Off a ways Moise Maheur watched with his own son, an angular boy with a protruding chin and squinty eyes, five years Jude's elder, about the same height. Hervé Hervé put his pipe in a pocket, lit a cigarette, froze each man with his one eye and proposed a second bet. It was a June day, wind lifting spray off shallow breakers as the crowd stood in the cool light and watched. The Maheur boy threw punches as if they were stones. Jude's came straight from the chin. The men shook their heads and looked away. Hervé Hervé counted up, gave Jude a penny for good measure.

Jude grew within the time capsule of this affection, an odd tableau for the fifties: the swarthy grandfather with his pagan eye, and his atavistic protégé, fighting, stripped to the waist, coarse reddened skin like a wet shirt against muscle. Hervé Hervé decided to train him, told him to

7

split wood, more than they could need or sell. Run, he shouted, pointing to the mountain. Each morning he gave him a jar of raw, fresh milk despite the disapproval of his wife, and Jude, stomach burbling, followed along to be weighed in.

8

For the people of the village, the fights were less amusing each year as small, plum-coloured bruises became missing teeth, black eyes, great cancerous swellings on the faces of their sons. Soon people were saying, Doesn't he know those times are over? Does he think this can go on forever? Jude's birth had coincided with the end of the war, and only a few years afterwards, electricity had reached the village. Power lines stretched over the mountains and above the potato fields so that, hoeing, they could feel the thrum in their bones. Salesmen soon arrived with new contraptions, and children crowded to inspect the fluffy contents of a vacuum bag or to let the metal wand make hickeys on their arms. There was something innocent, light about the age, the future destined to be better.

When Jude and Isa-Marie were ten, their grandmother, shocking village and curé alike, claimed that the ghost of her son had visited, some long-lost favourite of hers who'd fled west and never returned. In her stolid way she'd said that out there in the vast, English-speaking world she had other grandchildren that needed saving. Though Hervé Hervé tried to curb this madness, she left in the night with only her knitting and egg money, as well as some baby clothes and hand-me-downs, and was never seen again. The betrayal enraged Hervé Hervé, his bouts of drinking more violent, his sons and daughters less inhibited. Jude's grandmother, medieval in her devotion, had run the house firmly, and without her there was no one to save them from their appetites.

9

Soon even the youngest of Jude's aunts and uncles were gone, fled or married. The house became dirty. Clothes went unmended. While Jude and Hervé Hervé worked, Isa-Marie studied or read or clipped up discarded church magazines and taped the holy images to her wall: missionary priests, saintly house pets, jungle savages who'd joined the clergy, the scars of piercings still visible on their round, beatific faces. From time to time two married aunts came by, gossiped in the kitchen, cleaned and left bowls of fried eggs, bacon and potato that Jude and Hervé Hervé ate cold for breakfast, lunch and dinner. That spring another aunt moved in with her four children after her husband wrecked his rig on the north coast and was crushed by logs. The house became almost normal, hot meals, scents of baking, diversity of tastes. Even Isa-Marie ventured from her room to help, Jude hulking along at her side, learning to pin diapers and powder bottoms. In those years he became kinder, made an effort to piece letters together at school, eyes bobbing in his head as he tried to figure out where to put his hands on the book. He learned to write his name, and under Isa-Marie's supervision, wrote it often. In summer there were flowers on the table, berries picked and made into pies. During a February

blizzard Isa-Marie gave out Valentines, each a paper
heart glued with clippings of bleeding Jesuses, praying
Virgins and women's pumps from the Eaton's catalogue.
But Hervé Hervé's drinking increased. By autumn the
aunt had moved out with her children. The other two
resumed their visits: fried papery eggs, carbonized
bacon. They smoked in the kitchen and told stories:
fathers in drunken threesomes with teenaged daughters,
a pregnant woman who accidentally swallowed bleach
and gave birth to an albino.

Isa-Marie returned to the silence of her room.
Flowers dried on the table, stems rotting in brackish
water. Jude watched his aunts from the doorway. He
recalled the wild, innocent laughter of children. Before
that, what? An old woman with a jaw like a log splitter,
the way she'd held his collar as she scrubbed at his face.
His only memory of maternal love.

Shortly after Jude turned fifteen, Hervé Hervé started taking him to travelling fairs, pitting him against grown men
on sawdust stages after the shows had closed. Locals who
recalled the towering, wide-jawed Scots-American tourist
believed Jude was a fine fusion. Even as a toddler, he
couldn't be knocked down, simply rebounding like an
inflatable doll with weighted feet. Hervé Hervé had
trained him well. He bet heavily, treated Jude's cuts with
whisky, swigged and counselled in technique, to work
the lower ribs and solar plexus. Jude's only hint of softness was full, feathery lashes he'd inherited from his

mother, out of place on his red fighter's face though he was never mocked. He already weighed two hundred and twenty pounds.

Though Jude did his grandfather's bidding, fought well and never lost, his greatest love remained his sister. Ever since he'd been a toddler, he'd watched over her. If she was teased or berated, he was immediately there, strutting and bobbing, his punch-drunk face bleary with that unblinking, walleyed look. Only his aunts' talk of her frailty alarmed him, the way they clucked their tongues when she left the room. She often had colds and fevers, and she'd remained small, a pale girl with green doe eyes and tentative gestures. In church she prayed with her shoulders pulled forward so that she looked to be hugging herself, and often she sat in the sun, appearing asleep, or else she put her blankets on the floor, in the warm light beneath her window. The aunts commented that it was in her blood, that unlike Jude she'd inherited from her tourist father a southern predisposition. She wouldn't make it here, they said. There was a country for everything.

One afternoon, through the dark boxed rooms of the house, Jude overheard his aunts discussing the days when children were given away. They recalled how a man with too many mouths to feed might hand one off to a neighbour with a barren wife. Families who needed a girl in the kitchen or a boy to learn a craft would go to another suffering from abundance. Sometimes there were loans, agreements that the child would return when his oldest siblings moved out. Or there were flat-out trades for a garden cart or a saw. The aunts recalled those that Hervé Hervé had given away, a Jean-Felix, a Marie-Ange. It had once been a common enough practice in the peninsula, somewhat outdated when Hervé Hervé, ashamed of the runts, had taken it up. The aunts laughed. He'd bought men drinks and lied about ages, saying a six-year-old was four. Everyone had known that he gave away lemons.

Gradually, fear took control of Jude's simple mind, and he became certain that while he was working the fields or gutting fish, his grandfather would hand Isa-Marie off like a bag of potatoes. Though their long hours of labour were conducted in silence, at times, when Hervé Hervé drank, he spoke a little and Jude listened as best he could. Hervé Hervé mumbled about *Les États*, about sons who'd left with the thousands of others seeking a better life and the daughters who'd been stolen by tourists. *Même ta mère*, he told Jude. He spat and cursed the foreigners who took everything, the fish from the St. Lawrence, the village girls. Jude had heard some talk about tourists, that to keep them coming, shops had hired women to wear old bonnets and dresses, and to bring looms or spinning wheels down from their attics and set them into motion. Men were even employed to cure cod in public displays as it had been done for centuries. But Jude never considered that the silly, rich tourists could constitute another threat to Isa-Marie, that one might stop and toss her in the trunk of his car like a flat tire.

Now, as he worked, he considered the strangeness of the years, how he'd once been with her often, walking her to school or to church with their grandmother. He'd carried Isa-Marie on his shoulders, or clumped along behind her. But then he'd quit school to work. He'd stopped going to church, and she'd continued. With his grandfather, in the boat, on the slow rise and fall of swells, or cleaning fish, his scale-encrusted shirt like armour, he wondered where she was, what she did alone. When he saw her, they no longer touched. Evenings he sat at her bedside and gazed at her with his dumb, broken features, and she at him with her delicate pretty face. They had little games. She brushed her hair behind her ear, shrugged and smiled so that it fell forward again, ducked her head and brushed it back. He watched, and after sitting awhile, shifty with unspent energy, made a passable smile. He looked at his red hands curved halfway to fists, the veins between the knuckles, the nails the shape and colour of the tabs on soda cans. He often noticed her fingers on the Bible. Outside wind shook the leaves. Clothes moved in pantomime on the line. She watched him. He believed she was destined for something great.

13

That year, Isa-Marie was becoming a woman at last. She didn't have the rearing, dishevelled sex-appeal, the galloping bosoms of other girls, but frailty and lack of appetite gave her a slight, fragile beauty. Her shy manner, the way she peeked at the world past sweeping hair, incited in men a desire to embrace her gently, as if she were a childhood teddy, and simultaneously to ply the plush, stretch her limbs, toss her stuffings into the air. By becoming a woman she sanctioned the pedophile in sailor and school superintendent alike.

But that she ever knew the touch of a man, there was little possibility. Jude would have cuffed the curé for looking sidelong, and if the curé never did, it was because Jude made impossible all sins except those cherished in her heart. Among the village youths, the few who'd dared mock her or who, sitting behind her in class, had dipped the sun-blond ends of her hair in the ink pot, had received a slight shy gaze and soon after a roadside walloping that left bruises the size of horseshoes. But those months that her pale beauty became apparent, any man who so much as tried to speak with her was at risk, and once, when a tourist stopped his car for directions, Jude pelted it with firewood. Even the few girls Isa-Marie had as friends stayed away, afraid of Jude, who, like some mythical being, watched over her constantly. Often he came upon her as she sat alone, face to the fleeting sunshine, and then she'd hear him and jump. Cold made the skin around her eyes swell as if she'd been crying. She looked at the ground when he was near. She kept to herself or lingered after Mass. At home she made a crèche, though the curé told her that the baby Jesus did not have stigmata and a crown of thorns, that the animals in the manger didn't need halos.

The dry summer had passed, lilac and fireweed and the few wild roses withering in the headlands beyond the fields. Jude watched, drab clothes ghosted against dirt, an animal poised. On an October morning, as he went to cut kindling by the water pump, one of Isa-Marie's schoolmates was waiting on the road to Mass. The boy had rim glasses like those of the monseigneur and had once been praised by the schoolteacher for composing a sonnet on the life of St. Francis. He was holding a roll of paper bound in silk ribbon, which he extended when Isa-Marie stopped before him. He'd just begun to speak as Jude came down the hill through the trees with the thrashing of a bull elk. Without pause or warning, Jude leapt the embankment and carried the boy to the out-house, where he kicked back the board and shoved his head into the rudiments and slime.

That evening, a brief, cold rain fell, and in sunset's last silvery light, small pools shone as if the flat rocks of the coast had been strewn with mirrors. Isa-Marie had turned back on the road and skipped Mass. She'd gone home and into her room and hadn't so much as glanced at Jude when he came in to mug about. She lay in her bed, turned away. He sat and shrugged and cracked his swollen knuckles, his glazed, red face blinking widely, often, as if to communicate feeling. Finally, he went out-side and stood in the windy dark. The tide scraped the coast, and between a few isolated clouds a comet sketched a slow, bright flare. He stayed there until dawn lit the gradual contours of the eastern mountains.

Isa didn't leave her bed the next day. At first no one noticed that she hadn't gone to school, but when, two days later, she remained curled in her blankets, the aunts began to murmur. Jude felt Hervé Hervé watching him. Winter was coming on hard, and Isa-Marie had always

15

found the cold difficult. Dawns, when ice flowers sprouted from the stomped and rutted mud of the road, Jude returned inside and went into her room. She wouldn't look at him. She lay on the bed, breathing shallowly, turned to the window. What sunlight filtered through the dirty glass made her skin appear translucent, bluish veins in her temples and throat.

16

Now, as he did his chores, for the first time he dimly sensed all that he didn't understand. Because of his and Isa-Marie's silence or because she'd been born in his arms and their hearts had beat together so long, he'd assumed to know her mind. But perhaps she'd been in love, the moments before he came crashing onto the road the happiest of her life. He worked in a frenzy, feeding animals and mucking the barn, heaps of manure steaming in the pasture. A dry, crystalline snow fell and puffed about his feet. He gazed up at her window. He tried to understand her heart, to know what would make her better. He closed his eyes and saw sunshine. He saw the cup of the world spreading like a flower with dawn, wide and brilliant beneath the sun, then wilting into a fragrant dark.

The tourists were fleeing winter, their long cars passing along the road in convoys. Days shortened, the sky a cramped, closed space, low and grey, and in the gradual darkness the coast became a rim of ash. Only a few lingered with cameras and tripods, parking in the weeds and hiking onto rises to click shots of the sea, the turning leaves, the rough, exposed shape of the land. Jude watched them, these often thin, dapper men who wore their pants tight at the waist like skirts, and others, long-haired, sporting dainty glasses with coloured lenses. They ventured into his field, stumbling on the furrows, watching the swift, automatic motion of his digging as he brought up potatoes from cold, clean dirt. He considered them violently, twisting the shovel deeper.

17

Though it was hardly possible not to overhear stories of the U.S., Jude had never seen any point in joining the speculation. Talk of fine pay and cheap, easy living meant nothing to him. Maybe, for some, the stony earth and brief summers were not enough, but he'd wanted little else. Only now, for the first time, he wondered who the tourists were, where they came from, what they knew. His father had been one, and his mother had gone south, and so perhaps, he considered, they were his people, too.

When he returned to the house, the aunts had just arrived, quiet now. Isa-Marie's soft, persistent coughing came from upstairs. She'd always been sensitive to the chill—*frileuse*, the aunts had called her, *la frileuse*. She hadn't left her bed or eaten in days. Afraid to wake her, he listened from outside her room. The few times he'd gone in just to hear her breathe he'd stepped softly, opened or closed the door as quietly as he'd been able. Hearing her cough, he felt as if he was struggling against something invisible, suffocating and blinding, like a blanket over his face. He wanted to know what he could do, who to fight.

From the unlit hallway he listened to his aunts.

C'est triste. But she would never have married. It was only a matter of time.

Oui, it's sad. She should have gone to the convent.

Yes, the convent—she'd have made a good nun.

It is sad. *Tellement triste. Elle était si jolie.*

Jude stumbled outside. A grey sun settled faintly against a distant, watery horizon. Far off, the church's spire was a frail ensign between sea and mountains. The cold mustered about him.

At the docks he found Hervé Hervé. He asked what they should do—rare words, stumbling, *Qu'est-ce . . . qu'on devrait faire?* Hervé Hervé had been drinking. He'd just tied down the weir and put up the boats. He stopped and took in Jude with his single eye.

There's no point, he said against the windy silence. They die. People die. To call a doctor would be a waste of money. You can't change anything.

In the darkening chill Jude rushed against this rage. He went to the woodpile and grabbed the axe and swung. He split savagely, driving aimless, glancing blows until the handle splintered. He crouched, panting. Not knowing how to cry, he could only groan. Stiffly, he walked to the outhouse. It was set back in the trees. He opened the door and knelt as his grandmother had taught him in church years ago. He lifted the board. Without closing his eyes, he pushed his head inside, down through the thin layer of ice.

The emigration to the factory towns of New England had begun after the rebellions of 1837 and 1838, and increased

to a furor by 1880, the year of Hervé Hervé's birth. As a
boy, he'd watched for wagons in the grey light, the huddled travellers with collars pulled to their ears. He and
his father had sworn never to give up these lands. Their
hatred of those who left was perhaps their only point of   19
agreement with the curé. Several times each month, sermons described emigrants as lazy and self-centred. They
were weakening the Church's divine mission in North
America. They were corrupted by the desires of their
wives for luxury. *Aux États* they would lose faith and language. Understandably the first French-Canadians had
gone because of politics, for the lack of farmland and
opportunity. But leaving the northern winter needed few
reasons and had many: stories of the south, of busy sun-
lit streets and booming factories, the clear proof of
wealth that returned in the form of men with store-
bought suits and golden pocket watches. At the turn of
the century, an article in the paper said that there were
ten cities in New England with populations of more
than ten thousand French whereas in Québec itself
there were only five. Across the border relatives had the
wonders of running water, electricity and a steady pay-
cheque. Even priests began to go, impressed by the
wealth of the new parishes, realizing God's work could
be done elsewhere. The Sunday message changed: *les
canadiens* would spread the true faith. Doctors and
lawyers closed shop and headed south to open new ones.
But for those who stayed, the choice was as real as the
land's settlement, as if they were founding daily their
homes on a desolate coast.

A century of the same event is long enough for men to think that it is part of the natural order of things. So when the laws changed in *les États*, the end of the emigration and the closing of the border seemed strange to all—cataclysmic. Those who returned home to visit spoke of the Great Depression, a few families even moving back. It was only during the Second War that the myth of the south, not easily forgotten, was resuscitated.

Among the long-time tenants at the village boarding house was a man named Honoré, who, though very old in appearance, was one of Hervé Hervé's sons from the first marriage. Hervé Hervé never spoke of him but the story was familiar, dating back to before the Normandy invasions. The war hadn't been popular. The people of Québec felt no allegiance to England and hadn't the leisure to pity France. Still, there were the few hearts too big for village life, and Honoré, with his praise and war rhetoric, was soon called *l'Americain*. Troops were then being shipped west for war in the Pacific, and after telling the village how everything would someday be American, how they would all look like summer tourists with quiet cars and blond wives, Honoré packed his bags. Though Jude had never cared for stories, this one had been told too often for him not to know—how Hervé Hervé caught the young man on the way to the recruitment office and beat him with a broken shovel handle. Another son had just died in Dieppe and Hervé Hervé believed he was saving Honoré. But not a month later the boy, almost fully mended, left in the night, enlisted and rode off with a few plucked-looking fishermen to catch the train west.

As Honoré would later tell it, when the French-Canadian soldiers crossed through the Prairie provinces, the locals jeered. He'd learned that French-Canadian anti-war sentiment had roused anger from seaboard to seaboard. The Rockies hung colourless in moonlight. The train climbed, and before dawn, descended again, pausing at an empty station only hours from Vancouver. He hesitated, then left his wagon and kept on down the road.

Eventually he found a ride to the border with a truck of Polish immigrants. He crossed south on foot and enlisted again, this time as an American, and was shipped off, not to the Pacific but to the high deserts of New Mexico. He was sure a mistake had been made. His platoon marched and camped in the desert. They dug trenches and smoked cigarettes, and because of his nascent English, he couldn't ask questions. At night, the skyline lurid with bombs, he thought that perhaps the Mexicans had joined cause with the Japanese and Germans and soon would be streaming over the border in swastikaed sombreros and Hitler moustaches. Then one afternoon a detonation shook the earth. He'd been crouching, studying English with a rumpled *Superman* comic, and he looked up to see a light as dazzling and penetrating and white as what the curé had described as the seat of Jesus. He held his hand to his eyes and saw its fragile bones.

The summer after Honoré left, an old man shuffled into the village in too-large military boots, sweating terribly. He was stooped, bald and toothless, and the story he told was of a great detonation, how afterwards he'd marched back to camp and removed his helmet to find his hair glued inside. He thought perhaps this was from the sun heating the metal, but that evening his teeth started to go. He shook and sweated, hardly able to stand. When this passed a week later, he was discharged and given a ticket home. He still sweated, terribly and for no particular reason. Hervé Hervé refused to have him around, and so Honoré took a room in the village. He spent his days on the stoop, proving with time to be a formidable storyteller and brewer of potato alcohol.

After his return, many decided the U.S. was a terrible place, but this conviction didn't last. Somehow, looking at Honoré, folded and watery-eyed on the porch, they found themselves saying not *is* terrible but *used to be* terrible. It seemed, because of his great age, that the war and its struggles had been long ago. In fact Honoré had a regular audience and took up the role, dressing in a suit of old man's clothes, his mouth gummy and distracted.

On the evening that Jude went to the village boarding house, he found Honoré sitting in the parlour next to the stove, shivering and sweating at once, red pouches beneath his eyes.

C'est quoi alors . . . ces États? Jude asked. The old man squinched up his face and smiled. What is *les States?* he said with laughing gums. That is a big question, *hein, mon gars?*

Jude, who'd never looked at a map longer than it took him to realize it wasn't a picture, had no notion of a distance not lived in. He struggled to make sense of

Honoré's words, a strange war, deserts and crumbling red stone and plants with needles instead of leaves and snakes that played music with their tails. This human skeleton spoke on with toothless exaggeration, pausing only to slurp from his Mason jar. He described an elusive enemy, weapons that didn't kill but that aged you. New Mexico was a bad place, he said, too big and dusty. The good ones are California, Connecticut and New Jersey, and especially New York. He described a world of wealth and sunshine and nice cars, women with luminous hair, the absence of illness. He talked about the thousands who'd gone and who were no longer farmers but rich men with golden knickknacks. Jude nodded, understanding at last.

As he returned home, he realized that it made sense why his mother and most of his family had gone to *les States*. Emotion jerked in his belly like a big fish on a line. His aunts were right. Isa-Marie had not been born for this country. She wasn't a woman who would bear eighteen lineages. Few were. That was why so many had fled, though Isa-Marie would never have the strength or courage. Thinking of everything he'd heard, he wondered if there would be a place for him and Isa-Marie in the magical south. And if he followed in the footsteps of the thousands who'd left, what would he become? What of these mountains and sea? Villagers said that when you crossed the border, you were never the same. Sons who returned were strangers at tables. But he'd had enough whining and moaning, American riches, French-Canadian woes, poverty and exploitation.

Enough of a people whose wisdom came from suffering. Winter had set in, the high autumn tides long
passed, and the only solution was sunlight.

24 When he arrived at the farm, he didn't go inside. He
climbed the mountain path, the wind flapping at his
open jacket. In the potato fields he stopped. A few
unharvested furrows remained, and he began to work
though the sun was setting. By the time he'd raked the
last potatoes from the chill earth, clouds had gathered
in immense reefs above the gulf, black patches against
a reddening horizon. The festooned cables hung
between electrical towers like broad stitches. He stood
against the wind's gravity as the hard earth tilted about
him and the first stars flickered coldly. He stayed there,
perfectly still.

Just before dawn Hervé Hervé woke to the honking of
geese high above. For a moment he thought it was
spring, that yarrow had grown up outside the window,
but it was only flurries that had fallen, catching in the
dead tufts of flowerheads, lit by a setting moon. He lay
in bed, listening to the thrumming of the refrigerator
motor downstairs until it clicked off. He felt the stillness
of the house. Oddly his thoughts wandered back against
the years, the way he'd culled his children, building his
family like everything else, and the runts who'd died,
whom he'd known would die, the exigencies of the land
simply too great a law. He'd looked in on Isa-Marie
occasionally, with no strong emotion. She'd hardly

been able to open her eyes. Returning home drunk one night, he'd seen Jude walking the road in his underwear, asleep, mumbling, his bare feet gleaming against the packed and frozen earth. Whatever strange motherless, fatherless bond the twins had shared was too much. They'd both been idiots, one gentle, the other brutal, and while Isa-Marie had inherited something of Jude's strength, it now seemed the opposite, Jude's love no less an infirmity.

Hervé Hervé lay a while longer, remembering and hoping that he was wrong. The previous night, he'd gone into her room. He'd pulled back the sheet and seen that she was dead. He'd been about to leave, but something had touched him, pity for Jude perhaps. He'd drawn the blind.

Hervé Hervé listened. He was certain. Where would Jude take her? How far could he go? Hervé Hervé pushed back the covers and got up and dressed. He went downstairs and out to the barn. He broke the ice lids on the water buckets, then stood, watching the road. Perhaps he was the last thing his countrymen who'd left had seen or would remember, a large angry man staring with his one eye, waiting as they passed. For years he'd hated them, but he hadn't known how much it was possible to lose—not just his family but the power of pride and love and the easy law of violence. He couldn't imagine his children elsewhere or other than what they were. Did they carry with them something of this world, its land and sea? In the first dim emanation of that December morning, everyone he'd loved vanished along the road. They never ceased, constantly moving and vanishing against a grey light. The St. Lawrence thrummed the boulders of the coast, the wind as steady as gravity. He pictured those he'd lost as wood set into a fire, the south a country of ash, a land of ghosts.

Québec–Georgia
1961

The people of Gaspésie were a mix of Acadian, Normand and Channel Islander, Jersey or Guernsey, Irish and Indian and Scot, and though Loyalists had been there since the American Revolution, they set themselves apart. But the Hervé family could be traced back to Brittany, to a mute who'd given the strength of his blood and the name of a Breton saint. He'd somehow ended up in Québec when the cod industry was building towns for seasonal work. Stories had it that he'd never made a sound. A wise woman had rubbed his tongue with elder sap, put hot ashes in his palms, hung his baby teeth on the neck of a yearling goat and run it into the sea, but to no end—as a newborn he didn't cry or cluck, and as a man he lifted stones, received wounds and made love without a grunt. Why he should have been content to leave the banked homesteads of Brittany, his ancestors would never know.

In the century after his arrival his name became a quality of the blood, a tale too exaggerated to be true, making the Hervé men seem at once incomplete and too much. All through Gaspésie the name was known for giants because, in a forgotten past, the family had begun christening male children with the patronymic, hyphenating it to tell them apart. When each son became the head of a house, he claimed the title of Hervé *père*. Hervé Hervé's only departure from this tradition had been to let his wife give the runts the less illustrious but infinitely more appropriate appellations of martyrs and saints.

To many, a story is the endurance of human strength, but by the time Hervé Hervé had been born, the adventures of his ancestor had been forgotten, until then passed on only by others, the Hervés themselves too silent a clan. Though the original character was lost, for all the Hervés as for Jude, their name and the power of their blood was enough. He'd wanted nothing else.

Frost had sketched bouquets on the window glass. Jude sat a moment longer, then filled a bag with clothes. He put on three pairs of socks and went into Isa-Marie's room. The mound of blankets barely revealed the outline of her body. Someone had pulled the blind, and this angered him. He raised it even though it was night. He spread her blankets on the floor one by one until she lay uncovered, her nightdress twisted under her arms, her hips as tight as spools.

29

He lifted her. She hadn't eaten in days. No one had tried. He knelt and closed his eyes. Blood pulsed in his ears like bird wings. When the silence returned, he eased her onto the blankets. He didn't look at her face. He wrapped her, trying to be gentle. Everything he'd intended to take remained on the floor. He carried her downstairs. He left the house and followed off along the road.

The St. Lawrence stayed with him. The days were short, his step even, strong as if his training had been for this. He accepted rides but never put down his bundle or spoke or listened. The form in the blankets was so slight that no one could know what it held. When the sun was full, he lifted his face. There was Matane and Rimouski, a few churches, a cathedral, plenty of villages. A man in a box truck took him half the way. He rambled about the supplies he had to deliver before the snows. He offered Jude a cigarette and didn't mind being ignored.

At Rivière-du-Loup Jude hid among crates in the stockyard and climbed on a train. Bales of stiff, pungent leather crowded the boxcar, and he huddled among them, sheltered against the wind. This way he saw Québec, Montréal, the shores of the St. Lawrence now close enough for it to be called a river. Through the slats he glimpsed skyscrapers.

When he woke, a windy landscape shuttled past, pines black beneath ice and the deeper darkness of mountains. He'd crossed out of flat, winter-bleak fields. The Québec countryside had been tame, cultivated or recently fallow, sparsely wooded, here or there a few houses lining a throughway, a store and gas station. But only miles past the border, forest crowded the cargo doors. The train appeared not to move but instead the land swelled, erasing field and village.

That night he arrived in a stockyard, a maze of hitched wagons, sidetracks and crossovers and switch towers, coupled boxcars booming with the sound of bombs. Men tramped by, talking. A dog barked. He changed trains, the bundled leather now bales of cheap, single-stitched shoes. He created a space among them not only to hide but as shelter from the wind. He wasn't sure how much time had passed. He hadn't so much as folded back the blankets. He thought to look at her face. He didn't. Late in the morning, after jolting, the train began to move. The day wore on and away and was only just returning when he woke.

The sun had reached the horizon. The air was humid. The heat of his body seemed contained by the bales. He pushed them back and stood at the door. With one hand he undid his jacket. He inhaled, great gasps. Seeing the possibility of hesitation, he clutched Isa-Marie to his chest, and leapt.

When he opened his eyes, the tracks were empty, bordered by fields, trees in the distance and farther the blue smoke of low mountains. Gradually he looked down and unfolded the blankets. He stared and stayed there on his knees. Late morning, a raccoon came out and lifted its masked face. A groundhog and three deer all paused. Sometime before evening a storm blew through and puddled mud around him. Night came, the moon high, near full, the fields white and long and the mountains clearer, long and softly humped. When the moon was still setting, the sky began to grey. Ants probed weeds. Worms, pink and jellied in the rain, took shape and tongued the earth. His clothes might have rotted. He might have shredded them. Perhaps he'd been running days through fields and mountains. He recalled only standing to release the bundled sunlight, to let the blankets fall as he handed Isa-Marie back to the sky.

Weeks he wandered, starving, naked. He slept without consideration, woke to creeping insects or the patter of rain. He would never decipher those days, nor recall what had become of Isa-Marie or his clothes or even how he could have wandered so long in a country of roads and subdivisions. Years later he would see movies in which an event, a death or marriage or declaration of war, is followed by a shot of newspaper headlines or the sheets of a calendar fluttering from staples or even, as he recalled those days, a time-lapse with clouds whizzing past, suns flipping into the sky, shadows cast and snapped back. There had been the world of his childhood, clear and absolute, then the train and the same day over and over, the sun, night, hunger, time a wheel spinning freely and without consequence until he stepped through a windbreak into the backyard of a run-down brick rambler, one of a dozen similar houses on a narrow road, across from which were more fields. He saw a gold-painted can of Lysol in the weeds, clothes flapping on a line. He stared at the can and nudged it with his toe. A black beetle shot from beneath. Right then nothing seemed so normal as the houses, the clothes, the can and—as if a guardian spirit had taken the burden of his emotions and now judged him capable of receiving them—his anger. He went to the clothesline and came to a pair of red, white and blue Everlast boxing shorts and a flannel shirt, which he chose because the wind was blowing.

He'd put on only the shorts when he heard a door slam and saw a beefy man with a blond flat-top and arms the size of rump roasts. The man had narrow eyes, more piggish than bovine and chub from his ankles to the thick, sweaty folds at the back of his neck.

Them's my boxing gear. You don't know what you're in for, buddy.

He hurried down off the porch and advanced with heavy, bounding lunges. He wore polka-dotted briefs and was barefoot like Jude, a rim of fat jiggling in his singlet.

They came together on the lawn. Jude was weak with hunger but angry, longing back to those years of training, and whatever this man landed was no worse than what Jude's mother or the wharf brawlers had dealt. Dressed in roomy briefs, Jude planted his feet and struck as he would for years, not at the man before him but at a piñata loaded with loss and anger and loneliness. The man no longer moved, but the earth, the house and trees swayed. Jude had a cut on his forehead, and his blood did all the weeping that he could do. The man went down. A bird twittered, tweeted. Jude caught his breath.

A second man, this one old, came from the front of the building, hobbling a little, his shirt imprinted at the heart with hanging gloves. Hey, Boss, he called. He blinked watery eyes and followed Jude's gaze to the polka-dotted underwear limp in the uncut grass as if Boss had melted.

Jude tried to speak but succeeded only in making a sound like barking. He growled, swallowed, took a deep breath. No de English, he said.

No de shit, sonny, the man replied. He came a little closer, inspected Jude as if he'd been recently painted. He cast a glance at the supine man. What's your name, boy?

No de English. De Franch, Jude said after a bit more strangled barking.

Okay, Defranch. You need a trainer? How about a manager?

He and Jude just stared.

Okay, come on. My car's out front. Just let me get somebody down here to check ol' Boss out.

Jude stood there panting, and it wasn't until weeks later that he understood the man's name was Herb Carney, that he was Jude's connection to the boxing world and that within a few years they would be on the road to fame. You got some work to do, sonny, Carney later told him, but you got the moves. You're good.

Then began the training, the fights and Jude's dawning realization that he might find a place in this country and that the God so absent in fields and inarticulate sky, truant in grief, had made an effort after all.

Georgia–Louisiana
1961–1968

The U.S. was a wild place, Jude decided those years that Carney raised him like a son. The neighbourhood was no different than Boss's, a bit more crowded, bordered by a littered highway, scrub brush and fields piled with trash, a pitted and scorched no man's land where locals had tried to burn household appliances and failed. Jude lived in Carney's basement, slept on a green army cot next to a wall of gurgling PVC pipes. Though Carney had no idea as to Jude's age, he figured the boy could use a few years of good training and some time to learn the language. This wasn't simple kindness. He recognized a money-maker when he saw one. He appropriated a false birth certificate from a man in Atlanta, had known others who'd done the same for immigrant boxers and so worked his connections. Jude became Jude White, a safe name the man in Atlanta had insisted, no need to attract attention. Jude was now listed as being eighteen, Carney having wanted to make him legal.

During the day Jude did chores or chopped wood as he had for his grandfather, but now it was Carney nodding and dipping chew, spitting into the weeds and saying, Faster, sonny, faster. Jude sweated and heaved, shearing knots and burls, his shoulders burning. The rest of the time he trained in a gym Carney had set up with a few friends. He familiarized himself with technique subtler than his grandfather's, dipped beneath a rope strung across the ring and tore into the bags until they had deep dents and Carney made him wind them with duct tape. At night Jude lay on his cot, feeling his expanding body, the growth of bone and muscle that stabbed along his back and shins. He stared at the naked floor joists, heard the creak of Carney's frequent nighttime visits to the bathroom.

Jude knew things now: doctors were normal, poverty unnecessary. For each little cough Carney brought home pills, took an aspirin in the morning to stay fit, told Jude old age was hell and then some. After having lived so long in a leaning house of unpainted wood, drafts in the walls, leaks everywhere, Jude was impressed by Carney's rather shoddy home. He found it sunny, open and clean. But still, Jude realized that this wasn't the place he'd come for. The world that Honoré had described, that his mother and all those who'd gone south must have been seeking, was the very same that Carney watched each evening on the television. It wasn't that Jude desired this, but thinking of Isa-Marie or Hervé Hervé or the farm, he drowned in a sense of loss. Each morning, he woke, still worrying about Isa-Marie, struggling to realize anew that she was dead. He watched TV and tried to believe that he could find a place here. But at night, he dreamed the motion of the sea.

News came and Carney jawed on worse than a TV commentator. There was a man in orbit, some sort of missile crisis and a president shot in a parade. There were facts about the universe, satellites and probes and all that hooey doom. Jude ignored the broil of politics, colour TV and congressional bills. What English he learned was from Carney's endless diatribes, his talk of the old days and the boxers he'd lost to war. The man Jude had fought was named Hoss Jenkins, nicknamed Boss, an up-and-coming who'd defeated Lou-Roy Webster and Tony Salamba both in the first round with a hard left hook. After his fight with Jude, Boss had gotten up from the grass. Carney had replaced the Everlast shorts, but at the nationals Boss had lost anyway and was back on the farm, broken spirited, feeding orphaned calves with a rubber nipple. Carney used him as an example.

Don't fight with anger, he said. Dammit, sonny, you fight angry and there'll always be someone out there to beat you. That's the problem with old Boss. He didn't realize there was boys angrier than him.

As for his own rage Jude doubted this. He was desperate to begin, to get into the ring, but Carney was cautious, telling him that he still hadn't learned to box, that boxing wasn't fighting.

When Jude was eighteen, he started the amateur circuit. He cleaned up, abbreviating matches by breaking jaws, smashing ribs, lifting men off the ground with uppercuts. He went national, winning with ease. He now measured six foot seven, weighed over two hundred and sixty pounds and didn't have an inch of skin not bulging with muscle. Carney was always there, telling him he was great, measuring, weighing, prodding his flesh, collecting money from tournaments. After fights Carney took him to steakhouses for cheese-baked spuds and cuts of broiled and peppered meat. He fed him like a pet shark.

But Jude came out of each match unsatisfied. He was fighting poor whites, Hispanics and Italians and hulking blacks. In this world with so much sunshine, he couldn't help but think of what he'd lost to be here, and he considered that he might be happy with a family of his own. But though he searched the crowd for bright happy people, he saw crooked jaws, puffed lips, some bald, bearded fat men in oil-stained suspenders giggling over a downed fighter. Only at the nationals were there a few pretty single girls in tight jeans and leather vests, drinking beer and cheering. He watched them awhile, considering for the first time how this was to be done. They smiled until he'd lumbered close enough for them to see his boiled-fish head, his sparse, red eyebrows and the scaled, spreading muscles of his torso. Then they fled. Carney noticed his distraction.

Sonny, he said, we got the Christian religion today because Jesus didn't give in to girls like that.

Jude had been raised Catholic and saw Christ as the curé's business, a threat or oath or colourful laminate awarded at school for good grades.

Goddam, sonny, Carney said, you just keep the flesh strong. I've done invested in you.

And so Jude fought on. He swung his way through those months as if in a car wash, liquids spraying, great brushes whipping in like the faces and hair and gloves of opponents. He hoped that sooner or later anger and loneliness would be washed away and that he'd have no reason to return.

Though Jude won the nationals, the Tokyo Olympics had been the previous summer, and he wondered if Carney had kept him back to avoid an early defeat at the hands of Joe Frazier. Both agreed he shouldn't wait three more years and that he should go professional.

Don't lose heart, Carney told him, you'll be whupping Ali in no time.

All that fall and through the winter Jude fought, building a reputation, destroying ranks of middling boxers. Carney wasn't discerning. No purse was too small, no fighter or rundown showroom too disgraceful. The events were more often than not hardly newsworthy, and when the prize cash was on the table, Carney grabbed it up, shoved it in his pocket, gave Jude a crumpled dollar. In the hot spring of the following year, he booked a tournament in New Orleans.

40   Of the boxers there Jude was the only white, and the audience held more blacks than he'd ever seen at a match, boys stepping up on bleachers, girls tilting heads and making wry expressions. He couldn't shake his doubts about fighting these men also struggling to rise, but like that boy obeying his grandfather, he was resigned to victory. He climbed into the ring without show of any sort. He rolled his shoulders a bit and looked lethargic under the lights. The bell rang. His first match didn't last a minute.

On the second day he went in against Jerome Knight, a handsome man who swung over the ropes and danced about, pawing the air, then glided into long, smooth jabs, crosses and hooks, sharper as he bounded side to side. Pretty girls stood and called, Jerome, baby, you bring him down! You show him!

Air through the doors had been gusty all afternoon, a storm blowing in off the muggy gulf. As the sky darkened, the first raindrops pinged on the metal roof and with a wet sound like clapping hands the downpour began. Thunder boomed, the smack of landed jabs lost as Jerome shot in, wove and moved around. Jude kept his head tilted and took the blows lightly. He was surprised to see such expression in a man's face. When Jude connected, Jerome kept his feet and shook his head as if dealing with a child. He slipped in and landed his own more planned jabs. Then Jude began to fight in a blitz, inexhaustible and intuitive.

Lightning flashed in every door as Jude and Jerome, at the end of the second round, came together, ducked too close and struck foreheads. The rumble muted the referee's call for halt. The overhead lights died and Jude, blood on his face, delivered a hook that carried his entire body. In the unlit room a silver arc of sweat lifted from Jerome's head. The silence was startling. When the referee announced KO, his was a hushed, tired voice in the dark.

41

Afterwards Carney was quiet. He didn't look Jude in the eye. Candles and oil lamps had been set on shelves and about the edges of the locker rooms. Shadows played over the walls and at the ends of corridors. Carney confessed his concern for the next weekend. Jude's forehead had a gash as long and ragged as the fly of his pants.

You're going to have to sit out, Carney said. Call it quits for this tournament.

Jude opened and closed his sore lips. He looked at Carney.

It happens, Carney said bitterly.

A trainer whose fighter had already been defeated came to have a look. He was a short man, sweating profusely, wiping only his forehead so tears seemed to stand out on his cheeks.

That's one mean cut, he said. I'll tell you what. I'm going to call somebody for you. She might help your boy out.

Carney nodded and thanked him. The man told them to wait.

It might be a while. But don't get no doctor. Just mess that up.

This got Jude wondering. The doctor on call had given him a compress and ice but had left with Jerome.

Sad about that boy, Carney said and sighed.

Maybe an hour later Jude was brought back from dozing by the slipping of the cold pack. Carney had fallen asleep in his chair, chin to his collar, and now he woke and muttered, To hell with it, sonny. He spit in a Coke bottle and was standing when the hard clatter of a woman's shoes echoed in the concrete hallway. She came in from the flickering dark, big and brown. Her nose was as beaked as a Cherokee's. She was eating a hot dog and halfway across the room she appeared to see Jude all at once. She threw the rest of the hot dog in the trash.

I guess I'm here for you, she said. She glanced from one man to the other. She reminded Jude of his matronly aunts, though younger. Her lips were full, paler than her skin, and apart from a coarse, undyed smock, she wore baggy pants with a pleat down the front and a string of beads. Her look was serious and at the same time like that of the hippies who were appearing everywhere.

Carney pinched fresh chew and watched as she removed Jude's compress. Though Carney had occasionally voiced opinions on who ran what, who were the minions, the bosses, the landed interest—blacks Italians Jews—his racism had been tempered to respect by half a century of boxing. Jude wasn't surprised that he would trust her.

When does he need to fight again? she asked.

Next weekend, Carney said. What you planning on doing anyway?

43

Poultice. She spoke evenly as if to the wound. I think I can have him mostly ready by then.

How much?

People pay what they can.

All right. Hell, you just do your best.

Her name was Louise, and that week she treated Jude's cut. She carried satchels and jars of oil in a purse woven like a basket. Her hands, though as large as a man's, were careful. Three times a day she brought a fresh poultice prepared in linen. She massaged the edges of his wound, each touch like peeling a scab, the ragged flesh relaying sensation along his jaw and the back of his neck. A little pale and watery blood ran past the corner of his eye. He was silent, listening to her breathe. She spoke only to forbid him any activity other than walking.

Nights he wallowed in insomnia. He watched TV until programming gave way to black-and-white bars of various shades and emitted a shrill whistle. Occasional car lights shone through from the street. He recalled his grandmother who'd worked in the fields then dressed for church, her big hands awkward on the folds of her apron. Once when Louise was spreading ointment, he took the wrist of her free hand. Her strong nostrils curved. She stepped back, and he let go. He realized that she was younger than he'd thought.

A few days before his next fight he asked her for something to help him sleep. It was the first time he'd spoken.

Tu parles français? she said in a strange accent. She was looking at him.

Oui. He spoke hesitantly, not sure how his voice would sound now in French. He hadn't talked much to begin with. *Du Canada,* he heard himself mutter, not sure where this was.

Beaucoup de monde parle français ici, she said. Her voice had a hop in it as if she wanted to sing. *Mais tu ne vis pas ici, n'est-ce pas?*

Non, pas ici, he said. *En . . .* Georgia.

La Georgie. C'est triste pour toi. De ne plus parler . . . j'imagine.

As she made him the tea, she said a few things about the language she'd learned from her parents. Later, soon after she left, he was drifting below shadows and vague peaked shapes like cathedrals and trees. At some point he was in his childhood kitchen though the light through the windows was that of the landscape beyond the cargo doors when he'd leapt, when he'd first crossed south with Isa-Marie. There was a glimpse of her sitting on the edge of a bed, a piece of cardboard on her knees as she pieced together bright magazine clippings to make a word he hadn't bothered or been able to read. And again night. A dream of her bones and the field where he'd lost her. A dog rooting in weeds. He was running. Men in blue jackets lifted flashlights through the dark to find him.

When he returned to the ring at the end of the week, his wound was a tender, grainy line. He scanned the crowd and saw Louise. He'd have to fight at least two more times to win the tournament. Though he was stiff from inaction and Carney worried for his undefeated record, Jude felt calm. Carney had suggested they let this tournament go, but Jude had refused. He struck gloves. His opponent was long armed, young, hefty for his age. Jude watched the looping hooks, guarding his wound. He played the young man around the ring, jabbed and dipped and knocked him out cold in the second.

Goddam, Carney said. That was boxing, sonny. That wasn't fighting. That was boxing.

He was so happy he took out his chew and flung it down so he could speak. Jude looked around. Louise appeared later. She dressed his wound again, expressionless. She wasn't blond or lovely, but he'd wanted to impress her. He closed his eyes.

Ça va? she asked.

Oui, he said. *Oui.*

The next day he won the tournament though his cut opened and she came from the audience to treat it. They were in the locker room, Carney meeting with sponsors. The poultice she applied smelled pungent and made him faintly nauseous.

She seemed to be smiling. When she finished, she became inexpressive again. *Alors*, she said, *tu vas rentrer en Georgie.* Her irises were threaded with orange. He reached from where he sat and took her hand. They stared at each other. He let go and she left.

When Carney returned, he wanted to pay her. He didn't even have a phone number.

Dammit, he said. What's the meaning of these people just wanting to help? He sighed and sat and talked about Jude's career. By the end of the year, he said, you could be fighting Ali. He paused and seemed to think. Ah, that woman will come back later.

She arrived at the motel after midnight in a rattling Ford truck, the headlights shining unevenly against the folds of the curtains. Jude got out of bed.

Je peux entrer? she asked. Her hair was drawn tight in a bun with a few sprung curls. She neared, her brow at the level of his chin. He knew nothing about women. He hadn't paused from work or fighting for the usual rites of boyhood. She lifted her chin and placed her lips on his. She was such a formidable woman he hesitated. With her eyes on his face she kissed him. She stepped back, watching him, curiously, like a girl again. Then she began to unbutton her shirt. Her sloping breasts made her vulnerable. She lay on the unmade bed, palms up, shoulders back. The bedsprings crunched like beer cans as he joined her. She reached up to hold his big, sad face.

Jude had been relieved to get home to Georgia. Nothing had been stated between him and Louise. She'd left at dawn and he'd lain awake much of the night. There was something unsettling in the calm he'd felt with her. He knew he wasn't supposed to desire her or even this world, these rundown neighbourhoods, though there was sunshine enough.

Back home, Carney told him it was time to work the professional circuit in earnest, and Jude agreed. He saw boxing as his only means of completing this journey that he'd never wanted to begin. But before the tenderness had left his wound, a newfangled club outside New Orleans offered him sponsorship and full salary. At first Carney wasn't interested, but when he sniffed the money and heard his juicy part, he said, Hell yes, then sold everything, house and equipment. He and Jude headed south and took up in the guest suites.

The owner and mastermind of the club was Bill Watson, a businessman who'd dabbled writing sports for a conservative paper with limited circulation and had only recently meddled in training—in hopes, he liked to say, of saving American boxing. He was stocking his ranks with respectable men who'd fought for big schools, but he felt the need for someone sensational, an active fighter, a figurehead, and not only did Jude impress with his unbeaten record but he was, quite simply, Watson said, White. Watson didn't suspect a Catholic past or a fake name. Cleft palate, Carney told him when Jude spoke, no better explanation for that rough accent.

The plan, Watson told them, is to attract cultivated people to the sport. We build a gym with the most high-tech equipment, we bring in up-and-coming names, and we'll have respectable people involving themselves. Otherwise we'll lose the tradition. The Negroes and the wops will take over.

Jude listened to the dumpy, moustached man who paused often to primp his suit. After describing his philosophy, Watson gave them a tour of the Complex, a warehouse with several rings, racks of chrome-handled weights, bright blue punching bags, benches and mechanisms with levers.

We have the material here, he told them, to work every muscle in the human body.

Attached to the wall was a padded helmet hooked to hydraulic pistons.

Stick your head in this, Watson told him.

Jude did so.

Move it around.

Jude strained his head to one side. The pistons hissed.

Gives you a strong neck, Watson confirmed. Imagine what this could do for you in the ring. He took a handkerchief from his pocket and dabbed his forehead.

Back in their suites Carney warned Jude, You stay away from those machines, sonny. They'll slow you down. Stay fast, fight cool. Besides, I don't trust a man who always wears a suit. Don't make a damned bit of sense.

He admitted, however, that money was money, and Watson had offered more than a little. He confided in Jude that he had almost enough put away after the sale of his house to retire somewhere hot and quiet and live out his days in total boredom. Just better have a TV, was all he commented by way of redemption.

Training began the next morning. Jude's picture was on a few posters, WHITE in bold print below. A reporter came by to get the scoop. He asked Jude if he thought this move would alienate him in the sports world, if he had personal issues with black boxers, if he had long-term political goals. Jude shrugged, scratched at his flesh-coloured hair, tipped his blunt head one way, then the other, and finally answered, I don know.

Good work, boy, Watson later told him. Silence is always the best reply. They'll see.

That day a few local fathers paid so their sons could watch and learn. The slender boys with blond bowl cuts looked on in horror as Jude exchanged cracking blows with Red Benson, a man not unlike Boss in size, but more compact in build, his body having chosen the evolutionary strategy of eliminating neck and chin. Between rounds, Jude hawked and spat into the corner. Watson, seeing the strands of glistening mucus hanging from the ropes, told him, None of that, please. The plan, he said, is to elevate boxing.

An hour later Louise walked in.

Excuse me, Watson said, did someone send you?

Jude saw her and coldcocked his next opponent, a gangly investor in knee socks who'd come from Shrevesport and whose doctor had recommended more stimulating fitness than dressage and constitutionals.

Jude barrelled past Watson to meet Louise. They talked as if they'd always spoken casually, he in grunts, she in detailed sentences. She seemed younger, open. She told him she'd read about him in the paper. She asked if she could see him again. *Oui*, he said before he considered it. They planned to meet that night. Carney didn't seem to notice, only freshened his chew, and Watson said, We're trying to be role models here. A boy like you needs an image. You've got a career ahead of you in image. Boxing doesn't last forever.

50   That night, waiting for Louise, Jude tried to make sense of it, the simple pleasure of being with her, the way she looked at him. He stayed silent when she arrived. She drove him to where she lived, a small house north of the city on a piece of wooded land between farms. The rooms were clean and open, herbs drying from the ceiling beams, books and jars on shelves.

C'étaient toutes les choses de ma mère—my mother's things, she said. She told him her grandmother had been Creole and her father mostly Indian. She'd learned midwifery from her mother and grandmother, and French—*un français bien différent,* she added.

She paused, the persistent music of crickets and night insects filling the space. She told him that her mother had died not that long ago, too young, and that she herself had had to take over and do all those things she hadn't felt ready for. *C'est* . . . she began, but not finding the word, finished in English—lonely, she said.

Later they went walking. She spoke of what her mother had taught, things she'd alluded to, unsure herself of a tradition already lost. He and Louise followed a sparse woods, ancient trees around a collapsed house, pecans and oaks immense. They came out from the trail to power lines, a swath through the countryside, the galaxy so bright they could see the cables high overhead. The thrum of electricity was that of the fields above his childhood home. She touched his corded wrist. They pressed onto the ground. Her palms turned up to starlight. He dug his fingers through grass and root, throwing up clods like a running horse.

Later she asked about his life. Her breasts touched 51 softly against his chest, her hand on her belly. She closed her eyes as she listened. She was the first person he told about Isa-Marie, about her death and the journey south and not remembering what had become of her, and his wandering and even his dreams of her bones. He lay recalling the feeling of emptiness when he'd decided to leave, that wide gulf night on the mountain, fields and wind and standing against the cold. What had happened to that world and what should he strive for in this one? He saw the farm, the coast, the rugged sea. He wanted that simple work. He wanted Isa-Marie as when they were children, to carry her along the road and feel himself given over to this good. His terror was something he'd never known in the ring. Suddenly unable not to, he leapt up and ran. He rushed along the dusty lane between the fields and jumped a fence into a farmer's yard. Behind a shed, barefoot and naked, he grabbed an axe and swung into the woodpile. The farm was silvery, moon shadows beneath trees. Blood buzzed in his ears. He didn't want to stop now or think. He split until sweat released the heat from his body, until a dog barked and houselights came on, and then he ran away.

———

Those next months Carney and Watson conspired to book a string of fights. Too many, Carney admitted, but said it would make Jude tough and no matter, there was money in it. To Jude it seemed he was fighting every American who weighed in at over a hundred seventy-five. A few had beer bellies. One was covered with burn scars and missing an eye, another fresh out of prison, his back tattooed with the lewdest naked women Jude had seen. All went down fast, though a few show managers bribed Carney to make Jude draw out the fights then finish hard.

Despite the cat-and-mouse matches Jude was relieved. He needed time. He saw Louise between fights. When he visited, she was waiting in a bright dress, a meal on the table, rice and gumbo and fried okra, fragrant shrimp soufflés. They ate for hours. She put some giddy music on and later they relaxed on the sunny bed. He liked the familiarity, the brassy stretch marks at her hips, the bud of keloid on her arm from falling onto broken glass when she was a girl. Sometimes she made him talk and his few words felt so exposed that he pictured the curé next to him. But on buses or airplanes to Vegas, Reno, New York, he struggled against her within him. Before each fight, he stared at the elegant women in the audience, though when he went into the crowd, everyone withdrew, even grimaced. Afterwards, in the locker room, he faced the mirror. His broken features held nothing of Isa-Marie or even Hervé Hervé, and, ponderously, he considered his ugliness and whom he should look like, a mother or a father. His rage and frustration hardly felt expended. The pipes in the wall groaned, and he realized he was clutching the sink, dragging it from the concrete fixtures, trying, it seemed, to hold himself in place.

Those months, when he returned to Watson's ridiculous club, he reluctantly admitted his desire to see Louise. Though Carney kept the money from the fights, he'd bought Jude a side-swiped Falcon at the auction and had forked out a few dollars for driving lessons. Jude used the car to go only to and from Louise's house, crammed at the wheel. She spoke of her people, the journeys they'd made by or against their choice, of the mysteries that so many ignored and that ruled them. But one evening, back from an extended trip to New York, Jude saw that her belly had, as if in a day, grown round. He wondered how he hadn't noticed. After lovemaking he again walked out on the road. He knew the way she opened and touched. She'd said she'd learned from her mother to comfort the dying as if they were children, just by holding and touching. The dying longed for their mothers, she'd said, and this had scared him, had made him wonder how he could long for someone he'd never known. What had happened to all those who'd left the village—aunts, uncles, his mother, his father even? When he was a boy, men had discussed towns in the States where everyone spoke French, where curés and businessmen lived as they had in Québec, just wealthier, better. It seemed he'd followed in their footsteps but had found nothing. He thought of the village, the St. Lawrence. That world had ceased to exist, though at times he recalled it so clearly, without him, that it seemed he was the one who'd vanished.

In the humid dark he followed slowly along the road. The seasons here confused him. It was another magic altogether, the warm winters, the hot, ugly summers. He no longer knew how old he was.

54

Louisiana–New Jersey–Virginia
1968–1970

*I*t looks like Ali's out of the picture for a while, Carney told him the next day—still stripped of that dang belt for draft evasion. But if you show good on your upcoming matches, we can probably risk putting you in with Joe Frazier. After that it's history, sonny.

Jude hardly heard. He boxed but didn't follow boxing. Carney said it would be the money he needed to retire. He'd become thin in recent months, the bones of his face prominent, his eyes yellowish. But Jude could think only of Louise's belly, a line down it like that on a peach. The girl was gone. She was bright and strong and beyond his grasp.

One evening they walked the familiar lane between grown-up ditches and fields, a few pecans along the way, the shells of previous years in the gravel.

I know you're not happy, Jude, she said. I can feel it. You don't hardly speak and I don't expect you to, but . . . I am just trying to understand this. Is it because I'm pregnant—*que je suis enceinte?* Or is it me?

He watched his shoes scuff in the dirt.

Peut-être j'étais . . . I don't know . . . just lonely, she said. *J'ai pensé* . . . I thought I knew.

They came to a farm where they'd walked often. They passed the gabled plantation house at a distance. The night sky shone in the groomed pond. Near the barn he smelled horses and fresh alfalfa.

She paused. I love barns, she said. It's the lofts. I wished I had one when I was a kid.

The bay doors were open. A horse nickered and stomped somewhere inside.

Do you want to go up? she asked and looked at him. Her eyes shone. He regretted having ever met her.

T'es trop grande.

Non, she told him. Women used to do a lot pregnant.

Just inside she found the ladder. She tested the rungs and began climbing. He stared at her thighs, then followed.

The vaulted room was half-full, bales stacked along the ceiling. She lowered herself on one, and he sat next to her. If he'd never left Québec, he'd have been a farmer or a fisherman. He tried to think of what he was. A boxer. The muscles of his shoulders coiled.

It's normal to be afraid—*c'est normal*, she said. My grandmother once told me that accepting love or having a child is like accepting that you're going to die.

In the drone of sawing crickets something scuffed in the rafters, the sound followed by a resonant birdlike fluting. As she spoke she leaned close. She smelled of cut grass and the sweet soil in the roots of pulled weeds. Listening, he felt as he had leaving home, forcing himself towards a dream of sunlight that came only in flashes, knowing already that what he'd loved was dead. A pale shape moved in the air, and it took him a second to realize. It was an owl swooping, its spread wings catching the ambient moonlight. Louise called his name sharply. He struck out and the bird and his hand appeared briefly joined, and he struck again and it fell too softly onto the hay.

Jude, she said and took his hand. Blood shone darkly on her fingers where she touched him.

When he returned to the club and Carney saw the swelling hand, the torn meat of the palm and the gouged muscles, he just stared.

Well, he said. I guess I was pretty close to retiring.

They went to a doctor this time. After the sewing and the shots Louise gave her own treatment. Carney cancelled a few fights. Watson was concerned, his face red, the hair at his temples wet. The club hadn't been drawing. Some thought it wasn't competitive enough, others no more impressed with the white brutes than with the blacks.

The next night Carney died in his sleep. It was probably his heart. Maybe a stroke, the doctor said. No reason for an autopsy. Jude felt cut loose.

Those next days he stayed with Louise. He couldn't grasp the loss of Carney, the only constant in his life for the last seven years. Carney had just appeared, ready to take him in. He'd hardly asked questions, yet had chosen Jude's age and name, and neither of them had considered it—Jude desperate and half mad, Carney too used to the unexpected. Boxing, he'd once told him, is a world of what you can't see coming. Here today, gone tomorrow and sometimes good things, too. You can't make nothing happen. It's all got to be in you from the start.

But Jude had never fought for himself, except perhaps on that windy day when he'd met Boss at the clothesline. He'd fought for his grandfather or Isa-Marie or Carney, and now he wanted to understand what his reason was. He closed his eyes and tried to calm the pain in his hand, but he could grasp only loss, that he'd wanted to fill empty spaces. All that he'd loved had been there from the beginning and was gone. He saw no other choice but to fight and, fighting, to get himself somewhere where things were supposed to be better than before.

Three days later at the club he answered the phone. A man with a Jersey accent asked him to confirm a booking. You got it in you, kid?

Okay, Jude told him. Later, Watson, still sweating, offered to be his manager.

Those Garden fights do pay, don't they, he said. Both seemed to have forgotten the ballooning hand, the penicillin shots. Louise said it didn't want to heal. There's a spirit to everything, she told him, even cuts and scrapes. 59

The night after his injury she'd had a neighbour's boy climb into the barn rafters and bring down hatchlings. There were three of them, covered in down. She fed them grubs. Jude sat on the couch and feigned sleep. He'd tried to make love once after his injury, something he'd wanted in the night, but his hand had throbbed and he'd stopped.

Those weeks before the fight he didn't train.

You can't box with this for at least two or three months, Louise told him. He looked at her fawn irises, her lips. *Écoute*—listen, Jude, don't be crazy. You'll ruin your hand.

He studied his thick, corded fist. He couldn't understand how anything had cut through. He took to not answering her. He went days without speaking.

I was lonely, she told him. *J'étais seule.* I couldn't let the girl in me grow up, and you looked scared and alone. I didn't care you were white. *Ce n'était pas important.*

She waited to see if he would reply. When he didn't, she put his hand in a bowl of infusion and stood to leave.

I have others in my life, she said. *C'est assez.*

He'd never noticed anyone, but now that he was around more and the baby was due, the others became apparent, young black women, wiry men who passed without looking, as if they, like himself, couldn't figure out why he was there.

That Thursday, on the way to the airport with Watson, Jude gazed at the passing subdivisions near the city. There were a few clouds like strawberry blossoms in a deep blue sky and, on a cement driveway, a girl waving in the sunlight to someone he hadn't seen.

60

In New York he fought an Italian. The man attacked sloppily, had sticky feet. Jude didn't use his right hand. His heartbeat alone made it ache. He dodged and jabbed. The commentators said that though Jude had a powerful left, did he think he could take a seasoned opponent with one hand? They said he looked like a man practising his jab in the gym. The Italian landed a few mean shots but Jude took these lightly. It had never occurred to him that someone might knock him out or really hurt him. When the scores were tallied, Jude had landed far more punches. The Italian was in sore shape, and the judges agreed that Jude's was the stronger fight. The sportswriters claimed this insistence on the left was an act of defiance, of what, they couldn't agree.

During the match, Jude's stitches had torn. Back in the locker room he was sick. The wounds that refused to heal had opened. He wanted to slow down. Carney had been right to die.

Jude told Watson he would hang on to the money, maybe wait a year. Watson sweated, tried to make him see the possibilities of boxing left-handed. Jude barely heard, distant with pain. The next day, when he returned to the

club, padlocked chains and signs from the bank were on
the doors. Only a note, from Watson, that the club was
ahead of its time: People aren't ready for the plan. Watson
had absconded with the money from the fight. As for what
Carney had left, a few days after the funeral, his son,
Champ, a flat face Jude had never heard of, had shown
up with a truck, loaded everything and left. Jude agreed to
his last fight. Later, in the booker's office, contracts scattered on the desk, Jude struggled to make sense of all
these words. He recalled Isa-Marie writing his name for
him to trace, and he signed where he was told.

The contender was Leon Brown, big bucks, another
undefeated on the fast track to the heavyweight title. It
was impossible to play him the way Jude had the Italian.
After Jude took a beating in the first round, he tried to use
his right but it hurt him more than it did his opponent.
He felt the stitches split, the glove growing heavy. By the
sixth round the referee was on the verge of calling it
short. Jude's face was swollen, his lips ruined, one eye
shut, and Leon had taken just a few mean shots. Jude's
right shoulder was tired, the glove a solid weight on his
hand. Only when Leon delivered five driving punches,
his guard down because he was sure the fight was over,
did Jude strike. The soaked glove was like a stone. Leon's
head snapped back. Blood ran along Jude's arm, sprayed
the audience that leapt up, unsure of what had happened, of who had died. Later the rumour was that Jude
had struck hard enough to break his hand and Leon's
jaw. The papers picked it up. In the locker room the doctor cut the glove away as if it was something living,

revealing the embryonic fist. Jude collected his money. It was more than enough.

62   He'd been given painkillers and hadn't eaten in days. Louise had told him the baby was a girl but he didn't go look. The hatchlings were growing, lifting startled gazes at all who passed. What do you want to do now? she asked. The pills made his stomach raw. His throat burned each time he burped. *Dormir*, he said—just sleep. Her expression softened. From the way she looked at him she cared what had happened to his face.

He stayed in bed, his hand plastered into a club. Sometimes she lay next to him though she soon got up to breastfeed or do chores or walk in sunlight. He didn't approach the cradle with its mobile of beads and feathers.

I used to think I had to heal everyone, she told him, not checking to see if he was awake or listening. When I grew up, things were bad, but we weren't so poor. My grandfather—my mother's father—had a lot of French blood. I think he chose my grandmother for her beauty. I felt guilty for not being raised like other coloured people. I didn't feel coloured . . .

He lay there. She went to the crib and lifted the baby, a bare tinge of honey. He felt something odd, a spark of memory, those summer days coming down from the fields into the cool shadow of the house so that he could see Isa-Marie in her room studying Bible passages. He waited for Louise to go out to the garden. At the crib he tried to control the trembling in his good hand. He

lowered his swollen face. He wanted to touch his daughter, to bring his cheek to the calm, sleeping child.

That night he got up. He dressed and went outside.
His fist ached. He'd taken three painkillers. The summer
dark was hot and impersonal. He wondered briefly where
he could go and be just another man. Thinking of the
tiny girl, he was afraid that he might stay.

Fields were mowed and fragrant, and as he walked,
the moonlit roofs of farmhouses and a few lights floated
out across the dark. Eventually the road dipped to
another. A dog ran to a mesh fence, huffing and half
barking, then fled back into shadow. The moon set,
stars filling up the sky. He entered the deep ruckus of
the forest.

Where would he be if he continued? Back to that wild
self in the mountains? Again he tried to recall what his
people had understood about this place. On his way to
boxing matches, he'd seen dozens of cities, but his trips
had been all bustle and rush and busy streets, and there'd
been no way to stop.

Above the thriving night sounds an engine
chugged. At a slight rise, headlights fanned into luminous dark. He stood, conscious in stillness of humidity
and the sweetness of bloom, the ranging shadows out
along the road. The truck pulled close. A knocking
came from within.

Need a ride? a voice called with the rounded vowels
of a black man. Jude opened the door. The cab light
didn't come on. He climbed inside. The truck pulled forward and after a while his eyes adjusted to the faint glow

63

of the dash. The driver was thickset, his face fleshy and boyish. The truck hit a bump. The whole thing rattled. Seat springs creaked.

Where you going so late? the man asked.

I don know, Jude said—Mobile. It was the first reasonable city he could name, a place where he'd once boxed. His money and ID were in the trunk of his car.

That's a long ways away. Mobile.

Jude stared ahead. He considered saying something about his daughter. The well of headlights stretched out before them.

You okay? I seen your hand.

I . . . Jude hesitated . . . I am wid a black woman.

The man tilted his head. Sounds like a full-time job.

They drove a while longer in silence until, as the truck rounded a bend, something moved at the side of the road. The headlights kicked back, catching in the folded shadows of antlers and a dark eye. Jude braced against the dash.

Neither spoke as the man turned the truck around, one headlight dead, the other aimed into the ditch. He reached under the seat and took out a knife. They walked into the grass edging the road. The deer's breath rasped in its muzzle.

Somebody maybe will hit de truck, Jude said.

One antler was shattered, and the man approached the other carefully. He was large but nothing compared to Jude. His eyes were golden under the headlight. He took the good antler and pulled the head back and cut the buck's throat. Its eyes bulged. It tried to stand and died.

If you knew how often this happens. Like the Bible be saying, he told Jude, his accent exaggerated now—like the Bible be saying, this is a rich and plentiful land, always sending me sweet food. He paused. And you with a black woman. What you running from?

Whatever had been in the buck's eyes was gone. The man crouched and lifted a leg. He worked fast, sawing. Then he rolled his sleeve and slipped his hand in. He jerked his arm upward hard. Intestines spilled out. The smell was familiar to Jude, like that of home-made soap.

The man cleaned the knife, then stood and studied the buck's shape in the weeds. Jude touched the warm metal of the truck. He thought of lying in damp grass beneath the power lines and the way Louise lay back and lifted her hips, and his stomach ached to think another man might see her body say so much.

I am okay here, Jude said.

Now listen, the man told him. He gave Jude a long look, then nodded to himself and bent to lift the deer. He was dressed in slacks and an oxford. He glanced up at Jude and waited. Together they put the deer in the back of the truck.

He cleared his throat. I sure can't take you to Mobile. I can take you just a ways. Sweat beaded on his upper lip.

I am okay, Jude told him.

The man walked around to the truck door. Throw a stone, he said as if singing, and you'll hit an answer in Mobile. He looked at Jude before he got in. The single headlight cut up along the trees.

For years Jude would recall walking that night home. He'd understood that whatever Honoré had dreamed would not be found here. He returned to the house. A photo near the crib showed Louise's mother, chin lifted with pride or practised stillness, a braid on her shoulder like a bandolier. Because of the age or artificiality of the image her cheeks shone white.

Louise was sleeping. He was careful. He went to the owl cage. With his good hand he opened it and took each soft stirring body and crushed it. He took the baby from the crib and wrapped her as gently as he could. He never considered that she would cry, and she didn't. His hands shook and whatever steady pang of emptiness and loss faded and he was a huge gentle man holding her. He went to his car and started the engine and left.

He drove through what remained of the night. The next day he stopped for milk and fed the quiet newborn. He couldn't keep from looking at her. He was determined to take no risks. He would do it right this time and go where Honoré had told him. By morning he crossed out of Delaware over the long, low bridge to New Jersey. It was summer and cloudless.

The first days were difficult. At a bookstore he bought everything on babies. Unpractised with words, he studied the pictures, mostly of women breastfeeding. Not knowing what Louise had called the girl, he named her Isa, and she watched him with indulgent, even patient eyes. He bought her formula and new clothes, pullovers with sown-on feet, a yellow sundress. He paid a woman at a daycare to help him, telling her his wife had died. He ended up staying in a motel until he found a house to rent in New Jersey, a few streets up from a good neighbourhood. Though the rooms were cramped, the paint was new, and he could carry Isa down and see the big houses with their lawns and pools.

67

The feeling of wonder never left. He'd soaked and stripped away his cast so that he could place her on his gnarled right hand that was almost as big as she was while he fed or cleaned her with the other. Often he thought back to that year in his youth when the aunt had come with her children to live with them, the feeling of joy and the expectation of joy. But though Isa remained a calm, watchful baby with eyes lighter than her mother's, there were still the inexplicable weeping nights when he held her in his torn hands and sat in some too small chair not knowing when this pain would end. And there were the explicable cries too when he put her in diapers and accidentally jabbed her hip with the safety pin. One day he realized he didn't know her birthday, and so he picked a date, sometime in the weeks before he'd taken her.

Afraid of being found, he bought loafers, chinos and a blazer, and he lied to his neighbours about his name. Ey dere, he said, I am William White, which they, conscious of his absent wife, took for a makeover of Wilhelm Weiss or some such thing. He was even invited to a potluck. He held Isa and stood among his neighbours. One was a Hungarian, another a Pole, all awkward out of overalls. He drank a few, stared at the TV, said, Well okay, good night. He didn't know he was supposed to bring a dish. They never invited him again.

Though he had money enough, alone with Isa he tried to understand what would fill the years. Walking the wealthy neighbourhood, he saw men in suits heading for the train station on chilly mornings or returning, reappearing on the patio with sons and pigskins. Jude thought of the black man who'd picked him up in Louisiana, of that brief ride through dark woods. Jude hadn't wanted much, only to carve out a life.

That winter passed painfully slow. He bought a TV, a chair, a mattress. Isa was always in his arms, asleep as he watched episode after episode, as he tried to decipher books on how to raise her. The only instruction he didn't follow was to visit the doctor. His fear of being caught outweighed this recommendation. Louise appeared in dreams. She smiled as if they'd always been together, or slept deeply with her palms turned up, as though dead. When he woke, the array of houses beyond his bay window looked like a child's model circuited by an electric train. Often, nightmares of Isa-Marie's lost bones mixed with others of Louise's rage, the blue-jacketed men and weaving lights. She must be looking, must regret not having learned more than healing and midwifery from her grandmother. Briefly he wondered at giving birth. Louise was barely more than a girl, and he considered how she had suffered. He decided never to think of her again and gradually this lie against his emotions became truth and he didn't. But at times the split nerves of old fights jangled in his body, and lingering in sleep he felt her fingertips on his forehead, healing that wound, holding him there.

On the first warm, flashing day of spring, he began to walk. He didn't consider distance or direction, just plodded off with Isa in his arms, her bottle in his pocket so that he could pause on a park bench or the steps of some municipal building and feed her. He'd grown a beard and hadn't cut his hair. On the street, people paused to see him. Day after week he walked, always surprised to see the sun fall so quickly through the sky. Soon he sat her on his shoulders, these moments cast into her first memories, fingers in the red hair that she wore on her legs like a blanket or buried her arms in against the wind, avenues of sloping lights, city dusks and far off the skyscrapers of New York like a basket of jewels. He walked with a boxer's hunch and held her feet so that even when she slept, she stayed on his head. It was like some story from the curé's book, the wandering, the year passing into summer, autumn, ice crystals at dawn on the windows. He bundled her in clothes and scarves, carried her like a pod in his arms so that she blinked at snowflakes. Spring again and they went farther, crossed on bridges beneath metal girders, through interlaced sunlight and into Manhattan. He gazed at pretty clerks through shop windows, his looming reflection scary, the small girl laughing, her hair a halo of curly brass, a rein of his own in each of her fists. Into Brooklyn and Queens where black folk looked at him with silent respect for his ugliness and strength, for the simple joy on his face. Back out, Palisades Boulevard, Englewood Cliffs and Fort Lee, Edgewater, and home again at some lost hour, their empty house. To sleep briefly and leave. Unable to exhaust himself, he followed the river, kept the heaped city at the corner of his eye, the traffic across the water on Henry Hudson Parkway. Guttenberg or Weehawken, passenger ferries and again the ranked city. The branches of Central Park against those high, glittering buildings. Street lamps ran on. City dusks lit the river. Isa wore a sun hat, a mysterious thing she would still have years later.

Then one afternoon a police car followed slowly for ten minutes before it sped away. He realized through some fog of motion what a sight they were. He thought of the woman at the daycare who'd helped him from time to time. It was a miracle he hadn't been caught. He feared loss, heard doors close at night, prowling motors. He went to the window, then looked back to where Isa slept in the blankets. To lose this love, this simple silent world and all that streaked within him was too much now, again.

In the bathroom that night, he stood before his inexpressive features. The face held so much violence, and he wished he could ask it what he was doing here or could do, but he'd reached the point within failure when it is no longer possible to ask. He'd failed with Isa-Marie and boxing and Louise and even here, in the place his people had sought. All that remained was the tenderness of his child.

The next day, before dawn, he packed the car and fled. He travelled south through New Jersey, into

Maryland, Virginia, three days stopping in small towns, reading local papers for some idea of what next until he found a job on a horse farm. There, he was given an apartment above the carriage house and an allowance, and he could sit Isa in the sun while he worked. He saw that it was possible to be content in these quiet hills, mucking out stalls, watching evening long on the pastures and thinking, when he could, nothing, absolutely nothing at all.

71

Virginia
1970–1988

His name was Jude again, Jude White. He dressed in work clothes much like those of his youth, and the manure he shovelled was no different. It amazed him how easy it was to be absorbed by the country. Occasionally he heard people mention Ali or Frazier, and he thought of all he might have had. He never spoke of boxing, never set foot again in a gym. He hid behind his beard and gave his attention to the horses and his daughter. About daughters he didn't know much, but about horses he'd learned a fair amount from his grandfather.

Though Isa had been born into an America in the throes of Vietnam, she sensed not war but the eclipsing presence of a strength that cast its shadow, like, she mused as a child with her dinosaur cards, a pterodactyl. As she grew, Jude became more a mystery with his blazing hair and eyebrows criss-crossed with scars, his twisted and swollen hand keeping him up on cold nights. He was mostly silent, speaking French and English distantly so that she learned to mumble, I've gone English in the head, or to say, *câlice, ciboire* and *tabernac*, words interchangeable with *fuck* and *shit* and *goddam*, all of which she later used working with horses.

With time she came to sense her father's moods, the way the sky exerted its weight and slowed the world, a storm beyond the horizon. He'd be sitting, brooding, then go to the woodpile, upend a piece and swing the splitter until the raw fissures of his old wound cracked, uneven chunks tipping, wobbling where he stood them, making the maul ineffective, jarring his grip, blood now streaming. Winter was the worst. She couldn't imagine what he was thinking, couldn't see his tears or the hand bleeding onto the frozen earth as he crouched among scattered pieces, wanting to disappear.

Jude himself hardly understood his moods. He feared them and loved Isa fiercely. The first time she was sick, seeing her cough in bed he stood over her, trembling, trying not to yell. Glancing up, she saw this fear as anger, not just the part of it that was. He cranked the thermostat, brought a space heater and heaped her with blankets until after a day-long sweat she got better.

Eventually she learned to make herself small, and this worried him—this girl with all the threats of weakness. Shying away, she didn't understand what else he might want. But love lingered, a memory of something that wasn't quite either of them, those city walks, the way she'd held on to his red hair, or these fields, the sun through the stall door when he put her in empty feed troughs as he worked, and the soft, fragrant muzzles of curious horses brushed against her.

74

With time he left her to herself. He cooked a steak each night to ensure health—steak being among her first words. Steak, he said when he set it before her, a peppered, bloody chunk of meat. It had been a rough transition from formula, but she'd done all right. When things got complicated he deferred to the farm's owner, Barbara, who did what she called precision work, grinding aspirin before mixing it with orange juice, removing ticks or splinters. A rawboned woman, she'd come to Virginia from Scotland as a girl and had taken the farm over from her father. She hadn't married but seemed content and still spoke with a lilt. Isa had spied her in the house with men, more often with women, doing what she knew to resemble Breeding. When Isa asked why she'd never married, Barbara told her, I love horses— men would just get in the way.

Once in the slatted light of a stall Barbara removed her shirt for Isa, revealing two flat breasts and on her back, when she turned, the print from a horse's kick like the mark of a secret society, the skin there papery and strangely hollowed.

It's beautiful, Isa told her.

I know, Barbara said and put her hand on Isa's head, reaching her nails through the thick curls to scratch her scalp. Isa closed her eyes and purred.

75

Years passed with the speed of sameness, but at the first signs of Isa's puberty Jude withdrew. He got up to wiggle the coat hanger on the television when she spoke, or went straight outside. Barbara answered her questions about these changes by comparing her to a horse, which made it all seem not so bad. But Jude saw these new sunny looks, the way Isa stood at the mirror and brushed her curls or chattered with the men who boarded horses. He wanted to clobber everything, the horses she petted, the men who breathed on her, the women whose hair she practised braiding. Isa-Marie was there, the colour of frost, alone in school, alone on the road where the young boy had brought the poems. Jude walked away. Isa had survived this far. He recalled his grandfather's drinking against the pain of loss. He bought a dozen bottles from the discount rack, drank by will until it became habit, intent on incapacitating Isa's greatest threat.

Days fell from haze into oblivion, Jude never quite awake until his first drink, then working in that window of clarity. Occasionally he recognized a presence in Isa, as if her mother were looking through those intelligent eyes, seeing what a fool he was. But with his drunken midnight rages Isa's innate wisdom gave way to fear. Over the years some reel of logic told him he'd done what he'd failed with Isa-Marie, even as he blinded himself to Isa's inevitable loss. In his sleep he heard names in the harsh voice of his grandfather: Gaspé, Cap-Chat, Les Méchins, Ste-Anne-des-Monts, Rivière-à-Claude. He no longer had nightmares of lost bones and Louise's anger. He dreamed northern air, the St. Lawrence like bedrock, wide, wind-scarred water that decided the bend of trees, the sinuous road. He woke, gasping in stillness.

As Isa grew she went through elaborate rituals at the mirror that involved not makeup or admiration but the careful construction of a face that might have been her mother's. Her pale lips were a mystery, as were strange marks on one hip. She had Jude's lashes but more than this a scar on her nose seemed of her father, from a time when, four years old, she'd bothered him while he was splitting wood. Wanting to be fed, she'd stood too close, and a piece of wood struck from the block had glanced off her face. She'd cried, and he'd mumbled, I'm sorry, I'm sorry. She'd been afraid, seeing his look, that the cut was serious. He'd painted her nose with iodine from the veterinary box. Barbara had said she looked like a clown, but that had failed to make Isa smile.

Once, in the school library, she found a book on cannibals, and of everything she'd read this stuck with her, the information that—beyond rites of passage and manhood—they ate others to absorb power. She pictured looking into a cannibal's eyes after he'd eaten her and seeing a flickering light. What had happened to her mother's power when she'd died? Had it billowed like a sheet on a clothesline and drifted off, red dust behind

a passing car? If she'd eaten her mother, would she be
smarter and stronger and know whom she would
be someday with more certainty than the school aptitude
tests offered: librarian, secretary or technical assistant?

A few times, Isa had heard Jude mutter about uncles
and siblings, a grandfather's strength, wharf fights and
work in the fields. She'd heard French enough to understand it, even to speak it. Before holidays, when
classmates talked about family reunions, she was jealous.
What had happened to the relatives Jude described? Now
when he drank, she learned to time her questions so that
he'd talk. She listened inexhaustibly: fights, blizzards,
men who, because of Jude's mumbled delivery, seemed
like vagabonds. What he told her was at times so outra-
geous—siblings given to neighbours, uncles who
became old men overnight—that she doubted him.
Characters appeared like titans, grotesque within the sin-
gularity of their power. But gradually she saw the
workings of a better world, where everyone belonged.
She felt even a vague pride, that she'd descended from
hardier stock. She signed out an atlas and showed Jude
the map of Canada. He pointed to Québec. But where?
she asked, and he banged his blunt finger on the
province, the village not marked and, in his memory,
only a name, wind and fields and water.

But the question she asked most often was that which
had haunted her the longest.

Who was my mother?

He grumbled and waved her away.

Autre chose, he said once, nothing more.

———

By her senior year Isa was the tallest girl in school—taller even than most of the boys. She was sturdy and tanned from work, but popularity had a lot to do with clothes and attitude, and not only size but dreaminess and farm attire set her apart. She believed that in the place where Jude came from everyone was like her and that she would have to go there if she hoped to marry. Though she announced her plans to attend university, and her teachers encouraged her, she dreamed mostly of writing in a journal late into the night, of suffering like Jane Eyre. She loved the way the voices of women characters spoke into silence.

She didn't apply to university. Jude was in an accident. The tractor hit a hole and, drunk, he was thrown off, his legs run over. She stayed to take care of him and even when he was limping around, she couldn't picture him cooking his lousy meals. Barbara, who, by mere presence, had seemed a parent, also required help. Once able to punch a stallion to make it go weak in the knees, she'd had her own itinerary of heavy drinking and was in a similar state of dependency.

I might have fired your father, she told Isa, but he did his work well enough and fast, and I figured he had the right to get back to the ugly business of drinking himself to death. In fact he may have inspired me.

Jude had been convalescing, mixing whisky and pills, asleep or incoherent days on end.

He's useless now, Barbara said, but he's part of the farm, and anyway we've got you.

Isa let this sink in. The horses were her responsibility, the money once paid to Jude now given in an anonymous envelope. Her life was spartan, her room nearly empty, one photo on the desk—a girl dressed in Jude's farm clothes, leather boots to her knees, sleeves like wings. She couldn't recall the occasion, only that Barbara had taken it.

79

Summer chores eased into autumn, winter. Then the busy spring. She did her work, took the farm truck to the store, to the pharmacy, ate lunch with Barbara as they watched the few milky channels on the house TV. She told herself that horses were the love of her life. Alone in her room, done with the day, she perused Time Life books about ghosts and mysteries.

After his accident Jude aged terribly. He was haggard. Hulking bones showed in his frame, shoulders like knobs in his undershirt. His head moved as if on a spring. He recalled Hervé Hervé walking through the blustery sunlight to the wharves and the work that was the mechanism at the centre of their lives. On an August day Isa came in from the heat for a drink. He woke on the couch and saw her at the window.

Isa-Marie, he said. He stood in the unlit apartment. He hobbled towards her.

Sunlight through the window made the room seem dark. She backed away.

Isa-Marie, he repeated, *je m'excuse*. He hugged her and pressed his hands along her back with such an ancient strength she could barely breathe.

After that she avoided him. She locked her door at night. She hated the gassy scent of liquor and couldn't understand why one day he'd started drinking. She was twenty and didn't know whom to confide in, and she considered prayer. What little she knew about God she'd heard at school. She imagined Him as a voice like the weatherman's. She knelt in a stall where she'd replaced the straw. Dust motes hung like sparks in bands of sunlight, the summery odour all around her. She wanted freedom. But closing her eyes, trying to word the terms of her release, she felt herself verging on an act as real as violence, as if she might be capable of wishing Jude dead, and she stopped.

Afterwards she walked through fields and the dumb wheels of daisies, trying to forget her chores, to hold just the sky, pale and wide and empty.

A week later Isa saw a Jaguar parked at the barn. The driver was a thin elderly man, slightly effeminate, with sad, drooping lips that he nervously touched. He had faded brown skin and almond eyes and particularly black lashes. His hair curled loosely.

Excuse me, young lady, I'm looking to buy a horse, he said in a voice that she couldn't quite place, Southern though and stiff.

What kind of horse? she asked, thinking she'd have to get Barbara up.

I don't know. I thought maybe a Tennessee walker.

Oh, she said, you'll have to talk to Barbara.

He stared, his eyes big, his smile like on a toothpaste box. His teeth were square and perfect despite his age. Do you work here?

I live here, she said. He narrowed his eyes and lifted his chin. On the farm with this aging man in lapels she found it hard to believe that it was the late eighties.

Is this your dream? he asked. Horses? Many girls love horses.

No. I don't know.

He tilted his head. No, or I don't know?

I don't know, she said.

She told him a little about herself, that she liked to read but not what, and that she loved horses though she hardly thought about them when her work was finished. Suddenly wary of revealing how paper-thin her thoughts were, she agreed to show him the horses that were for sale. He confessed breed wasn't as important as beauty and that he could return when Barbara was more disposed.

What's the horse for? Isa asked.

He hesitated, then told her, Aesthetics. He described his farm, how he thought a gentleman's farm always looked good with a fine horse, maybe two so one didn't get lonely.

What about shelter and food and exercise? she asked, impressed by his concern with aesthetics.

Maybe I would hire a girl to come take care of them.

Because he was old, she wasn't worried. Though he barely reached the height of her shoulder, she felt like a girl and talked like one. His name was Levon Willis, Pronounced Live On, he told her, and in the course of that day, walking the pasture, she learned about his farm and big house and his hobbies: reading and contemplation and self-cultivation.

I used to want, he said. Now I think.

She so enjoyed the conversation that she looked forward to his next visit. She never mentioned him to Barbara, and he never asked about buying horses again. He was a harmless old man, she decided, kind and intelligent, and surely from someplace far away, where a person could look with trepidation at a grazing horse, extend a hand and say, I would like to pet it.

Only when she asked how he became rich did she feel briefly unsafe, as if he'd admitted to being an ex-con. He told her the story of his farm, passed down for generations through his family, and how for years he'd barely been able to pay the taxes but couldn't bring himself to leave it, not knowing where else he might go. At fifty he'd come to hate the meaningless work. He reduced taxes by putting most of the farm into scenic easement. He sold his livestock and machinery, and he began charging locals to use his land as a dump for construction materials. He burned what he could in the fireplace and sold scrap to salvage yards. Those years he progressed from reading the encyclopedia—Something I always meant to do, he confided—to books on investing, which, with patience, he was soon attempting. One winter a local demolition company was hired to dismantle and ship away the beams of a defunct water mill whose foundation had washed out. Local legend had it that the young George Washington had kept an office in the basement

of the original structure when he was surveying the picturesque town, which was a short drive from the capital
and also bore his name. The beams went to a rich man's
weekend house in Middleburg, but the trash and shattered wood, everything that had fallen from floor to floor,
lodged there for centuries, ended up at Levon's. The
crew cleaned to the stone foundation and brought frozen
mounds of dust and splintered wood, nails and glass.
Levon hadn't wanted this sort of trash, but in the spring,
raking it out, he found his first coin, an 1802 Draped
Bust. Within the week he had several more, all of that
same period. He purchased a metal detector and discovered coins in value from forty dollars, such as the 1943
Steel Penny, to others—he could list them—1853 Liberty
Gold Coin, 1917 Mercury Dime, 1877 Indian Head, 1839
Coronet Head, 1808 Half Cent, and many more, among
them a dozen other Draped Busts, minted in the first
decade of the eighteenth century, each worth thousands.
The demolition, he supposed, must have knocked them
from their hiding place. He read up on numismatics and
eventually sold them to collectors. He invested in a spree
and not long after a few of his stocks soared. His years
were numbered, and he was fashioning the life that
remained as he thought it should be.

Isa listened in awe. She, too, she told him, had felt she
was different. She explained that her father was French,
that she'd never known her mother and that she'd been
an outsider at school.

Ah, he said, it's that dark French blood you have. I
had wondered.

It must be, she said, considering that this might be the *autre chose*, the other thing—Dark French. She repeated it softly, testing it for suitability.

On his third visit Levon seemed nervous. He always came at the same time, and it occurred to her that no one else was ever out then. She'd been telling him about her frustration, her feeling of being trapped. She was surprised to hear herself use the word.

It's a prison. I must have been meant for more than this, she said.

Levon hesitated, then told her he had a proposition in mind. He cleared his throat and brushed fingers against moist lashes. His tone was businesslike.

You are unhappy, he said in his over-articulated English. You would like to see the world. Now this might sound odd. I am also a lonely man. I have been so for years, and what I have with you may be my first true friendship. I have thought about this. It is possible only because you are too young to have presuppositions. You accept me. What I would like to propose is a business marriage though not really business. I feel a great love for you, but I know I must repulse you. I am very old. So what I offer—what I propose—is that we marry. There will be no consummation. No sex, he added, looking away, as if unsure whether she understood. You can travel, go to university. I will pay for it. I will even buy you horses. It's as you like. But it would be a friendship to carry me through my last days. Will you say yes?

Isa felt as she had with Jude when she'd decided not to go to university, that she had the power to save, only now there was the possibility of escape. She liked Levon, nothing more. He was short, skinny, and dressed like a very old man. He had a silk flower in a buttonhole.

All right, she said. But we have to go now and do it. His eyes widened. I mean, soon, and I don't ever want to come back. I don't want anyone to know.

She tried not to think of Barbara asleep with her scotch and water, Jude watching TV in a daze. People would be angry. The farm needed her. Jude and Barbara needed her. She would be fine if she could forget what she'd done and never see them again.

As planned it was an escape in the dark. She packed, wrote a note, then snuck from the apartment and walked out the gravel driveway. She tried not to think of Jude deciphering her words, his big, flickering eyes rolling back over sentences. This farm was the only place she'd known, and she feared now that every familiar scent or sound would remember this. Jude's drinking would be worse. He'd have accidents. She paused and looked about her, not sure she had enough courage. The lights of an airplane moved above a dead oak, its branches like nerves against the star-lit sky. She expected a sign, that some aspect of the world around her would indicate what she should do.

At midnight Levon met her in the Jaguar. He looked tired.

I don't normally stay up so late, he confided.

A few days later they were married. This, too, was businesslike, though she refused to change her name, having read that women no longer did and thinking it would break Jude's heart. Levon appeared annoyed. She moved into her room, the farm far enough away that no one would know where she'd gone. He kept true to his promises and bought what she asked. But soon she had the feeling, when he began bringing home Southern-belle dresses and insisted that they sit on the porch or walk in the evening, that she, like the sleek horse in the pasture, was for appearances.

God was frequently the topic of conversation. I often contemplate God, Levon said. Sometimes I think of spaceships and extraterrestrials, and this all seems important in the question of God. One of the pleasures of being married is sharing my thoughts. There was nothing worse than thinking about God alone. It was very lonely.

He could talk for days. This was difficult for Isa after so many years of silence. His age showed more, and he often wandered the house in a terrycloth bathrobe like a short, emaciated Hugh Hefner. They would lie on his bed, and he'd talk, a wise and ancient child. Then he'd doze, and she'd go about her day until she heard him calling.

There's a story I have been wanting to tell you, he said. I just wanted to make sure you understood me. Otherwise you might think it silly.

It was evening, and they were on the porch with their books. He had introduced her to many startling and philosophical works, his favourite on how the Bible was a record of extraterrestrials, how all holy scripture encoded a war in heaven fought by gods, really our superhuman predecessors who genetically engineered us. It was fascinating, she agreed. It made her want something to happen, aliens to arrive or a comet to crash into the earth. But as often was the case, he'd interrupted her reading to tell another story.

You see those woods? He pointed beyond his acreage, 87 down a slope to a collapsed stone wall.

Those woods, he said, have been there since I was a boy. The government owns them, I guess. No one really knows. There's a creek there, and across a ways a rather busy road, so if you go too far you see the trash people have left. But the trees are old and it's dark, quite scary.

The story he wanted to share regarded an evening when he'd been sorting his scraps and had taken a bucket of nails down, figuring they'd rust faster in water. He'd gotten only a bit into the forest when he saw the man and the girl. The stream was running high and loud, so there was no way they could have heard his approach. The man was tall and wearing a black suit.

He was incredibly pale, Levon said, the whitest man I have ever seen. The girl looked a bit younger than you. She had on a thin dress even though it was cold. She was lovely, and I couldn't help feeling for her. But it was late and the man was scary, very, very pale. They just stood there, minutes at least. His face was against her throat, and her head lay on his shoulder. He was so tall it didn't look natural. I watched them for as long as I could bear it. The girl appeared to be falling asleep, the way her hands started slipping down his back. I got frightened and returned to the house. I locked the doors that night.

Now I do believe in God and Jesus and the truthful-
ness of the Holy Bible. There, in the woods, I saw great
philosophical questions for the asking. If pure evil could
exist, then so could God. I went out every night after that
to look for the man, thinking if I could find him, then I
could believe in the deepest of ways. I've stopped going
since I have married you. I did not feel it safe, and I did
not want to leave you alone. But I think I should go
again. It took all of my courage, and I believe it takes all
one's courage to look for God. One risks finding nothing,
and one is always face to face with death.

The following evening Levon resumed his nightly
vigil, standing in the cool air off the stream, watching
the shadows. The story had unnerved Isa, and she'd
asked if he'd read the papers after what he'd seen. He
had, but no young girls had gone missing. Evil, he'd
told her, might not be so simple. She'd thought of
everything that had eluded her about her life, of the
way she'd chosen to save herself and run away, and of
what Jude must feel alone.

Isa had been living there several months when she
heard about Levon's nickname. She was at the general
store, and the clerk asked if she was the one who lived
with the Mexican.

The Mexican? she repeated.

Oh, I guess they just call him that, he said. I've out-
right forgot his real name —

Levon Willis.

Yes, that's it. The clerk chuckled. He's been called the Mexican for so long I forgot.

From this conversation and from what Levon had told her about himself, Isa was later able to make sense of the nickname. Levon's forefathers had been mixed, and he'd come out of the muddle relatively pale. The last of his relatives had died or moved away to become white, and he'd considered himself too black to marry white and too white to marry black. His entire life he'd stayed on the land rumoured to have been a slave's forty acres. He'd turned into something of a hermit, alone in a house built by an ancestor who'd done well, and which, in the years that Levon ran his dump, began to lean. Later he'd had a new one built and hired landscapers to beautify the farm. He'd dressed expensively, drove a Jaguar and kept to himself. It seemed only natural to give a man as inexplicable as this a nickname. Thinking of it, Isa wasn't sure whether she should pity him or be ashamed.

That fall, Levon bought her a Honda so she could attend university. She was old for a freshman, and she had no sense of what was popular or what other young people liked. Instead, she took an interest in her heritage. But when she tried to research the White family name, she discovered nothing like it in French Québec. She didn't know how it could belong to any family not English. Regardless, she practised her French and decided she would do a degree in that language. But even in this her frustrations grew, her professors not sure why she was interested in Québec's dowdy past, why she didn't want to study abroad in Paris.

Over this year and through the next, Levon changed little. His body was resilient, his mind active. He walked and read and talked until she began to hate him. The only questions he asked regarded her ancestry. Her igno-

rance about her mother concerned him. You could be anything, he said and looked at her carefully. Then one day he startled her.

Do you think it is right for us not to have consummated our matrimony?

Though she tried to appear calm, her sudden pallor was answer enough. He got up and walked away.

All that week he stayed withdrawn. They no longer talked in his bed. He dressed formally, with a gold watch and cufflinks and tie clip. He had gold rings on his fingers. Only when tired days caught him off guard did he shuffle about in his robe. Those weeks he appeared shrunken. He'd met with a lawyer, she knew, most likely about a will. Then gradually he came to treat her pretty much as before, though with a sort of watchful propriety.

Each month they saw one another less. When not reading, Isa walked the steep pastures. She cultivated an obsession with the past, sensing how, when she mentioned origins or repeated the stories Jude had told her, she became distinct. Through her unaimed tenderness she divined a lost family, the pleasure of winter nights when snow hushed the world and noth-ing could be done but wait. What of the mother he'd erased within his silence? How had he come here and fallen in love?

Sleep wasn't easy. She woke confused, thinking she was back in the room she'd known most of her life. With her eyes closed she had actual vertigo, a sense of falling or floating. She practised French until dawn, occupying insomnia with cassettes and films that left her with a feeling of sophistication and a Parisian accent of the 1960s.

part two

Virginia
April 1993

Isa turned twenty-five at the
end of a sopping April. The frostbitten grass had washed
to raw earth, and what flowers bloomed along the fence
were few and small. Five years now she'd lived there,
reading or making excursions to the university on the
long, twisted beanstalk of the highway. She brought
back books with a ritual sense, carried them into her
home like the fruit of a day's labours. An upstairs room
had become her study, and she cluttered it, knew every
volume crowding walls floor to ceiling. Though she'd

taken a degree in French, minors in history and litera-
ture, she wasn't interested in teaching. She liked old
words, immortal ideas. She had no love for money or
the young.

With time she and Levon had learned to coexist, and
while he rambled—extraterrestrial civilizations, theories
of Atlantis and invisible planets—she put on silence like
an armour. These, what she was reading, were the real
books, and she knew him to be a dabbler. But he possessed the longevity of a fool, and though each year he
thinned, withered, hardened, he stayed true to the pho-
netics of his name: (lĭv) (ôn). He might become some
stiff, scary looking thing from an import shop, bought on
a whim, propped in a corner, but he would never stop
talking. And while he diminished towards that far line of
horizon, Isa crowded the foreground, and the
unsketched space around her she filled first with words
and history, then food. Soon Levon's savings went as
much to annotated additions as to jars of marinated
artichoke hearts, caviar, fancy breads and cardboard
boxes loaded with pastries, chocolate-filled croissants.
Her horses sighed under her weight and stood spraddle
legged, sad eyed and mugging about like old dogs.
She rarely rode them though occasionally took them
on walks.

But evenings she spent in regret, looking out at the
dark landscape, the seismic shift of night. Downstairs
Levon watched TV and reviewed his stocks. The econ-
omy was bustle and freight, and he was doing well,
laughing at sitcoms. Only her size loosened his grip. She

was no longer the proud possession, the showpiece, and though occasionally he still sat next to her, he appeared to consider her less as a romance than as a frontier he might someday brave. But well after he'd put away his lunar charts and star maps and gone to bed, or on those evenings when he stood by the stream, waiting to be killed—when he'd come up the pasture and nodded his still-living head in her door before retiring—she sat in her study and, quite simply, wished. She read her favourite poems as if casting spells, testing how she might sound in another place or age. She put her books on the floor, cleaned dust from the shelves, alphabetized. She cried. One night she saw a bud of firelight on a nearby pasture.

The next morning, as she was leaving the house, she noticed a few ratty camping tents on the adjoining property. They'd been pitched between the trampled bull's-eye of a bonfire and a brown van, a trail of crushed grass behind it, JESUS painted in bulky white letters on its sides. And that afternoon, as she was leaving the grocery store in town, she saw the van again, parked at the far end of the plaza, near the Blockbuster Video. A small crowd had formed and a man dressed in black like a Plymouth pilgrim and wearing a dark, wide-brimmed hat was preaching. She opened the hatch of her Honda and put her groceries inside, then crossed the parking lot. The man gesticulated. His white, uneven hair bristled at the brim of his hat. Because she stood a head taller than the crowd, she had an easy view. He looked at her, then again, his glance tangible, like a spark from a wire. She thought she had imagined it, yet, in the moment, she was certain he'd recognized her. He watched her even as he spoke.

And Jesus will walk among you, he was saying, as he himself began to walk into the crowd, . . . and touch you one by one on the shoulder . . . , which he did just then with a gentleness unlike the strength in his voice, . . . and you will kneel and take his name into your heart.

Soon so many were on their knees that those still standing looked conspicuous and crept away. Though Isa had missed the sermon, she knelt, caring nothing for religion but curious.

We are men of God, he said. We are carrying God's message to a country that is losing its values, to the children of a country polluted with sex and drugs. But we depend on you to want us, to tell us to continue our mission saving souls.

He gestured towards the van, to where a man sat on the asphalt with a boy on either side. Then she realized that the boys were in fact young men, that the man between them was enormous.

The message of the Gospel can go deep, the preacher said as the giant stood.

With a grabbing sense in her gut Isa felt his size. It was a bodily motion like gravity. He appeared even larger because everyone was kneeling. He wore jeans and a sweat-stained oxford, his face broad as a shovel, dark, uneven sideburns halfway down his jaw. His chest and throat and even the backs of his hands were matted with hair. He ducked his head and glanced about at the crowd.

Barthélemy, the man said, is an orphan from the far north. As a boy, he was found wandering in a blizzard. His parents had frozen to death, and only because of his sheer size and strength, and truly because of the will of God, did he not perish. For years no foster home would take him. He terrified people. Nor could he speak. The doctors believed that the cold had destroyed his vocal cords or that perhaps the sheer terror of seeing his parents die shocked him to silence. When I met him he was still illiterate. I took him with me, and it was with the Bible, the true Gospels of our Saviour Lord Jesus Christ, that he learned to read. This child had been seeking a home, and as a man he has found it in the word of God.

Until then the crowd had seemed interested enough, but now all eyes were riveted on the giant, who stepped forward hesitantly, each of his hands as big as a man's head.

Barthélemy will go among you, the preacher said. He will seek your aid so that we may continue our mission.

The preacher then took a felt bag from his jacket and handed it to the giant, who withdrew slightly, looking about him, his fear evident now, his eyes wild. Isa could see the waves of compassion and worry pass through the crowd.

Be calm, my boy, the preacher said. Seek the Christian generosity of these good citizens.

Isa was amazed that such things still happened. People emptied their wallets. The way the giant pulled his mouth taut with nervous fear and averted his eyes as he held out the bag touched her. Only when he stood above and she gave a few dollars did she sense the element of threat, that she might not want to know what this fear could become at its limit.

98   Afterwards the preacher began a lengthy exhortation. The two young men at the van went among the audience to whisper prayers. Isa received and repeated her own, then another, that she composed just then, invoked silently, eyes on the giant.

It rained that evening, the fire in the nearby pasture extinguished, and when the storm had blown over, insects began to whir and faint steam rose from the ashes into the washed and moonlit sky. Isa sat on the porch. Levon had come up from the stream early. His vigil was occasional now, more a means of keeping appearances. He'd spoken a bit about new research on biological engineering that disproved evolution and showed that every plant and walking thing had been concocted then set upon the earth as if into a showcase. She listened, smiled, and he'd gone to his room. His light had clicked off exactly one hour after the official time of sunset, Most appropriate—he liked to say—and most in concordance with the circadian rhythms. She'd waited, then went in and took two bags of soft cookies from the cabinet.

The road glistened, and as she crossed into the pasture, her pant legs grew heavy with moisture. One of the young men was coaxing the fire, and the other, who'd taken out a guitar, tuned and strummed it and sang softly, Jesus. Then Barthélemy appeared from the direction of the forest, his arms loaded with sticks.

Hello, she called as the fire lifted into the dead wood. The man in black wasn't there, just the two who'd gone among the crowd offering salvation, one seated on a plastic bucket, the other on a stool.

Hello, they both said, and God bless and words of thanks as she passed the cookies around, and one sang—For you, he told her—about Galilee. But Barthélemy sat in the open door of the van and began reading a dog-eared Bible though every cookie passed his way he devoured and only when she stood near and held the bag did he look up with a veiled if not indifferent expression.

I'm Isa, she told them.

My name's Andrew, said the guitarist, a young man with a pale complexion that the firelight made hysterical. He introduced Morris, the other, then pointed and said, That's Barthélemy. We're in town a week or so. We'll be giving a service this Sunday at the Lower Macedonia Baptist Church. You should come.

I will, she told them. What you're doing is wonderful. Well, goodbye.

They waved and said God bless again, the too-happy, Archie-faced youths, though the giant only glanced at her, a little too long but still indifferent.

That Sunday the man in black—Reverend Diamondstone, the minister introduced him—gave the most compelling and strange sermon Isa could have imagined, of archangels and wrecking balls and his personal narrative of failure and loss and finally salvation, how he'd gone from being a sinner to a man of the cloth. He described a dream in which he ascended a narrow mountain road in a '57 Chevy convertible. Everyone in the car was laughing so hard they could barely lift their heads.

Then I looked up, he said, and a black eighteen-wheeler was coming down that road, honking and honking, and we didn't slow down and there wasn't even space to turn around. I woke up to honking and saw the archangel Michael. I knew then that I had to leave my wealth for the kingdom of heaven.

The rain started again, drumming the peaked roof. It lasted through the barbecue and singalong and a congregational jubilance that undoubtedly would have finished in starlit prayers without it. Musical instruments and Bibles were held under jackets, white bread soggy, gravy thinning out, the fire hissing like an angry audience.

Though Isa tried to manoeuvre herself near Barthélemy, he stayed close to Diamondstone, who—she could no longer believe she was imagining it—kept an eye on her tack from buffet to picnic table to church porch when the rain battered down, drilling up the loose earth. She might have gone home sooner had she not seen that the giant, too, was watching.

All the while the congregation gathered around Diamondstone, and she wondered at his power. She could sense him as if he occupied a place of greater density, drawing her gaze the way a black widow on a wall once had when she was cleaning. His prayers were at times long and Byzantine, at others as simple and hokey as country songs, but they always seemed appropriate. He had the ability to slip formidable lines into casual conversation:

In the future we will turn to Jesus as our one sure link to the past. Otherwise we will get lost in the chaos of time.

The fear is not that the earth is invaded by inhuman aliens but that with technology we become those very insectlike invaders ourselves.

Hearing Diamondstone's coreligionists applaud, Isa doubted her intentions. She was educated, falsely married, and Barthélemy was mute, perhaps half mad and among loony spiritual company. She'd had crushes, once a towering professor, another time a linebacker whom she later saw with his girlfriend propped on his knee. She never passed big men without glancing up, in department stores or in the street, measuring their heft, matching them against her own, against Jude's. Barthélemy dwarfed any she'd seen.

Only once was she able to get close to him. The clouds had temporarily blown past, sunlight glittering in the late-afternoon sky as if vast and invisible cobwebs had caught raindrops. The congregation strolled the lawns, discussing politics and the Rapture and even guns, though the preferred subject was the eternal sanctity of marriage and its threats. Diamondstone was working the crowd like a socialite, and she wondered what he had to gain. Then the thundering of an approaching storm resonated in the earth.

Her patience was almost exhausted. She'd been listening in on one circle of conversation after another and
decided it was time to leave. But the rain came suddenly,
and while others ran for the porch, she found herself
beneath the shelter of a gazebo. A second later
Barthélemy stepped in next to her.

The downpour shut them off. It was as if they stood in
a round windowless room. He opened and closed his
hands, his musty odour not unlike that of dry fields in the
first minutes of a long-awaited rain. He no longer
appeared afraid, his gaze distinct and measuring.

I'm Isa, she said.

In the dark of falling water his eyes shone. Her head
barely reached his shoulder and she considered the
size of a heart that would suffice for such a man, that
could push blood through so much body. What might
it want? Desperately, she wondered what to say or do,
but he was already turning, stepping through the wall
of rain.

That night Isa woke suddenly. She'd been dreaming
of Jude though had no one image of him, just a sense of
immensity, the way someone might recall the mountains where she'd been born. It took her a moment lying
in the quiet dark before she realized that something else
had roused her, not the dream. The night was calm and
without wind, and she listened until she heard the low

creaking of the porch beneath her window. She got up and looked out. After a few seconds a swatch of shadow shifted near the driveway. A black bear was nosing around the shed where she kept the trash. Often enough in the spring, they came down from the moun- tains, hungry after the winter. She should have known it was this to begin with. But lying in bed again, an hour passed and it was one in the morning before she admitted to herself that she wouldn't be able to sleep. The horses had begun to whinny in the pasture, and their skittish hoofbeats were oddly loud. She got up and dressed and went down to the porch. The bear was gone, and she crossed the yard to the stables. Only when she neared the door did she smell the heat of another body. She'd been downwind of bears after hibernation, and she thought of this. Then all at once she placed it.

What do you want? she managed to say, trying to catch her breath.

He came into the moonlight, the edges of his eyes pale.

I'm Isa, she pronounced carefully, considering whether she should run. She pointed to herself.

I can speak, he said. He took a step closer. His face was calm enough. I'm sorry I scared you.

Her heart clamoured in her chest. What are you doing here?

I followed the stream up. I've been going into the forest for firewood, and I found a path here. I really didn't mean to scare you.

It's okay, she said. Her fear had given way to a sudden, breathless sense of hilarity. And how about French? Do you speak French?

No.

Did . . . did your parents really freeze to death?

No, he said and glanced off. Then they just stood, not quite looking at each other.

How long have you been . . . with the reverend? she asked.

A year or so, he told her and moved his lips as if to say more.

Isn't it sort of dishonest to pretend you're a mute French orphan giant or whatever, just to make money?

I am a giant. Besides, it's for a good cause.

She tried to think of something else to say, but the way he faced off conveyed no interest. She was afraid he was going to leave. Are you hungry? she asked. Regardless, she herself was, insomnia and adrenaline being powerful aperitives.

Barthélemy, she said.

Bart, he corrected. You can call me Bart. Yeah, I'm hungry. I mean, I guess I'd eat something if you did.

Will you wait here? I'm going into the house. I'll be back in a few minutes. We can eat in the stables.

Inside she felt giddy, as if she might any second burst into laughter, though she was terrified. From the pantry she took two family-size bags of corn chips, three jars of salsa and three cans of meat ravioli. From the fridge, half a block of smoked Italian cheese and a crispy baguette spread with congealed garlic butter. As quietly as possible, she put it all in a grocery bag. She added a pan of tiramisu, Parmesan and a two-litre bottle of root beer. On the way out she snatched a bag of chocolate-covered coffee beans.

Crossing the yard she began to feel ridiculous with so much, but half an hour later she wondered if she should return to the kitchen, only a little root beer remaining. The tack room had a hot plate, and she'd heated the ravioli. She was surprised at how easily they fell into conversation as they began to eat.

Where are you from? she asked.

Maine. Originally from Maine.

She waited for a question from him, but when none was forthcoming, she told him that she'd studied Maine's history for part of her graduate research.

Do you read a lot? he asked.

She smiled. Any excuse is good.

What are your favourite books?

Nervously she named a few, trying to think of something that wasn't a classic.

Oh, he said. I used to like Thomas Wolfe and Kerouac. I've only had the Bible for a while now.

Watching him eat, swiftly, unconsciously, his gaze abstracted, she thought of Jude, but unlike Jude he talked almost dreamily. In the light of the single lamp, she studied his heavy features. He seemed too docile for his size. His hair was roughly cut, and she wanted to touch the sharp, clumsy angles made by the scissors and feel them against her hand.

He didn't quite tell what he'd done in his life so

much as enumerate his journeys and the books he'd read. It seemed he'd been everywhere, and getting lost in the names of places he repeated himself, as if he'd travelled the same routes many times. He rambled, and

she considered that, having to pretend he was mute, he'd stored up years of conversation.

In turn she told him about her studies, the history she'd carefully reconstructed. It always surprised her how easily she described events that hadn't touched on her life though had no doubt affected the arrival of Bart's family in the U.S., which she told him. She said that the French population of Québec would be double what it was if it weren't for the emigration. She didn't say that she'd never been there.

In the quiet of the stables, horses shifted in the stalls or nickered softly. She'd paused a long time, not able to mention Jude by name, afraid that somehow all this would lead back to having to talk about Levon.

Bart cleared his throat. In a subdued voice he said that he also liked to read about history. He told her that his mother had given him books about the Roman Empire and ancient Egypt when he was a boy, and how he'd believed those places still existed far away.

Are you close to your mother? Isa asked.

He didn't speak at first. Sometimes, he said, I think I read just to know what a person can become. I probably don't really understand what I'm reading. I just think about what it means to me. It's like I'll have to read it all over again later, when I know more.

She wasn't sure what to say. They sat against the wall.

The digression had surprised her. She looked over. He held his clenched fists in his lap.

Yes, I've thought that before, she told him, and she considered how the simple perceptions from the mouths of strong men sound like poetry.

Sometime in the night Bart said he needed to go before his absence was noticed, and she invited him to come again the next evening.

He looked at her and hesitated. Okay, he said, but not so late.

That's fine. My . . . my father doesn't bother me when I'm in the stables. I'll meet you here. I'll bring better food tomorrow. But don't let my father see you. He's particular. Vaguely, she explained something about intolerance.

The stables were set back in the trees, the tack-room window facing the mountains, and Isa felt confident that Levon wouldn't notice anything. They'd lived too long oblivious to each other, and ever since the stables had been built, there'd been an unspoken agreement that only she went there. The tack room had a kitchenette and a couch with a fold-out bed. It had been her refuge, its scents and familiar silence recalling the life she'd abandoned with Jude.

Isa's lie about her father weighed on her all through the dawn and into the next day. She managed to sleep a little in the afternoon, and later she drove an hour to the built-up suburbs closer to D.C. She stopped at several restaurants and bought party-size trays of take-out sushi, spicy Thai soups in styrofoam tubs and bags of spring rolls as well as burritos and chicken enchiladas and chili. At a bakery she chose a lemon meringue pie, a sponge cake and a half-dozen chocolate eclairs, after which she stopped at the grocery store for soda and milk. She took it all to the tack room in a feed bag.

The rest of the afternoon she sat in her office and tried to read, but she could hardly focus. What did she want from Bart? And why was he with Diamondstone? Oddly—amazingly—he hadn't mentioned religion.

A little before eight, she went to the back of the stables and sat under the cover of trees. When he arrived, it was from the stream, on the same forest path Levon used. He appeared nervous and wiped his sweaty palms on his pant legs. Only as they ate did he fall into the mechanisms of conversation.

I can't believe all this food, he told her.

The spiritual life must not be so . . . epicurean, she said.

He didn't comment on this, but the food vanished quickly, stacks of greasy tins and styrofoam containers on the floor, fingerstreaks on icing-smeared cake cardboards. After half an hour of crunching and slurping in a general silence of suppressed belches, they both sat back and rolled their eyes and moved about to get a purchase on their innards. Bart held a two-litre of pop. He twisted the cap and let the air hiss out. He tightened it, swished it a little, let out the fizz. He took a drink.

How did you meet Diamondstone? she asked.

I was living in Louisiana, he said and swallowed. I had a guitar and amplifier and I sold them so Diamondstone could have his van repaired.

He sounded proud, she thought, like a child, but he furrowed his brow. I was thinking about everything you said about your family and my family. It's true, you know. My mother's name was Amy Beaulieu. It's like you said—a lot of people in Maine have French last names.

Does your family still speak French?

Some of them. My grandparents do.

Isa wanted to say something about Jude. She wished she hadn't lied.

Kerouac was from Maine, Bart added. I read somewhere that he spoke French before he spoke English.

The rain had started up again, its patter filling the space. Isa had the sense that she'd invented Bart. She was seeing him just then, his expressions as he spoke, lines and angles from ruddy flesh. His clothes were worn and stretched, and she could imagine them holding his shape after they'd been washed, the way Jude's had.

Is everyone in your family as big as you are? she asked.

Some, he said. My father was. My mother was pretty big too. I remember when my growth spurts began. It hurt more than you can imagine. My mother told me that if I took a bath the pain would go away, and maybe because I believed her, it did. It got so I even thought standing in the rain would help. She'd go out with me and we'd just stand there.

Do you miss your family? Travelling like this?

He looked up. My mother's dead. I never really knew my father. I mean, no, I never knew him.

Isa had the impression that he'd only just considered sharing this and might not have. She thought of everything she'd never told anyone.

I was raised by relatives, he said. I'm still in contact with them.

He seemed to be hovering about his words. He cleared his throat. Mostly, I remember my mother's tattoos. She'd let me copy them on paper. I remember when I learned I had a soul. I pictured it like a tattoo of blue light under my skin.

Isa wanted to tell him about Jude but instead she spoke of her mother. I don't know anything about her, she said. My father wouldn't—won't discuss her. The only thing that he told me was that she was . . . something else.

Another race?

No . . . No, I don't think so. I mean, I think she was dark French, perhaps.

Bart was watching her. She'd sensed the shift in his interest, this, too, like a memory of Jude, a sort of atmospheric pressure.

When I was a girl, she said, I used to try to understand what a mother was. I would stand at the mirror and I thought that if I looked long enough, her part of the reflection would stand out and I might see her.

Wind carried rain across the roof in a slow pulse.

Why didn't you know your father? she finally asked.

Bart remained silent a moment longer. My mother left him when I was born. I saw him just once, in the street when I was with my stepfather. We were Christmas shopping, and a gigantic homeless man started following us. A few days later, for what seemed like no reason, we moved to North Dakota. It took me years to find out that the man had been my father.

Bart cleared his throat and forced a cough. Diamondstone, he said, once told me that only pain seems real because human love can't last. The only power greater than suffering is God's love.

Oh, she said . . . How did your mother die?

She died when I was nine . . .

He paused for so long that she realized he wasn't going to add to what he'd already said. He looked about. I should go.

Now?

The rain had lulled. It was as if they were coming back to themselves, their voices returning to these big, tired bodies propped unevenly against the wall.

I take walks, he said, but never this long. The others will notice.

He stood and went to the door. Can I see you tomorrow?

Again? she said with pleasure though she'd meant, Of course, and she said it now. Yes. Of course. I'd like that. I'll bring more food.

For a while after he'd gone, the stables felt empty. Then, little by little, the usual gravities exerted themselves, the horses and the stalls they occupied beyond the wooden partitions.

She pushed herself up. Her body felt old. Outside she

was surprised that so many lights were on at the house. Levon never stayed up this late. As she was climbing the steps, she saw him in the living room. She stopped. He was seated across from someone else, and though it was obvious, the black, the pale complexion and white hair, it took her a moment to realize. Diamondstone held his hat on his lap. He was looking out at her, smiling as if she was expected.

Isa, Levon called when she opened the front door. Please come in here. I want to introduce you to a gentleman who has been telling me the most fascinating things.

Virginia
May 1993

When Bart arrived that evening, Isa expected him to know everything. The previous night Levon and Diamondstone had stayed up talking long after she'd gone to sleep, and all the next day Levon had sought her out to tell her bits of their magnificent discussion—Magnificent, he'd repeated, a truly magnificent connection. A profound meeting of two minds.

He said that Diamondstone had recognized him as a recluse and a seeker of the truth. He explained Diamondstone's various outlandish interpretations of the man at

the creek. Isa wanted to cry, not because of the absurd-
ity of all this but because of how pathetic their lives
were—Levon's loneliness, his desire to speak to another,
to anyone.

114   And us? she asked, feigning ignorance about
Diamondstone. Did he ask about us?

No. Why? He simply wanted to discuss God's mission
on earth and the many ways He sends His messages.

Fantastic, Isa later repeated to herself at the wheel of
her car, even while composing the dinner that she wasn't
sure would be consumed—Fantastic, she hissed, this
being her replacement for Magnificent. At some point in
Bart's listing of his travels, he'd told her that he'd loved
everything about Louisiana, especially the cuisine, and so
she drove forty minutes to find a Cajun restaurant, where
she ordered a survey of the menu: jambalaya, dirty rice,
beignettes and alligator piquant, seafood gumbo and crabs
Lafitte along with two gallons of crawfish boiled with corn
on the cob and small tender potatoes red with spices.
Fantastic, she told the boy at the counter when he offered
to carry the boxes to her car, though she didn't believe Bart
would arrive to help her eat it.

But when he did, he never so much as mentioned
Diamondstone. At first she was suspicious. She didn't
trust Diamondstone and wondered how Bart could not
know about the previous evening's visit with Levon. As
they ate, their conversation progressed from where it had
left off. He talked about his family, and she found herself
reluctantly trusting him and soon telling what little she
could about her own just so he would continue. Despite

herself, she liked his stories, how on his lips English became an old language, filled with sighs and long pauses. He described the close-knit clan, the holiday gatherings, the quiet childhood. He'd told her he was twenty-six, but he seemed older.

They still want me to move back, he said. That's how they are. And maybe I will, later.

He explained how, when he was a boy, he'd believed that he and his parents had moved away because of his mother's tattoos. His stepfather had been an account- ant, an overly conventional man who'd mysteriously married Bart's mother when, after a year in Boston, she'd returned home with dozens of tattoos and a new- born. Among Bart's earliest memories were the frequent requests that she dress differently. Skimpy tops showed a black Tinkerbell on her breast, barbed wire on her arms, a heart of melting ice in blood-red flowers on one shoulder.

My stepfather didn't complain so much when it was winter, because she wore a lot of clothes, but . . . Bart paused, gazing at the dark stable rafters.

There was . . . she had a tattoo on her wrist. It was the one my stepfather really hated. It was just black writing, but it said Barthélemy. That was my father's name. I thought it was mine.

Isa knew that if she told him about Levon or Jude he would understand. But the history that she'd explained the previous night meant nothing—colonization and set- tlements, wars and capitulations. None of it touched her life: the overshadowing Church that would proclaim divine mission, that Québec was to maintain the true Catholicism otherwise lost in France—agrarian society and work the vessels of preservation. Still she found herself again talking about how the French-Canadians ended up in New England. He, in turn, described summer festivals and singers who came from up north, the snippets of a language he'd heard from his grandparents.

I haven't been to my mother's grave since she died, he said suddenly. Isa was growing used to this, the way he switched subjects. She tried to decipher the paths that his emotions took.

I always thought about going back, but I never did, even when I was in Lewiston. It was as if I couldn't. I can't explain it.

Is that where you're from? Lewiston? She knew the name from the history books. It had been important though the details eluded her.

Yes, he said. She realized she'd interrupted.

After a brief silence, he again began to speak of the winter when he and his stepfather had seen the homeless man, how they'd packed and moved. A week later, in North Dakota, while his stepfather was at work with the car, his mother walked to the store for bread and never came back.

He paused, distracted as if seeking through what he'd said. He told Isa he'd spent nights trying to remember, to close his eyes and see the homeless man, the shabby green military coat with latches like curtain hooks, the hems curled like fallen leaves. His relatives had claimed to know nothing about him. Bart could never quite recapture the face, the wet, breathless mouth with the moustache growing into it, the hard, dark eyes. During his travels, he'd studied the homeless men he'd met.

Telling all this, he repeated details often. He spoke with such clarity and immediacy of emotion that everything seemed recent: the loaded U-Haul, the drive west, nights in cheap motels. Hours after Bart's mother had walked to the store for bread, his stepfather had returned home pale and stricken. He ignored Bart's questions and closed himself in the bedroom with the phone. Only in Maine did Bart's grandfather tell him what had happened—that she'd been hit by a snowplow. Before that there was the silent drive: fields lost beneath snow, cities distant in updrafts of mist. Strangely these were the details Bart couldn't leave off—an earth that repeated with the mauled ridges where the interstate ran through, towering signs of Exxon and Citgo, fast-food restaurants and warehouses on bypasses. It was burned in his memory though he could recall no names, only emptiness, repetition, that nothing could be still in the rushing country, the weaving chains of tail lights, blue plains sinking along the dark curve of distance.

Tentatively, Isa put her hand on the muscle of his neck. He smelled of sweat. She kissed him. Her thoughts were spinning. How should this be done? It was both clumsy and too careful, and it amazed her that she'd never kissed anyone before, had married but hadn't so much as dated, too big or lonely or unable to speak to another. Was love something she'd read about so often she'd come to believe in it? She held her face to his shoulder. She unbuttoned his shirt and moved her hand over the soft hair of his chest. She uncurled his fingers from a fist and brought them to her. They breathed against each other's necks. She'd never considered this as it would be, the touching or how quickly it would all become automatic and strange, the weight of their bodies, layer upon layer of muscle and fat. She wanted to let herself stop thinking. His face was against her shoulder, his eyes closed. She put her fingers in his hair. Afterwards he lay next to her. The stables were strangely silent.

They got up and in the cool dark they walked down the centre aisle. A bulb hung above a concrete slab where she washed the horses. She held the hose, chill water running to her elbow. He looked like a man from another time, his coarse features, the sideburns, the nose with its split lobe, heart-shaped. Water flashed in his hair, along his neck and shoulders. It captured the light of the bulb so that it seemed she was looking through his skin at the bright shape within.

They returned to the tack room and lay on the mattress that she'd taken off the fold-out bed and put on the floor. She thought about where this could lead. The room seemed cavernous with the rhythm of their breathing. She closed her eyes. A breeze moved in against the humid air. She dreamed of setting out: she and Bart in dark glasses, a plaid suitcase crammed with cash.

They stayed there until the grey pre-dawn gave the smudged window glass a battered look. She thought maybe he'd fallen asleep, but his eyes were open. He was gazing at the ceiling.

Later they dressed and she walked with him down the pasture. The stream rushed, and they stepped through the shadows to the collapsed stone wall where Levon often waited. She thought of what Diamondstone knew and that she hadn't truly questioned Bart's duplicity, the evangelical show, the mute giant.

My heart's not in the religious stuff anymore, he said abruptly as if she'd spoken and he was simply responding. Because of the way his voice fell away, he sounded as if he might cry.

Maybe it's more than that, she told him.

Somehow she knew he wouldn't affirm this, that he wouldn't be able to.

Trying to think of what to say, she realized that she'd dropped her suspicions too quickly—the magic of the giant appearing, fulfilling her longings. She was already seeing this in the past. She told herself that she'd survived being Jude's daughter, survived Levon even and her guilt, though she'd aged too quickly. Beyond the trees, the sky had begun to grow light. She thought of how you could miss the gravity of a presence.

The next morning, not long after Levon told Isa that Diamondstone had again been there the previous evening, Diamondstone returned. She heard their insistent voices through the floor and went down to the kitchen to eavesdrop, hungry with nervousness. She composed two clubhouses with chicken fried in the bacon's fat, tomatoes sprinkled with spices, yellow homemade mayonnaise with a pinch of cayenne whipped in. As she prepared it, she ate a wedge of cherry cheesecake from the wrapper. In the other room Diamondstone was trying to persuade Levon to join his mission.

120   This could be home base, Diamondstone was saying, a camp for re-education and training young minds. I have served my years, and God has brought me here. He—He brought me to you, a man who has lived alone so long in contemplation. How can I simply leave? Was all that you have worked for so that you can spend your days alone in a house, this house? Alone, in this house on this land that God gave to you, cultivating your wisdom for no reason?

And, Diamondstone said, and, forgive me for saying it, but I cannot help but see. With a wife who does not love you but simply lives off your wealth.

Fantastic, Isa muttered, suddenly ravenous and all at once knowing that Diamondstone had overestimated his rhetoric. Levon was greedy, and despite his fanciful words, the point of his life wasn't wisdom so much as appearance—to have what he could show, wisdom or wealth. And so, as she licked the spiced mayonnaise from her fingers and picked strips of chicken from the toasted bread, she waited for what could end only badly. It wasn't that she underestimated Diamondstone. She feared him even. It was simply that Levon's greed was a more tangible thing. It had the intensity of revenge, and to the people who, for decades, had called him the Mexican, a Christian living camp, in all its glory, would be ridiculous. Most likely Levon had already devised a denouement for his wealth, a disappearance or mystery. Perhaps he'd interred grand sums, pirate treasures buried around the house as on the shores of a deserted island.

When Diamondstone finally left, Levon was not in great humour. No doubt he'd seen something he might like in the portrait Diamondstone had painted. He refused to look at Isa as he went up to his room. Perhaps he was also in agreement with Diamondstone's assessment of her worth, though Levon was in no position to oust his one miserable companion. Still, she wasn't convinced the story had finished. Soon enough Bart would know who Levon was. Perhaps he did already. Perhaps none of this was absurd, the meals consumed in the stables while the grand questions of life and men's fates were determined in Levon's living room. The mute giant might not be Bart's only act.

She considered what meal she would make that evening, but nothing came to mind. She found her car keys and left the house, but halfway across the driveway she heard a cough. Diamondstone was standing in the shadow of an oak, his arms crossed.

Good afternoon, he said and glanced up past the branches at the sky. If you don't mind, I'd like to have a word with you.

It was odd, she thought, seeing him step close, how much larger she was, how, if she wanted, she could crush his bones simply by falling on him. It might solve many things, and what judge would find a towering, obese woman guilty of tripping—an act of God, if you will.

Diamondstone walked with her to the car and then a little beyond, as if both were aware that they needed to put as much space between them and Levon as possible. They stopped where the graded driveway gave onto a descending pasture, beyond which was the stream and, distantly, the van parked at the end of its track of beaten grass.

The boy tells me everything, Diamondstone said.

The boy?

Bart. He's very innocent. There's nothing I don't know. He's clearly in love. Nobody has ever showed interest in him before.

What do you want?

Diamondstone lifted his upper lip as he considered her, his teeth small and glittery.

I want you to help convince Levon. He's a fine talker. He'll talk all day. But he won't give so much as a penny to the mission.

He might not have as much as you think, she said, and as soon as she'd spoken she realized how true this could be. She hadn't shied from luxury these last years. She'd raided every gourmet-foods store within a two-hour drive, swiping away with his credit card. She knew Levon invested a lot but he must have losses, too.

Listen, Diamondstone said. I have no ambition to bring you to the love of God. I've spoken with Bart, and the educated are the last to be saved and the first to burn. But maybe your judgment will be more lenient if at least one act in your selfish life furthers the Saviour's mission on earth.

And if not?

Bart will find out that you're married.

Okay, she said, knowing already that she had no choice. I'll do it.

You will? The querying tone was barely discernible, his words sounding like an order but for a faint treble. He moved a finger along the band of his hat. The day was somewhat humid, the lulling breeze a premonition of summer, but Diamondstone didn't appear to be sweating. His skin looked cold, his sunken eyes no colour she could easily place. They gave her the impression of not having seen clearly, that she should look again. She'd never noticed that he blinked.

She got in her car.

Wait a minute, Diamondstone said. We haven't discussed—

It's as good as done, she told him and closed the door.

That afternoon she stopped at a Chinese restaurant and a steakhouse: sweet-and-sour pork, prawns and rice, ducks in foil, two surf-and-turf platters, lobsters and steak and buttered spuds. By the time she returned home, Levon was gone. He had a calendar of events on his office wall, and she checked it. There was a gallery opening in D.C. He'd been attending such things more and more, no doubt enjoying the aura of sophistication, and he always returned with decorative pieces—art being, he'd told her, the only truly sound investment.

When she met Bart at the stables, she invited him to

eat in the house and said her father would be away for several hours. She showed him the rooms, and afterwards, as she heated and set out the food, he stood at the window, silhouetted against the blue vista of dimming fields.

I can't imagine . . . he said though she couldn't make out the rest of his words.

She came to the kitchen door. What? she asked. I didn't hear—

I said I can't imagine having all this. A place like this.

She leaned against the doorjamb. She was going to ask why, but that was stupid—the tableaus of abstract art, the expensive couches in earth tones, the vases and Turkish rugs. Her first night there, she'd thought the rooms looked like pictures from a catalogue, and no doubt that had been the inspiration. Only in the morning, when she'd seen the farmland in the windows, had she felt she could live here.

Bart turned towards her. What are we going to do?

She tried to think of how to begin telling him everything.

I don't know, she said. We could go someplace together.

Slowly he faced back to the window.

Maybe, she said, we could live near your family.

I don't have money like you do, he told her. It isn't easy. You've never done anything but read books. You don't know how hard it is.

What is?

Life.

That's not true.

It isn't?

No, she told him too fast, listen. Listen.

She felt suddenly exhausted. She dragged a chair out from the table and sat. I lied, she said. She told everything then: Diamondstone's conversations with Levon and later, with her, in the driveway. She didn't pause for Bart's reaction. She continued: no longer the contemplated past, the vague economic reasons, migrations and mill towns, but the chaste marriage to an old man, the naive girlhood entranced by the willed age of a father whose recollection was silence.

No lights were on, and now, in the darkening room, Bart spoke. His voice had an odd quality, trying, it seemed, both to hurry, as if there were little time, and to slow in order to give an impression of earnestness. He repeated things he'd already told her, his mother's death, how he'd been handed off between relatives, that his mother hadn't been so close to the family.

For a while I lived with her younger brother, he said, in Louisiana.

That year had been a rare calm spell during which the uncle taught him to play electric guitar, Bart dreaming of being a musician. They'd listened to Motorhead and Iron Maiden, spending entire days flopped on couches, staring at album sleeves as if they were the spirals and symbols of Hindu mysticism. But the uncle had been in love with another man and had left a note to that effect. Bart never would have guessed. The uncle hanged himself. Then there had been foster homes and detention centres, and sometime during that period Bart had been taken with Kerouac's America. He'd envisioned freight trains running misted coastline, car trips into Mexico. It seemed the only way to redeem his life.

126 He paused on this, and she considered that these might be stories he was used to telling. He was twenty-six, and he'd been with Diamondstone little more than a year and from before that the only thing he'd clearly conveyed about his life was travelling. He'd tried to make that period sound like one adventure after another, at times down-and-out but always chosen: living in a rat-infested mansion that had been for sale for years or in a seasonal cabin on a frozen lake where he'd eaten icy canned foods. She'd enjoyed the stories, but what had brought Bart to someone like Diamondstone couldn't have been simple.

I had a lot of adventures, he said. I guess by now I've probably done more travelling than Kerouac ever did . . . But I had some hard . . . months. I remember once, I was stranded in the middle of Nevada. I slept for a few weeks in an abandoned dinosaur park, in the belly of a brontosaurus. I got so hungry I imagined I was a holy man in a cave.

From the way he chose his words she could tell that he wanted her to believe him.

I was homeless, he said. Things weren't always good. I mean, I wanted all that at first. I thought it would be freedom. I don't know. I guess I thought about my father a lot. It's just, when I met Diamondstone, I didn't think things could be better.

But I knew, he said—I know about what you told me.
I knew that Levon was your husband.

She was confused only briefly. Everything that Bart
was telling now was his justifications. He'd wanted her to
understand what had gone before.

We always do it this way, he said. When we get into
an area, we look for rich recluses. Diamondstone, Morris
and Andrew, they're all good at finding things out. And a
guy that everyone calls the Mexican, I mean, we heard
about him right away. It was just a matter of getting per-
mission to camp in the field down there.

He blinked slowly as if tired. She wasn't sure why he
was telling her this.

A lot of lonely rich people give us money, he said.

Have you ever seen it?

What?

The money.

He considered. No. I haven't. But Diamondstone
isn't bad. We're not pretending to be religious. He
always tells us, You believe, but you have to put food on
the table. People are . . . too greedy to give willingly.
But they'll go to God with lighter burdens and fewer
sins even if we were to rob them. But we don't. It's like
in Job—

Actually, she said, it sounds more like Robin Hood.

You don't understand. Diamondstone did a lot for
me. It's hard to explain. Whenever I tried to make my life
better, I felt guilty. It was like I was leaving my family
behind. And I did try to get jobs but look at me. When a
little man is angry, it's okay. When I'm angry, people see

a monster. And I was more angry than I can describe. For years. That stopped after I met Diamondstone.

But who is he? Where's he from?

She hadn't noticed the colour coming into Bart's face, and it startled her to think that he might cry. Slowly he pushed back his chair and stood.

I'm sorry. I wasn't pretending. He hesitated, then added softly, I'm as stuck in this as you are with your husband.

He walked out to the porch. His footsteps stopped. She didn't have the strength to stand or call him back. Then he went down the stairs and she was alone in the quiet house.

There had been luck in all this, she told herself later, that Bart had left and she hadn't tried to stop him. Levon had returned shortly afterwards. She asked where he'd been, and he told her he'd planned on attending the gallery opening but that his heart had gone out of it. He'd turned around on the highway. He stood in the hall, slight and stoop shouldered. He was wearing his best suit with the perennially flowering buttonhole, the gold accoutrements.

I can't stop thinking about my conversation with Diamondstone, he said. I'm not a fool. I know he wants my money. It just made me think. That's all.

He stood a moment longer, then climbed the stairs to his room.

Isa went onto the porch. Could love and fear exist

together, just one of many combinations, like greed and piety? Hadn't, for her, love and fear always been joined?

She was surprised to see Levon come outside. Without so much as glancing at her, he descended the steps. He walked almost gingerly as he made his way down the pasture. She watched until he disappeared. The moonlit bands of telephone poles hovered out across the dark.

How odd that what was animal, what was physical—simple attraction, lust—could draw two people so close. When she'd lain against Bart, she'd imagined telling him how similar their lives were: to be haunted by a family that was impossible to grasp or let go. His restlessness and contained energy was Jude's. But perhaps her fear was right, and Bart's stories meant more than she realized. Still, had she come so far from Jude, whose life could have been no better? How much might Jude have been able to tell if there had been someone to love him?

She went up to her room and waited for Levon to return so that she could go and find Bart. It frightened her to think she could be that brave.

She didn't know how long she'd been sitting when she looked at the clock. She counted the minutes as if to test the continuity of time. She went into Levon's room. She walked through the house, seeing—foolishly, she thought—it was so obvious—how afraid she'd been to give all this up for a life like the one that had shipwrecked her and Jude. She gazed from the porch. It was well past eleven, the sycamore by the well house invisible, the stone wall a faint border. Levon had never stayed at the stream so late. She sat until long after midnight, the spring air warm and faintly humid. Around one in the morning she went in and called the police.

Virginia
May–December 1993

Two police cruisers and an ambulance arrived not long afterwards. Isa spoke with an officer on the porch while in the woods below, flashlights swept in along the trees, catching across each pale trunk like a slow strobe. When she'd first realized Levon hadn't come in, she'd felt a twinge of relief, afraid only of seeing him brought up, dead of some natural cause. But the officers returned and told her they'd found nothing. She walked down with them. The older of the two, a greying man with a trim moustache, asked if she'd seen anyone around, and only then, with the cold bracing of nerves, did she consider the degree to which Bart was suspect. She explained the story, that each evening Levon waited by the stream. She tried to make it sound believable.

Excuse me, the officer told her, but that's absurd.

I know, but he believed in things like that.

The officer asked her dozens of questions. Why had she married? Who were her friends? He said he would look in on the farm where she'd been raised. She told him about the religious group living in the field. Later he radioed the information back. She made out the words *missing, yeah that guy, the Mexican, who would believe?* Another police car arrived as well as a red pickup with a few men from the volunteer fire department to help search. The rain had started again.

One officer had been to neighbouring farms, and he returned with descriptions of the religious group, which, he said, had disappeared. The older of the two asked her more questions based on this, and she told him only that they'd been around and she'd known them a little. His concerned, friendly attitude was gone. The rain had become a downpour, pounding the fields and house, driving in against the mountains so that the searchers gave up. He told her to lock her doors.

Keep a phone by your bed. God knows what this is about.

The next dawn she looked from her porch. The fields glistened. There was no trace of the van, barely even a hint of its beaten tracks. She heard a knocking at the back door.

She went slowly, not quite afraid now but tired. Bart filled the windows, his shoulders bunched. He was pale and soaked. She opened the door.

Diamondstone left me behind, he said.

What do you want?

I saw the police and I . . . I didn't know where to go.

Levon's missing.

She studied his face. A giant, she supposed, would always look guilty. She thought of Jude and the degrees of betrayal.

Look, she told him. If you didn't do anything—

I didn't.

Then okay. The police will be back in the morning. I guess . . . I guess we need to hide you.

She took him to the cellar, a low room with exposed pipes and insulation and heating ducts, a furnace at the centre. When she opened the crawlspace door, rust sifted from the hinges. Bart was sweating in the cool air, wiping his palms on his jeans. Dust speckled his forehead and the backs of his hands.

Wouldn't the attic be better?

You're too big. They'd hear you moving around. She handed him a flashlight. I'll be back as soon as they're gone. She tried not to look at him as she closed the door.

There was a larger search party this time, the entire volunteer fire department and various locals, though she figured they'd come mostly out of curiosity. When the forensics team arrived in the afternoon, whatever clues

D.Y. BÉCHARD

might have been imprinted in the mud had either been washed away or trampled beyond hope. She heard a man swearing about incompetent hicks. Others wandered the woods and fields, and the officers gave a quick look-see, they called it, to the stables and house. By evening they'd found nothing. All day, on the road, cars slowed past. She stayed in a chair and thought less about Levon or even Bart than how Jude would react when the police contacted him. She was stronger, and after so many years she would understand him better, perhaps be able to make him speak. She'd never let herself think about this, and now that she did, she was startled by how much she longed for it. She waited near the front window as the sun's light moved in and along the wall and faded.

Again the officer questioned her. She told him what she knew. Regarding Levon, she spoke of friendship but not love.

Diamondstone didn't have another name? he asked.

Not that I know of. Can't you track down the van?

The van, he said and sighed. This is a big country. You don't know how easy it is for people to disappear.

When he left, he gave the same warning as the previous night. He seemed disappointed that he hadn't found any reason to think she was guilty.

We'll keep an eye out, he told her. There's not much we can do now but wait.

It was almost midnight when Isa went to the cellar.

Bart's face was smudged, and she stood back as he climbed out.

I'm sorry, she said. She'd turned off the lights throughout the house and drawn a few blinds. Come upstairs. Quietly though. Just in case.

Tell me what happened.

He listened gravely. His breathing was laboured. Each time he wiped his sweat away, he rubbed more dirt onto his face. I need to get out of here, he told her.

We need to wait. Maybe they'll find him tomorrow.

I'll be blamed.

We can't do anything until tomorrow night. The police will be back soon. It's almost dawn.

I didn't do it, he said.

I know.

In the hour before sunrise they ate silently though neither was hungry. She asked if he wanted to take a bath, and he nodded.

In the end they didn't discuss what he would do. She went to the fridge and gave him some fruit and a bottle of water. He stood at the cellar door, wet hair pushed back from his forehead. She wished she'd dried it, but she was worried that the police would return or that someone was watching.

This might be long, she told him. He nodded, then stooped into the cellar to hide.

The police came in the morning and there were more questions and searches, and again, that night, lights out and blinds drawn, she went down to Bart. He said he'd lost track of time in the crawl space. He hadn't slept.

I need to leave.

I know. I'll take you somewhere.

She went to Levon's bedroom. There was a safe whose combination he'd had her memorize years ago when there had been trust between them. He'd kept ten thousand dollars of what he'd called crisis money—Not much, he'd said, but the banks have failed before. It's in the history books.

Isa gave it all to Bart.

You can wait for me somewhere. I'll join you as soon as things calm down.

Where? he asked, looking away from the brick of bills he was holding.

Go to Maine. I'll come and meet you.

In Lewiston?

You can call me every now and then, she said and touched his hand. Besides, you have family there. And this should get you—us through for a while. I'll bring more. Okay?

He wasn't looking at her.

Bart, she said. She tried to stand against him. Bart. Is that okay?

I should go. He sweated, smelling strongly.

Wait, she said. She told him what they should do though she knew it was humiliating.

He went outside and climbed into the hatch of her Honda. It was after midnight. She stood on the back porch. Across the pasture were the still figures of horses in moonlight. Realizing that she believed in Bart's innocence, she thought of how frightening it would be to return.

She drove more than an hour to D.C. At the station she let him out. They didn't touch. Loose queues mostly

of black people were in the hall below. Bart, she said and
he looked past her, then around. He lowered his eyes and
turned and hurried down the stairs.

The paper never mentioned murder, only disappearance. It ran a photo of Levon from years back that on
newsprint was grainy and too dark.

Barbara called the next day.

Jude passed away a year ago, she said, bless his soul.
He couldn't have been fifty. He got old so fast. We
wanted to find you. And you only two counties away.
Who would have known? We still have his ashes, bless
his heart. You should come get them. It would make him
so happy.

Yes, Isa tried to say and hung up. She closed her eyes.

She stood and went into her room and lay down and
stayed there until morning.

In the days that followed neither Levon nor Bart
seemed to have existed. She woke often to her own crying. She recalled waking in the barn apartment to the
sound of Jude calling out hoarsely in his sleep. She tried
to think of something tangible, his savage, scarred hand,
sunlight in his red hair. She slept entire days. Dreams
were glimpses of nameless avenues falling to distance,
those first urban skies as she rode on his shoulders, clutching his hair, the faces along the street lifted as if looking
at the sun. She woke to the full, silent moon and walked
outside. Whatever passing had been his was the quiet
enormity of nothing, and she gave herself to this shadow,

as if the pterodactyl of childhood had swooped low one last time and vanished.

The police came by again. She lied about everything, not caring or believing that any of it mattered. Occasionally, she felt guilty for Levon, that she'd brought Bart into their lives, but then she recalled that Bart and Diamondstone hadn't come for her, but for Levon's money. Otherwise, there were days at a time when she didn't think of any of this at all.

One afternoon, she drove to the farm where she'd been raised. It was in disrepair, weeds high, most of the horses gone, likely removed by their owners. When she knocked, Barbara called her in. She was sitting, feet on a footrest and wrapped in blankets, her change from strong and rawboned complete. Her face was red and swollen, and her hair had been cut so that it frizzed about her head in that way of older women.

Come in, she hollered. Come in. I'd get up to give you a kiss but they had to go one of these days, my legs, that is.

Isa went over and offered her cheek.

I mean, Barbara said and kissed it wetly, I can walk. I just don't like to. It's too much work. My feet get all confused. Something to do with drinking, permanent, you know. She looked Isa over and commented that she wasn't a little girl anymore. She talked a bit about the farm—Hard to keep it going, she said, and you so close, married to that black man? Her damp eyes focused briefly through her plastic glasses. You'll be staying, won't you?

Isa hesitated. How did he die?

Hell if I know. I didn't see him around for a week. I sent someone over. I suspect he starved or drank himself there. I mean, it wasn't anything violent. But who knows? Who knows? He couldn't hardly have been fifty and drank like a . . . like a . . . Anyway, after a week you can't always tell.

I understand.

But you ought to take a look around. It's been hard getting good help. I keep thinking about selling it. She wet her lips. But dear, I am sorry about your father. He was a good man. When he went, the police dealt with it. Then I called Mindy. Remember Mindy, the trainer? Right, well, we drove down to get his ashes. She liked Jude and used to think there was something sad about him, that he was probably in love. We went and picked up the box. It was terrible. I got the giggles. I don't know why. Mindy had bought these roses. Pink roses, I think. She said it guarantees a safe journey for the soul. I don't know. We got back to the barn, and then Mindy started laughing too. We were both laughing something terrible. She said how heavy the ashes were, what a big boy Jude was, and we decided to weigh them. We went into the feed room and used the scale.

Isa listened as long as she could. Where is . . . are they? Barbara had become quite red in the face, her front lip lifted like a rabbit's as if to breathe through her nose. She was clearly trying not to laugh. He's on the shelf in my room. I figured he could keep me company.

Thank you, Isa said and went to get him. There was

also a box with boots and folded clothes, the old farm rifle and some papers. In it she found several identity cards: Jude at eighteen, shaped like a gladiator. A driver's licence: Jude White.

May gave onto a windy, mild June. Honeysuckle sweetened on the fences. Now there wasn't even small talk at the gas station or country store. She was the Mexican's widow. A suspect, too. They studied her aloneness, surely eager to know what she would do, or else wondering why she didn't also disappear.

Unreal weeks gathered into months. The house became a roomy extension of the sky. There was something else she'd been thinking. She'd never paid her body much mind and gave herself fewer ministrations than she did the horses.

She forced herself to change clothes and drive to the pharmacy. She bought a pregnancy test. Home, she locked the doors and used it. She sat. Nausea radiated in her like a sun, though this was just fear. She tried to picture herself transformed. But she felt cut off, insubstantial, her entire life something she'd heard from another, about someone else.

Isa thought of Bart more and more. What she'd felt for him was gradually coming back to life within her. Perhaps she'd made peace with the possibility of his guilt so that she could reconcile her own. Or simply, she didn't want a child with a missing parent. She recalled how, as a girl, she'd imagined the family she'd never had. She'd reread the part of *Jane Eyre* when Jane leaves Rochester and wanders through the woods to find her true family. Bart's appearance had something of that magic to it. Perhaps desire was a form of prayer, and through Bart, the divine had economized, a two-in-one ploy, murder and love.

141

Though the police still stopped in every now and then, they no longer seemed terribly interested, and similarly, Levon's death had ceased to matter for her. But even in death he kept her. He completed her isolation. She sensed his piddling ghost browsing bookshelves, threading phantasmal arms through bathrobes. She read late to reclaim the night, but he hovered at her door, bereft of the gold he hadn't been able to take to the next world. She tried to banish him with fantasies of a new life, but only that immense shadow drove him off—Jude and all that had gone before, eclipsed even her feelings.

She told herself she needed to plan. She opened a bank account. She began putting aside modest amounts that she withdrew from Levon's account with a card he'd given her. She would meet Bart. She reminded herself of details, wondering when he would call. He's very religious, she said, not sure if she was trying to be convinced of his existence or his innocence.

Alone in her room for hours, she closed her eyes. An inaccessible region of her brain was constantly turning, thoughts dissolving into images as she verged on sleep. She tried to see herself as self-sufficient. What was she lacking? Philosophers had written that there was no unrealized essence waiting to emerge, that identity was actual and had to be cultivated. There would always be temptation to exist when another turned his eyes on you, to live for love or against tyranny, to find meaning as a victim. All this had appeared simple when her fight was to stand against Levon's rule, read eat write all night, think up something like poetry in the mountains. But with Levon and Jude gone, freedom was absence, and nothing, not even freedom, had meaning in itself. Bart still hadn't called.

142

July and August passed, mercifully temperate, hardly summer, it seemed, the rains still occasional. By September the evenings were cold. The answering machine received a few calls from professors wondering what had happened to her, mentioning seminars or asking if she was still considering graduate school. She never listened to them through. Her belly had grown, though she carried the weight easily. She hadn't been to a doctor. She gave all this little or no consideration. A few times she'd felt movements within her but somehow couldn't think that this would be a child. Familiar silence occupied the house, the fields encroached upon the windows, the verandas were hung with a cloth of mountains.

Levon's lawyer had called a few times. He explained there were laws regarding disappearances but that by now death could be assumed. Isa met with him in the kitchen. It was a sunny late-October afternoon. He gave her a summary of accounts and assets.

Wow, she said without inflection.

But there's a stipulation. He was a middle-aged man in the preserve of impersonality, lines on either side of his mouth, black frame glasses, a Clark Kent without softness. It seems, he said, that your husband loved you very much. He unfolded a letter. It began as she might have expected . . . If you are reading this now . . . but then startled her: Here is my vision for your life after my death. Fashion yourself as a Southern lady. I have always admired them though they have all but disappeared. Sit on the porch and read. Join a literary discussion group. Cultivate distinction, not eccentricity but conscious distance so all will know the depth of our love. Though, my dear Isabelle, I cannot enforce these things, I can make a few demands. My holdings have been placed in trust. You will be granted an allowance, but if you remarry, you will cease to receive this. You will lose everything. I hope only that this measure does not matter and that you cherish my memory of your own free will. Yours, Levon J.

She lowered the letter to her lap. Clearly it had been composed years ago.

And if I remarry?

His legacy, the lawyer said, will go to the creation of the Levon J. Willis Municipal Parks.

Parks?

Yes, he has planned for one, each with a bronze bust, in all of the nearby townships within reason of funding. If you decide to marry at seventy, there might be just one.

He smiled. When she didn't, he explained her allowance and excused himself.

Beyond the windows the sun set in a sky the colour of struck ice.

She was suddenly awake within this anger: Levon's future, her corseted, a frou-frou of lace beneath her chin. As if this were all of life she had a right to.

She went into the yard barefoot. That year's rains had worked nails and glass shards free of the earth. The wind blew and lulled, dark clouds shuttling past a slight moon. The heads of wild grass clicked along the fence. Slowly she crossed to the stables.

In the aisle between the stalls she listened to the soft shift of hoofs in straw, all three horses come out to watch, nodding and tipping ears. They'd always been in her life, so present in disposition that riding lessons had never been necessary. She'd simply climbed on and observed herself at harmony. Had she chosen anything? Years had passed in attachment, not love.

On a bench lay the rifle that Barbara had given Jude. He'd used it on stray tomcats, on groundhogs or rabbits in the garden. She found the box of shells and worked in the glow of houselights through the window.

Nearby the stallion gazed at her. He was a silver Arab that Levon had bought and pastured near the road. She touched his neck. She stepped back. She put the stock to her shoulder as he lowered his nose, his ear above the rifle's muzzle. She tried to recall the kick from when Jude had taken her to the field and had let her shoot into the trees. A bat darted in through a stall door and up to the rafters. The horse didn't spook but continued to watch. She felt for the trigger, wondering how subtle the movement would be, recalling her only jerky shot, the drab sky resonating above an ocean of leaves. She'd thought that the force of the bullet needed something strong in the hand. The stallion shifted closer to the barrel.

145

She let the gun down, then took out the bullet. She put her hand on the stallion's warm neck and brought up dust with her fingers. Slowly she returned to the tack room. She wanted Bart, to lie against his chest until whatever seed of destruction, hurt or loneliness went away.

She pulled a horse blanket from the shelf, then unfolded the couch into a bed. In sounds and smells and memories, everything was here, the hours she'd spent with Bart, her youth watching Jude work. She just breathed, lying still until her mind was half coaxed by sleep. Once Jude had come in with the rifle. She'd been watching *I Dream of Jeannie*, and she wanted to show him how much she could be like this. She tied her shirt at her waist. He was sitting at the table and she put a red plastic bead in her navel and turned, her dress spinning out. Her spontaneous smile and confidence were strange to both of them, the brightness that she felt in her own eyes. He stood, all at once kicking his chair away, and she jumped back, arms crossed before her. He went out and through the grass, leapt the fence into the field and strode to where, in the evening, it disappeared towards forest. He shot three times at the sky. Then he swung the rifle, long turning arcs, distant and strangely silent, steady as his ragged form dissolved into the dark.

146 The last fitful and evocative days of autumn had come, shaking the trees. On a cold afternoon, the officer stopped by to see how she was doing. He asked how far along she was, though she hadn't thought it obvious.

At least your husband has one on the way, he said. Nothing worse than leaving this world without a child to carry your name.

She imagined people in town saying, The Mexican's child. Oh, yes, that one's a Mexican, too.

She saw then what it would mean to stay. Levon had been going to the stream for years and, in the week that Bart was there, had disappeared, and she accepted this. Murder no longer seemed so savage. There had been too many absences and unknowns. Her child was going to need a father.

She went into the kitchen. She ate more than she had in weeks. Then she listed materials for sale on pieces of cardboard and paper, the prices ridiculously cheap. She drove to the post office and the country store. She pasted the signs anywhere she could.

The next day her property was crowded. She sold it all: the Jaguar, horses, every relic and piece of electronics. She let locals strip the house of furniture and counters, pine cabinets and oak flooring. All that week she watched the fences go, the stables, the entire building given up for eight hundred dollars, dismantled and removed. She hired an investigator to find out who her mother was and gave him copies of Jude's cards. She was almost pleased at the extravagant cost, as if being married had had a purpose after all. She told him she would be out of town and would contact him. Bart had never called. She slept in the only room that she'd left intact. She kept some clothes and books and Jude's ashes as well as an old Polaroid camera. She imagined a trip to Québec with Bart, spreading the ashes, starting her life, not over but at last.

The evening before she left, she filled trash bags with what remained of Levon's possessions, his suits, collector's editions on UFOs and geometric studies of crop circles. The window glass flashed with the electric blooms of a far-off storm. Finished, she undressed and scrubbed her face with her damp shirt. Her belly was large, and she felt its hardness as she pulled a sweater on. She went out and carried the bags down the pasture to the stone wall. The flowing pools held rusty nails, from the mill, she supposed. Trip after trip she threw in books and documents until the stream was a roiling mud of paper and old clothes. She stood in the chill silent dark, not knowing what to expect or whether to be afraid. She didn't need proof, not of God nor gods nor evil.

Maine–Québec
December 1993–January 1994

*I*sa arrived two days before Christmas. She stayed in a hotel in Lewiston and told the clerk she was looking for an old friend. He suggested she ask at a few popular bars, and though she was doubtful, everyone at the first place knew Bart. When she'd entered, the talk had fallen to an uncomfortable silence. It was a sparse afternoon crowd, mostly older men, but between them they were able to tell her exactly where he lived. She wasn't sure if the silence had been because of her belly or her height. She

considered that if she wasn't pregnant they might have
told her more.

The apartment was on the edge of town, one of two
above an abandoned convenience store. December
had been temperate, warm enough for her to wait on
the stairs. She'd had no reason to be certain Bart would
be in Lewiston, but she hadn't been able to imagine
where else he might have gone. And if he wasn't here,
she'd told herself, or if she couldn't find him, there
would be his family, and even then she could simply
continue north.

He arrived in the afternoon, driving a rusted-out Ford
Bronco with new tires. His clothes were muddy, and he
walked halfway to the stairs before he saw her. Already
she could smell the alcohol. He simply stopped.

You're working, she said. For the first time she truly
grasped how long it had been. His face looked heavier,
older, his eyes bloodshot.

How did you . . . get here?

I asked at the bar.

He hesitated. I thought it might be dangerous to call.

She shrugged. Maybe. Anyway, I'm here.

He looked at her, then up at the apartment. I can
show you where I live.

She was relieved not to have to speak. She watched
his hunched back as he climbed the stairs. The ceilings
were low for them. There was a mattress on the floor, a
table with two chairs. The fluted dish of the ceiling light
had filled with dead flies, and the only wall decoration
was a dusty dead clock in a laminated slice of wood.

Dirty boot prints made the yellow rug look strangely like leopard skin.

He stared past her and shifted from foot to foot, the floor creaking like a ship at sea.

Were you still thinking of me? she asked.

Yeah. I've been working. I've just been staying here and mostly working. The money got stolen. I . . . I bought the truck and what was left of the money got stolen here. But I have a job.

She was silent. That's okay. I have money, too.

With the deliberate motions she'd become used to, she sat. She felt oddly detached, like a monk. I'm tired, she said, and then, after a moment, when he didn't speak, I'm pregnant. I think it's been almost eight months.

Later, to ease the tension, she asked that he show her the town. The calm between them felt like a lull. Clouds rafted against a sky the colour of aluminum. They walked aimlessly. She'd brought her Polaroid but felt ridiculous now for having done so. She noticed that people, usually men, paused to stare.

How's your family? she asked.

He didn't respond immediately. I've been working with my cousin Zy. He operates and repairs log skidders. He was doing helicopter repair for the army in Korea and just came home last year. He's the one who got me my job.

What do you do?

Just stuff for the logging company. I'm working my way up.

She was about to ask if he'd seen his grandparents, but he pointed out the railroad station.

The French-Canadians all arrived through here. I remember . . . my grandmother told me that they came after a spur was built to the Portland–Montreal line. All this area from here to the river was called Little Canada, I think.

She glanced at a sign: Lisbon Street.

He had a pained look on his face. You said you have money?

Enough . . . to get by. She'd intended to say, For us. To say, To have the child and get started. She wondered if he would continue working if she were to give him what she had.

We should buy groceries for dinner, she told him. To celebrate.

He'd stopped and looked away. He turned back. Let me take a picture of you, he said.

She stood by a lamppost. She tried to look calmly at the camera. The sky was almost dark. He snapped the picture.

They waited for the photo to develop, shoulder to shoulder in the last flare of light.

I was wondering, he said. Was your . . . was he found?

Levon?

Did they find him?

He wasn't really my husband, she said. Just legally. And no, he wasn't found.

He hitched his thumbs. The photo's probably ready. Why don't you peel it?

She did and turned to show him.

It's perfect, he said. It's really good.

152   They went home without groceries. She was suddenly too tired. This had been happening more and more, bouts of exhaustion that had her asleep almost before she could lie down. She took off her shoes, the floorboards cold from the abandoned convenience store below. She stretched on the bed and thought of those first days when she and Bart had lain together in the dark stables. She wanted to speak now like they had. Her throat hurt.

What do you think we should do? he asked.

Do? she repeated. We need to worry about simple things.

He sat next to her.

Come here, she told him. Feel it.

It was as if she'd taken a stranger's hand. She held it to her. There had been entire days she'd refused to acknowledge this. She closed her eyes, then forced herself to open them and look at him. He was staring at his hand.

When I was boy, he said, I used to hate my hands. They were so hairy. I remember one of my teachers said that hands were a symbol of human beauty or humanity or something.

Isa let her eyes close. Drifting, she could sense the weight of his hand, its heat like that of a sleeping creature. Later, she realized that the pressure was gone. She heard the creaking floor and gazed from the bedroom through the dim living room into the kitchen. Bart's head almost touched the ceiling. Lamplight bruised the declivities in his haggard and fattened face. Neither spoke. He was holding a bottle, now reaching for the counter like an old man.

In the morning he was gone. She couldn't recall him returning to bed. Vague sunlight came through the windows. She put on her coat and sat on the stairs. Across the building a boy came out. He checked the thermometer, then wrote in a journal.

What are you doing? she asked.

I'm keeping a record of temperatures, he said matter-of-factly. I send them to my cousin in Mexico City, and she sends me the temperatures there. It's sunny now, but the radio says it's going to snow today, so I'm checking every hour.

Oh. She tried to smile. For the first time she considered what her child might be like.

Are you Bart's wife?

Um, yes.

I'm Miguel. Bart told me he's going to be a writer someday. It's a coincidence because I'm a writer too. But I write about the future.

The future? she repeated, considering Bart as a writer, that he might see himself this way.

Yes, mostly about intergalactic travel. I'm working on a book about a world where body parts are replaced and nobody dies. This world as we know it, he added, will soon be obsolete.

Obsolete?

He looked at her sharply, perhaps annoyed that she kept repeating.

Exactly. Everything we do won't matter anymore. We'll stop aging, and work will be done by robots. People will get to enjoy their lives forever.

Like children.

In a way, he agreed. But better.

Later, still waiting for Bart, Isa considered this future. Would she sacrifice a little of herself for certainty: nobody forgotten, a bar code on her arm, a number on one of a million identical doors?

She slept through the morning, then began cleaning. Work clothes were piled in the closet, the mud on them dried to a fine dust. Empty whisky bottles cluttered the space beneath the sink. She thought of Jude. The weather had turned, and snowflakes struck the glass. Traffic sounded hushed. She watched the wet halos of car lights. She didn't want to run away again.

She went into the bathroom and pulled back her hair. She held her hands to her belly. Her body had changed so much. The child moved often.

She found a phonebook in the kitchen. When Bart had first told his stories, she'd made a mental note of his mother's name. There were quite a few Beaulieus, but on her third call an elderly man said that Amy Beaulieu had been his niece, and what was the research about?

Just a genealogy, she told him, and soon she knew which of the remaining numbers was Bart's grandmother. The listing read Bill and Evelyn Beaulieu, but he told her the grandfather had passed on. The wife lived alone. Isa let him finish. She thanked him and wrote down the address.

She put on her jacket and took her purse.

Snow fell steadily out of a dark sky. A few Christmas wreaths shone on lampposts.

She started the car and turned on the defrost. Sitting in the cold she felt a pulse deep inside her. Snow had gathered around the tires, but after a few attempts she was able to back out.

The house wasn't far. She rang the doorbell and stood, pulling at her jacket. She'd been afraid to call and lose momentum. A stocky man with a moustache answered.

Yes? he said.

Hello, I'm looking for Evelyn Beaulieu.

Right. She's here.

Who is it? a woman's voice called. She came to the top of the stairs inside. Her cheeks had spots the same iron colour as her hair. She took off her glasses and held them a bit in front of her face.

Can I help you?

Isa touched her jacket over her belly. She wondered how she looked. I'm sorry to come by so late. I'm your grandson's wife.

Which one?

Bart, she said.

Evelyn mouthed his name. Bart? she repeated. He's around?

He lives nearby.

Come in. Come in anyway. I don't know why we're making you stand in the cold.

Evelyn put water for tea in the microwave, then sat. Isa told her where Bart was working, that they'd been living in Virginia and had moved to be closer to the family.

Evelyn furrowed her brow slightly. I lost track of him a long time ago.

I know. But he's here now. Isa tried to smile.

Oh. I see. Well, apparently he had a very bad time growing up. He wasn't one of the lucky ones.

He'll get settled.

Yes, Evelyn agreed.

They sat. Knit doilies lay on the coffee table and mantels, under the telephone. Framed photographs showed brides and heavyset grooms in tuxedos sitting sideways and smiling into the camera. The man hadn't spoken. He shifted in his chair and pursed his lips.

I was hoping to know more about the family, Isa told them.

Well, Evelyn said, a few of us were together today. We just came back. This is Mike. He drove me. He and Bart would be cousins, I think. She lifted her hands as if to shrug and put them back on the armrests. It was never a very close family. And the children who do stay around are parents, grandparents some of them, and they have their own to deal with. But Bart's mother never had much to do with us. I think I saw him only two or three times.

Isa glanced at the photos. She tried to connect the youths with the men, the girls with mothers.

Do you have any pictures of Bart?

Evelyn hesitated. No, she said. No, I don't think so. There was no reason I would.

Isa struggled to breathe. She felt herself being looked at. I'm pregnant, she said.

Evelyn lifted her eyebrows with a sudden motion, like the wings of a bird. I can see that. Will it be a boy or a girl?

I don't know, Isa said. She wasn't sure why she'd come. She'd wanted some way to help hold her and Bart in place. I don't want to keep you, she told them. In the kitchen the microwave binged loudly. She tried to calm her breath.

I need to go.

That's okay, Evelyn said. It's been nice meeting you. If I'd known you were in town, we would have invited you . . .

Thank you.

Evelyn stood and sat again.

I'll clean the snow off your car, Mike offered.

Isa followed him into the drably suburban street. A wind had blown up, ice crystals tinkling on the windshield.

I'm sorry, he told her. He kept his hands in his pockets. A few of us knew Bart was around, but we had no idea . . . He lifted his chin . . . about you.

It's okay.

When I was young, it was like we got used to seeing Bart come and go. He couldn't stay still. He was always a nice guy. Nice to me anyway.

He likes to travel.

Yeah, he said. He cleaned off what little snow had gathered on her windshield. There wasn't enough to warrant this. He couldn't quite look at her. Listen, he said, I know things probably aren't okay if you're here alone. I . . . I've heard a few times what Bart's been up to, but no one's mentioned you. If you need help, my wife and I have an extra room. We'll do what we can. There's still some family. We're not very close, but we all help out.

She wanted to ask about Bart's past, but it seemed unfair. Besides, what was there to know. The alcoholism couldn't be new. She could guess other things from Bart's stories, or from Evelyn's hesitation and surprise.

Thank you, she said.

It's no problem. We'll be in touch, okay?

All right.

Good night.

She sat in the car. She felt what she was, a huge woman, pregnant, maybe even pathetic in their eyes.

On the drive through town she passed a shop with TVs in the windows, large images that she immediately recognized as New York's streets at Christmastime. She felt that the world on the screens in no way belonged to hers.

Bart's truck was there when she got back. Just inside she smelled him. The floors creaked in the bedroom. He came into the doorway, positioned so that the light from the kitchen showed the stubble on his jaw. Briefly she paused, lost in the moment, the gassy odour a familiar ghost.

He shifted closer. Where've you been?

She turned on the light. She tried to hold herself

steady and look at him. Bloodshot veins banded his eyes. Did you kill Levon? she asked.

He rocked slightly and turned away. It was an accident, he said. He put his forehead against the wall. He appeared odd, large and unshaven and holding his face to the wall like a punished boy.

159

I went to see your grandmother, she told him, wishing he'd lied, that she'd never asked.

Slowly he straightened. The reek of alcohol was overwhelming, and she noticed that he held a bottle. She couldn't make out the label, and if she hadn't been trying, she wouldn't have realized he was going to throw it. She screamed involuntarily.

You can't do that, he said. You can't.

From the way he stepped forward and back she understood he was forcing himself not to approach. She moved to the door. He swung and broke a chair effortlessly against the wall. She thought of words that might have power or meaning. But seeing how easily everything came apart, she knew that all they could try was hopeless, and she fled.

By New Year's she was in a hotel in Québec. She stayed in one after another, the humming resonance of travel inside her even as she slept. The northern sky seemed wider. Sunset came too soon, some evenings yellow and vast, others a faint red mist. Often she couldn't recall if she'd showered or eaten. The highway was streaked with mud and salt, and she followed it.

It was strange she'd never been here before. She'd read so many books, had collected old photographic studies of the regions, quiet terrains that she searched for hints. She cast Jude's stories against the landscape, but there was nothing of the cartoon past, its blurbs and silences. He hadn't belonged to the recognizable currents of history the way Bart's family had, even if Bart had lied about what remained. Jude had come too late. His death hadn't left a single clue.

160

Was the desire to return natural, like that of a creature spawning? How long before it ceased to matter? She'd tried to make sense of what Jude had sought. Was it odd that a place she'd never known lived on within her?

She stopped at lighthouses and cathedrals. Repeatedly she was mistaken for *une parisienne,* for the accent she'd relearned in university. She was a foreigner here. Like all the others, she parked on the sides of roads and walked to outlooks where vistas offered what they could: a landscape with a few souvenir shops, or evening's postcard on the sea.

For two weeks she stayed on the coast of Gaspésie. She rarely ate. She woke early, preferring this light. She thought of Virginia, the way the house had given her the space to dream and become something new.

At the nearby town she bought boots. The mountains, without leaves, showed the deep lines of their creation. Walking a frozen road she came to a place where trees had been felled and split, the tang of wood still in the air. Once Jude had sat and held his puckered hand, thinking himself unseen, in the barn loft for hours. Hidden, she'd matched his stillness until after dark, calming what she felt in her breath for him.

Her body ached. Her guts cramped. Her feet were swollen, and veins bulged in her legs. Though the cold made her return to the hotel, she felt she could walk off in such a way that the world would forgive her.

Mid-January a strange warm front arrived, announced on the radio. The sky seemed to unfurl, blue upon blue. Sunlight was on everything, itching in her sinuses. People stood outside, not talking, jackets shaken by gulf wind. Even in Virginia this weather would be odd for January: half a day of crystalline rain, hot winds, snow melting from grey outcroppings. Ice floes crowded into the gulf. What was Bart feeling now? It seemed a lifetime ago that they'd lain together, talking about their mothers. What had happened to that part of them?

She decided to leave. She packed. Indian teenagers were out hitchhiking in jeans and heavy-metal T-shirts.

That afternoon she found a stretch of empty beach strewn with boulders. She took Jude's ashes from the back of the car. The tide was coming in, washing against raw coastal mud. Slanted isles jutted from the sea, grown with grass and forest and looking, in the heaving water, like pieces sheared from hillsides, like parts of the world cut off and set afloat. There was no ritual she knew, no means of returning him to a place he'd left and which had kept no trace. Finally she undressed, naked, one hand on her stretched, aching belly. She wanted to be there completely. Her breath came shallowly. She threw ashes against the wind. Shattered, dry bits of bone fell away, and fine powder blew back onto her face. She touched her lips, the scar on her nose. She recalled the book on cannibals she'd read as a girl, and she moved her dusty fingers onto her tongue. They tasted of ash, faintly acrid. That was all, and she sat and held her belly. Regretting a last gesture, she thought of her mother, of what other ceremony there might be. She'd assumed her dead, had never considered, even when she'd hired the investigator, that it might be otherwise. She lacked the strength to dream her life over again.

In brisk sunlight she dressed, startled movement within her, pain. Touching grey hands to the boulders, she stumbled back. That night she parked on a stretch of shore, wind rocking the car, heat in the vents. She turned off the lights. She woke to moonlight on disturbed waters, a sense that this could be anywhere, any country but her own.

In Montréal she took a room. She left the Honda in a car park. She walked the blustery city: riotous karaoke, Irish pubs, Japanese kids in arcades, old Jews playing chess in a dingy café. Her love of the past had no place here, sleek cars and club music, boutiques of exotic knickknacks, *Depart en Mer* and *Dix Milles Villages*. Even the day before, Québec, the Plains of Abraham, the old town and picturesque inns—it had all been meaningless. She couldn't go more than a few minutes without having to sit. She wanted sleep. People wavered like old ghosted TV tubes. They stared. She could see herself towering over them.

Where a street angled up against a city vista, a black woman stood in sunlight, holding a baby. Isa was con-   163 fused, tired. She had a sense of loss. It took a moment, standing there, to realize how many things it might be.

Each morning she touched the closed venetians. The sun shone against them, and they shimmered like water.

Hunger woke her. She tried to hear her story told carefully by people she didn't know. She stood at the mirror without her shirt and touched her breasts, her abdomen. She'd once read that the Spartans had treated childbearing as sacred as soldiery. All in the days before overpopulation.

She would gladly accept Miguel's vision of the future now. The past, her suffering even, were obsolete. She could easily follow philosophy to that point. A place of letting go.

The snow had begun again, sweeping against skyscrapers, silencing the city, wet streets turned to ice. The radio was calling for a cold front, clear arctic skies. As low as minus forty. The weatherman warned people not to go out longer than necessary.

She slept constantly, it seemed, and never more than an hour at a time, pain frequent. She woke not knowing where she was. She wanted familiarity. She got up well before dawn. She dressed and went out and warmed the car. She cleaned the snow off. In the city's glow, the air felt sucked up away from the earth as if the atmosphere had expanded. Even as she drove the cold radiated through the windows, the heat sapped from inside, the car's suspension stiff and jerky. During the hour to the border she was drowsy, her thoughts distracted, and in the bathroom there she washed her face and throat. On the empty interstates south, the stars shone a path between the trees. Briefly, she had a sense of grief, for all that had been lost or stolen, for the family she could no longer let herself imagine. Was she dreaming or remembering Virginia now, white fields, the way moonlight dissolved against the humid dark? Or those first evenings on Jude's shoulders, endless galleries of sky and the lit city, the dark faces gazing up, sharing her wonder? The cold felt as if inside her. She wanted to sleep. She dreamed it was dawn. The grey sun dropped from a horizon of clouds. She closed her eyes and waited to be lifted from stillness.

Maine
December 1993–January 1994

Could he stop again? What reason was there to make this effort now?

He drank constantly. He hadn't showered or shaved in weeks. People jerked their heads when he passed, and the men on his crew commented among themselves. He knew how easy rage would be. When he tried to make sense of things, it seemed that only his fear of his own anger held him in place.

The last time he'd stopped had been at a halfway house in Louisiana, his possessions a beat-up electric guitar and amplifier, and a grocery bag of books. Later, the director found him work and lodging on an old farm that was being converted to a nursery. There, dogwood and pawpaw and magnolia bloomed in the fields, each shift of wind fragrant, and he hadn't minded his daily chores. Though his rages still came, sudden and inexplicable and making him want to drink, instead he dug, sweated, heaved at the earth. His pores released an animal smell that was neither bad nor good but which he hated.

One evening, as mist gathered in the trees, he walked an overgrown farm road into the woods. He'd finished work but was restless, and in the fading light he followed weedy ruts to where he'd been told there was a cypress swamp. Bleached trunks rose from land as irregular as a crumpled egg carton, exposed clay red, the water covered with leaves and pollen and seed fluff. Grass had turned beaver dams into bridges of spongy earth. The sky above the blasted trees seemed faint and far. The silence was voracious unless the wind set up, though oddly the silence remained. He stood in the presence of the marsh, the thick rank settling air, and breathed.

Sundays were no-work days, and late the next afternoon he loaded his guitar and amplifier and a gas-run generator into the farm truck and drove back. On the bank of the swamp he set up to play, then worked into the songs he'd loved best as a teenager, *Iron Man*, Metallica's *Fade to Black*. Though he'd seen himself many ways, often as characters in books, poets or writers or explorers, music had been the only thing he'd given any effort. There had been a time when he'd memorized the fretwork of songs and practised them for hours. He tried to find satisfaction in the crunching rhythms, the dull chop of palm-muted power chords. He sang, his voice grating. He wanted the noise to be raw, the way 167 he'd first heard it. Sweating against the urgency of spring, he stared at the crowded waters. He lifted his hand to strike the guitar but stopped. A man was standing across the swollen murk, on a hummock, dressed in black and holding a wide-brimmed hat.

Just a minute, son, the man said and began to make his way over the marshy earth. Don't leave, he called, all the while lifting his knees like a heron, stepping for solid ground.

Close, he looked Bart over, up and down a few times as if just now perceiving the sheer size and perhaps the potential danger.

My boy, he said, what a gift! The Lord has blessed you with the voice of a shepherd. The voice, he added, as if shepherds were not known for hollering, of a leader.

Now, don't get me wrong. I thought I heard cries of pain. I myself came here to work on my preaching, but I can tell you have other reasons and I have heard those records played backwards. But the Lord wouldn't have brought you if He didn't intend you saved. I can see you have it in you.

He paused, his face tense, hawkish, gaunt, the skin like frost beneath the thinning hair. I can see you've been seeking. I can see you have the power of the Lord God in you and you don't know how to express it.

Reverend Diamondstone, he introduced himself—
said it was a self-invented name and that he'd been told,
street preaching in New York, that it was a Jewish name,
but hadn't believed it. He will tell you anything to turn
you away. He said, *he* will, with special significance, low-
ering his voice as if this *he* was not only lowercase but
squiggly and smudged. It was not the He of his Reverend
Lord Jesus.

168

That Sunday, Diamondstone talked until mosquitoes
swarmed over the stagnant water and darted at their
faces. Bart listened, wasn't asked but rhetorically.
Diamondstone told of days street preaching, businessmen on Wall Street who fell to their knees and wept and
gave him donations of a thousand dollars to continue his
mission. The Ecclesiastical Manger of the Holy
Tribunal, he said. I suppose that's a good name, but any
will do, just so people don't think I'm another Baptist. I
am a Baptist, though. He told Bart he'd been homeless,
living in a ditch in West Texas, then had a visitation of
the Lord, the terrifying angel Michael who'd cast down
the fearful legions with the strength of the Lord's right
hand, and he, Diamondstone, had started preaching
right there in the ditch—converted, he said, a lady walking home with her groceries.

Diamondstone took a long breath that he balanced in
his chest. Yes, he said, Jesus found me. Jesus found me in
a ditch in Texas and decided I'd done my suffering. He
gave me a dream and turned all of my evil to good. But,
son, listen now. Do you know why I suffered so much?

Because I desired. I wanted the world. I wanted to be

there, on the mount, instead of Jesus when the devil tempted Him. I would have failed and not known it. That's why Jesus died for us. That's why He defeated temptation. My pain took Jesus. And what you are suffering will take Jesus, too. We all know. We all see. Give everything to desire. It will never be enough. But within every hunger or want or need there is a moment, a space of desire that contains all desires. Just to be satisfied, and that, if you understand it, is desire for God. Take your longing to Jesus and the rapture will be real, the satisfaction eternal. 169

Bart looked off into the dark as if some faint light had been lit between him and the reverend. The sun was near set, a soft glow against treetops. Diamondstone sighed. So how about it, boy? The world could use a voice like yours.

Bart understood all that they had in common, the homelessness and drinking. For the first time, the path seemed clear, the restless power of his anger no longer such a force.

Anyway, Diamondstone said, I will not be returning the way I came. I will follow you to be sure you are not weak.

The marsh was nearly invisible though Bart could sense its presence, as if the density of mud and clotted water generated a stronger gravity. It was pretty obvious that Diamondstone had been led by the music and had no idea of how to go home.

Bart loaded the truck, and together they rattled back to the farm, Diamondstone swaying with each bump but holding neither door nor dash for balance. When they arrived, Bart's employer was at the dinner table with his wife. Bart entered dutifully and said, I'm really sorry about this, but I have to go. I want to thank—

Before Diamondstone, filling the doorway like the wide, moonless night itself, stepped in and began to preach the beauty of his conversion.

Those first weeks travelling, the country seemed innocent again. Morris and Andrew were already part of the team, and as spring gave onto summer they gazed out the broad windshield, the changing earth their mystical experience, tableaus of prairie sky, blue with a single lazy stroke of fading contrail, endless fields that made them realize how easy it would be to lose one another and drown.

Our God is an almighty poet and painter, Diamondstone said.

Amen, they hollered.

Amen, Bart repeated softly as an afterthought, looking out the window, testing the space in his heart to hold the bigness of the world.

Each day they stopped at college campuses and Christian living camps. They crossed the country town by town, though Diamondstone preached and the others collected from the audience. When the spirit came on him, he hollered, This is the place, and pulled the van flush with the sidewalk, the tires squealing against the curb. He'd be preaching before he was out the door.

Though Bart found comfort in Andrew and Morris's

presence, he shared little with them. Andrew was pale, with a soft, annoyed face, and Morris, a Floridian, had the neat haircut and rim glasses of a prep but the beady eyes of a possum, and was either too happy or too angry, then saying Jesus saves, Amen, thank the Lord for this meal, praise Jesus for the good weather, for the good interstates, God bless McDonald's. With time, Bart knew everyone's stories, Diamondstone's theories on dressing in historical black to make people see, not just hear, him as an agent of Jesus, and Andrew's drop-out from state college to live in a Christian commune where he symbolically burned everything he'd previously owned — including, he told ruefully, six thousand dollars in unread comics, among which were X-Men numbers one, two and three.

171

Though Bart listened and commiserated, he felt that his own hardships were of another order, even at times that happiness would be a betrayal of those he'd lost. But whenever his doubts grew, Diamondstone seemed to sense this. He asked about Bart's life, encouraging, reminding him that the depth of wisdom came through pain. It wasn't long before he took Bart aside one evening. Morris and Andrew had appeared nervous all day, and Bart sensed them watching as he and Diamondstone left the campground.

Son, Diamondstone told him, we're running out of money. Now, there are some sad facts to being a missionary in the world today. Sometimes, he said — sometimes people need to be persuaded. They simply don't know what's best for them, and a little . . . let's call it theatre, is necessary. Now, I have an idea. This might not be what we intended, but we have to eat and the world is a miserly place.

In this way, Diamondstone revealed his plan, and soon thereafter Bart became mute for the purpose of fundraising. He considered that Diamondstone had found him howling at the swamp and had heard the voice of a leader, but he also understood the need to sacrifice. In a way, he was relieved not to have the responsibility of preaching.

And so for almost a year, they plied their long, indirect trajectories cross-country. It surprised Bart how easily the anachronism of a travelling religious show was accepted. His role was not a difficult one. He'd never been talkative, but strangely his silence made him want to speak. And though Diamondstone had explained that they were fighting corruption, moving towards something better, Bart's restlessness crept back. He told himself that he was taking from a world that had wronged him, that this was a spiritual quest. His rages now rarely tormented him. Despite his act, he felt that they had found a sort of innocence.

But gradually, the mission began to seem like the homelessness he'd once lived, public showers and meals in parking lots. Night highways cleaved, great armadas of blustering semis, runs of billboards flocked by wind and dust, silos and processing plants all with a look of neglect and history. Nearing Oklahoma City they saw lit crosses soaring above the dark disc of the plains. Dear Lord, they said, and Amen. What a blessing! Closer, they realized that the illusion was created by office buildings with lights left on to form a cross on each side.

This disenchantment was gradual, coupled with the theatre of salvation, archangels and businessmen and perilous '57 Chevies. Diamondstone never stopped talking. Soon Bart and Andrew and Morris could do no more than sigh a tired Amen. It was twenty-four-hour evangelical television right there at the wheel of the van, practising sermons, telling of his dreams, his decision to make a name like Simon's, the Rock, with the hardest rock in it, the one eternal stone, made from pressure. I was coal, he said, and they were all fast asleep, immune to sermon or soliloquy, cradled by the jouncy van.

Eventually, Bart stayed only out of fear of the life he'd led before. He'd never told Isa how truly bad it had been. Though there were periods of rehabilitation and work when he swore never to fall back, he always did. Loneliness and drinking seemed inevitable, then the wandering. He'd slept off the side of the interstate, in gullies and ditches, the dry culverts and arroyos of the Southwest, beneath crumbling, moon-battered cliffs. Weeks, he'd been able to give nothing its name. He'd wandered past burr and shrub and cactus, through yellow and magenta deserts. He never understood how he lost track, layers of self like that red, broken strata: the simple desire for love and that drunken sense of floating, then grief that gave on rage. He beat a man for trying to rob him. He robbed others. He picked through trash. Supermarket glossies were rare and elegant depictions of life in better places, Rome to the Visigoths. He found books everywhere, in sidewalk free-boxes, on vending machines, propping windows or in weedy yards, rain-swelled, stiff as scriptures.

174

Bart hadn't intended to be drawn close to Isa. Diamond-stone had wanted him to separate her from Levon. The convenience of her love had been too much to pass up, but somehow, listening to her talk of her mother, Bart had found himself wanting to speak. He'd learned to fab-ulate from Diamondstone, to use the parts of his life most pertinent to the listener. But this had felt wrong with Isa. What was strange, what truly surprised him, was that he'd continued to lie though his intentions had become sincere, that she find what she dreamed of in him. Brief warm rains blew through, clattering on the stable roof. He'd studied her pale lips, the scar on her nose, her contained gestures, watching for a sign of what she would believe.

Still, there had been truth to it, too, the childhood passed around as if given away, the years after his mother's death and the way he'd read indiscriminately, days on end, hardly sleeping so that at twelve he'd had the puffy face and baggy eyes of a trucker. Through nov-els he'd learned to picture his unknown father as a silent, road-wise man at a bar, frozen and turned away, unable to reveal all that he'd suffered. Like Isa's, his life had seemed determined by those who were absent.

Though he'd met his grandmother on only a few occasions, it was these visits he'd drawn on for his stories.

The first time, she'd appeared uncomfortable and had talked in a detached manner, far too polite, cold even. Nice getting to know you, Bart, she'd said. Together they'd walked through town, and she'd shared a bit of the history. Her mother had been Irish and her father French, and though he hadn't understood much of what she was telling him, she'd talked of old animosities between the cultures, especially where work was concerned. Many of the French had eventually changed their names. She knew a Mr. Beauchamps who'd become Mr. Fields. She mentioned the first years that the French schools were closed, and the places her cousins and brothers had gone to work, Manchester and Woonsocket and Fall River. But he'd never considered any of this the way Isa did. Once, in Louisiana, in a boarding house, an old Cajun man had told him that teachers used to make boys lie on the damp earth under the school building as punishment for speaking French. Bart had never felt French, or cared.

Perhaps the only strong memory of a family had been the funeral. His grandfather, a near stranger, had finally told him what had happened to his mother. He'd sighed and mumbled about the Lord's ways with little conviction. Later, before the viewing, he went out to speak with the stepfather, and Bart found himself alone. After the frozen streets, the warm hall felt detached and foreign, vases with roses in the corners, a bouquet of white on the closed lower half of the coffin. His shoes touched silently over the carpet. He neared and looked inside. He hadn't expected it to be his mother. He must have known but was startled as if this meant she wasn't dead. She had on too much makeup. He said her name. Amy, he repeated. He lifted her hands and moved them from her chest. He undid the buttons on her blouse. He let his weight rest on the side of the coffin. Tinkerbell was visible just above her bra. Her tattoos had never been so vivid, and he'd wondered what would happen to them in the earth.

The evening of Levon's death, Bart had left Isa's no longer sure of his intentions. He'd told her the truth and wanted to change everything, but his fear had been too much. Outside, in the dark, he tried to make sense of it. If he turned against Diamondstone and she rejected him, he would be alone. Under the cover of the forest, he stopped to consider Diamondstone's order from that morning to frighten Levon at the stream. The plan had been simple, entirely in keeping with their theatrical tactics. Diamondstone and Andrew and Morris had discussed how to awaken Levon's fear of God and the strange man he'd seen. Though Bart felt he'd switched loyalties, he'd lacked the courage to refuse.

He was sitting on a rock, trying to decide, when he heard Levon's car climb the driveway. He hadn't expected him to return so soon. He listened, the highway not far beyond the forest, the constantly fading traffic sounds so much a part of him. Finally, he started towards the stream. He told himself that he wanted to see Isa's husband for himself, to know if all that she'd said was true.

The rushing water was loud, and as he crossed the rise above it, the moonlight cast his shadow. He'd been thinking of a hiding place, but Levon was already there, gazing at him. They faced each other for what seemed like a minute. Bart had thought he was being sized up, and this made him realize how foolish he was. Levon's heart must simply have stopped. A moment later he collapsed. Bart waded the stream and crouched. Levon's eyes were open, the muscles of his throat clenched. Bart touched his chest, then his wrist. He lifted him and started towards the house before he realized that he would be blamed.

177

Cold sweat began to drip in his armpits and along his back. As gently as he could, he returned to the stream and stepped in. Rains had kept the current high and muddy, and he followed it up the mountainside. He came to a place he'd been during his walks, a wide pool with low stones at the centre. He lay Levon in the water. His hands trembled. Sweat dripped from his fingertips. He chose a stone that was slightly larger than Levon. He bent and heaved until it came up, the water sucking in around his knees. He took the body and studied the moonlit face. The eyes seemed to have glossed faintly. There was no question. What Isa had told him was true. He pushed the body under and pulled the stone back. He took a few steps and turned in a circle. Perhaps in the summer, when the water was shallow and clear, someone might notice. He went back down the mountain, not leaving the stream until he came to the place where Levon had been waiting. Carefully he crossed through the fields to find Diamondstone, knowing that if he stayed, he would be caught. Sooner or later a muddy footprint would give him away.

Every decision from then on passed in a fog of terror. As soon as Diamondstone found out what had happened, he told Bart that he and Morris and Andrew would accuse him if they had to. The departure was without ceremony. The tents went into the van, and they left him in the field. Bart walked into the forest and waited as the rain began. He heard the cars arriving and saw the ambulance lights. He knew that his size alone would mark him as guilty.

Those months afterwards, in Lewiston, each time he wanted to run, he drank. The responsibility of his actions was with him constantly. He'd lived through too much that he'd never chosen, and only with his drinking did this feeling go away. When Isa arrived pregnant, his confusion and rage was involuntary. It hurt him to see her fear. He'd known that by telling her he'd killed Levon he could make her leave. But when he said it, he wanted to see if she would stay, though he didn't give her that chance. His rage was too much. Christmas morning, he woke sober to a breathlessness like pain, as if he'd been struck in the chest and felt the heat of an injury that would never rise to the surface.

All that day he expected her to return. He'd felt that she had no claim on him after so long, but the child was his. In the evening, not wanting to drink, he went out and drove. He crossed the Androscoggin to Auburn, then followed the reservoir back. Christmas trees lit windows, and he recalled picture books he'd received as a boy— those sunny histories and the way he'd dreamed of empires, of those in tune with struggle and the satisfaction of struggle. He wanted to fall through, to feel whatever was holding him fall away and disappear. The frozen gusting leaves, the occasional traffic and few pedestrians all seemed driven by some pain of memory. He stopped the car and closed his eyes.

For the first time, he questioned the power of his recollections over him, those winter afternoons, when the sun set too early and his mother would bathe him. She'd sat him in the stuffed laundry basket and undressed, her shoulders and thighs like the pages of a colouring book. She held him to her belly as she washed him. The black Tinkerbell shone on her breast, the linoleum on which they lay glistening with moisture. Afterwards, she put him on the toilet's tufted purple seat cover and drew on him with bath crayons, red and blue slashes at first worrisome but that soon became pictures like those she had, hearts and serpents and flowers. Then she wiped the mirror and held him before it until it misted over again. He thought of the power of absence. Her death was an image of him at nine returning across the Midwest: the dull humming of the U-Haul cab and beyond the windows, winter's blue and cradling distance. He thought of himself, or of a child, alone.

Back home he tried Isa's number in Virginia. It was disconnected. He called the police and was put through to a man who told him that her name wasn't on the system.

Bart took a bottle from under the sink. He found the Polaroid. He considered Isa's high, strong cheekbones. She reminded him of the Creoles in Louisiana.

180   He knew he'd abandoned others too often, learned to stop caring too quickly. Diamondstone had told him that only God could lighten his burdens, and Bart had believed this.

But then he'd simply walked away—because love had brought him closer to his innocence, and there was no place you arrived in the search for God. Still, perhaps Diamondstone had been right and all desires gave onto one. Perhaps Bart believed in salvation, even now, as he waited, as snow silenced the world and he considered what a person might do to bring meaning into his life.

Mid-January, a warm front arrived, deepening the blue of the sky, snowbanks revealing gravel and trash and filling the streets with mud and melting ice.

His job was as a grunt on a skidding crew. That Levon's money had been stolen was a lie. He'd spent much of it on the truck and apartment and at the bar, but had lost the rest playing cards at a party. Zy, a cousin he hadn't seen in years, had kept him drinking and talking about his father throughout the game. The next morning Bart had counted what he had left. He'd thought about leaving and not paying rent. Instead, he'd asked Zy for help finding a job and was hired a few days later. His duty was to hook a heavy chain to stumps or trees or to carry things for the other workers, though mostly he just stood in the mustering cold and waited.

With the thaw, everyone on the crew was fed up, the ground unlocking, leaving them shin-deep in mud. Then on Friday the radio began calling for a cold snap, expected minus forty. Arctic air and clear skies, the announcer said—With all this water, Maine is going to be the biggest hockey rink in the U.S. of A.

Bart had forgotten mud season, the scents of earth, warm wind from far away, the way sunshine made him sneeze. His mother had laughed when he'd stomped in. He thought of Isa and their child. He could hardly contain the rage of self-hatred. He felt he could pull the skidders by the chains and haul back the forest and hills like a sheet from a bed. At lunch he took a bottle from under his truck seat.

Later, after hauling the chain into place, he yelled at the operator to go before he'd taken his hand off. The links crushed the tips of two fingers. He roared and men gathered, and he punched the operator, who'd been apologetic but insistent that Bart was at fault. The foreman sent Bart to the hospital and told him not to come back when his worker's compensation finished. Two fingertips and nails may as well have been removed, they were so thoroughly crushed.

Back home, when he parked his car, Miguel was sitting on the steps. Bart hadn't seen him in a while.

You hurt yourself?

Yeah. It's nothing. Bart knew that his pallor betrayed him.

My dad's done that. Lots of times. I guess it's normal when you work with machines.

I guess. Book going okay?

Yes, except my mom and dad are fighting.

Oh.

Where's your wife? Is she at the hospital to have her baby?

No. She's with her family.

Glittering water dripped loudly along the eaves.

Anyway, Miguel said, you probably need to rest. See you later.

Inside Bart didn't take painkillers or drink. His fingers pulsed. Sweat gathered along the elastic of his underwear. He sat and let sensation build, a nerve in his arm like a live wire. It was as if every emotion he'd known was in his hand.

The first time he'd kicked drinking had been at a state park near Natchitoches. He'd slept for a week under a picnic table. He'd forgotten how hard it was. He wanted to tear everything away, to dress in fresh clothes, eat, lie down and sleep, start over. He wanted to wake up from all of this, to decide. Had he always been afraid to act? He knew how easily he could be eclipsed by emotion.

He got up and began to pack. He would go to Virginia and find Isa. He took the Polaroid and in the closet he came across a bag. It held one of Isa's notebooks and some old ID cards: Jude White. Even from the head shot Bart could tell the size of the man, the flattened face and goggle eyes, dumb and powerfully innocent, not someone who could be anything other than what he was. Bart suddenly felt exhausted. He needed to lie down. This ugliness burned into him and filled him with sadness, a sense of helplessness before the inevitability of their lives.

He slept fitfully and dreamed the swamp, mud whose depth he could sense beneath him. In the ambient night he knew another person was there, and at first he thought it was Diamondstone. But the presence had the gravity that a child feels with an adult. He couldn't move, waiting, recalling even in his sleep the father that memory had held unchanged all these years, the huge man staring at him from across the street. He wanted to escape, to plunge into the dark water.

He woke. The lit window had frozen in a scrim of ice. He opened the door, the cold a searing band at his temple, up into his hair. The sky seemed too brilliant, the moon oddly distinct, full but for a faint crescent as if the white had been blurred against the vivid blue. The world looked tilted, stark, naked with cold, a vague garden of ice sprouted from the sopped parking lot. He returned inside. There was half a bottle of bourbon in the cupboard. He poured it into the sink and went back to bed.

Again he dreamed the swamp, the sprawl of silent mud. He was kneeling, gazing into the water, thirstier than he'd ever been. He woke and stood and reeled against the wall. His hands shook. He made it into the bathroom. He turned on the light. He hadn't shaved. His skin looked rutted and old. He held to the sink. He was barrel chested, arms swollen from months of exertion.

He stared at the serious imposing face. He'd killed a man and would be, was perhaps already, a father. How was it that he'd still felt like a boy?

He went to the door. Snow had started falling. He picked up the phone and called the police. This time a different man confirmed Isa's name. He was abrupt and told Bart he would call him back. Twenty minutes later the phone rang. Now the man spoke slowly, pausing, now repeating, it seemed. Bart didn't respond. The man spelled out an address in upstate New York. Then to Bart's surprise he continued speaking. Gradually, Bart understood that this was about a child.

He changed and put his jacket on. He took his bags down the stairs. Ice cracked over the frozen mud. The truck's heaters beat at the air. Only the pain held him. So many times he'd wanted to disappear into a last sudden movement. He drove carefully now, going into slight fishtails then slowing before he accelerated again.

He considered self-hatred, or was it simply responsibility? All that a person might claim in a life, all that had to be claimed because it couldn't be undone. He passed the cemetery, then turned around and pulled off near the gate. He left the engine running. He got out and walked through the graves. Snow creaked beneath his boots, the night a cavern at the corner of his eye. He'd once told Isa that his father's name was Barthélemy, but that had been a lie. The day of his mother's funeral he'd seen a tombstone in the old French part of the cemetery. Barthélemy was written on it. Because he'd never known his father's name, he'd decided this must be it, that his own name must have been taken from this. Perhaps he'd simply liked it better. It had been a boy's lie.

He tried to keep his mind still. He had a vague memory of flowering trees and a stone building. He saw it now, set back against the forest. His hand ached in the cold. The thaw had exposed most of the stones. After a while he found it. Amy Beaulieu Gray 1951–1976. Gently he knelt on this hidden, untended earth. He'd thought of Isa as someone who could save him. He touched his mother's gravestone. She'd been twenty-five. He counted the years. And then he realized she was gone.

Virginia–Louisiana
February 1994

The interstate south past
D.C. was extraterrestrial, military, walled with concrete
barriers and embankments, the sky yellow, the colour of
lights in a highway tunnel, bypasses with suburbs clus-
tered about like galaxies. The city was eerily empty.
Sunday. Every street looked the same, squat buildings
like bunkers. His dream of that old, innocent America
was far away. He had never felt so aware of pain. He'd
thought he would be the one to destroy himself.

An aging doctor in the hospital had explained it.

Afterwards there had been blood tests, papers to fill out. Words and lips, the echoing hallway. For several hours no one had noticed the car stalled on the meridian, no snow-banks to stop her. They'd done all they could. For years Bart would seek words to explain this until he gave up, forever dreaming that she was closing her eyes, seeing the night sky. It's a miracle, the doctor had said—the way things give back.

Bart had to stay two weeks for the paperwork to go through. For the first time, it was effortless not to drink. The nurses made him spend entire days with them so that he would learn. They packed a bag, clearly worried, not letting him leave until they'd explained everything. There were boxes of formula, books even, a child's car seat that one woman brought from home.

It was a miracle, he repeated to himself. He recalled something Diamondstone had said—We ascend by affliction. Then he didn't think for a while.

In Virginia he stopped at the house. The door was unlocked. The hollow pulse of those first steps froze him. The place was a shell, rooms stripped to the joists, hanging wires and insulation. He'd thought she would return here. He'd risked coming with the hope that he might find something of her that he could keep for the future. There was only a manila envelope on the floor, from an investigation agency.

He continued south through the day, stopping to mix formula or to soothe whatever unrest and tears. By that evening he'd reached warmer weather. He crossed into Louisiana. He felt steadier, strong even. Later he took a motel room. She was a quiet baby.

He watched her sleep for a while, then went out. Night sounds emanated from the swamp across the highway, the darkness staticky, lit with phosphenes. He was twenty-six. Power lines hung against the sky, barely visible. He crossed the empty lanes. A truck passed, a clapping sound under the hood. He stood at the edge of the mud, in the grass, the gleam of water through the trees. He knew this place. Everything suddenly seemed clear and simple, the emotion he felt for that tiny child that was a part of him. Perhaps Diamondstone had truly believed that the only power greater than worldly suffering was God's love. Bart was no longer sure. Another truck went by, piling up the darkness and letting it spill in, fuller than before. The humid air rushed over him. He waited a while longer, just letting himself breathe. Then he went inside to sleep.

BOOK TWO

part one

Québec
1918–1963

The rest of her life Georgi-
anne would return to those first years, pausing over the
Bible, gulf wind and white cedar, the sound of river ice
on waterfall rocks. As a girl she'd never been more than a
few miles away: on land, the clapboard houses scattered
between embouchure and a waterfall the height of a barn;
or at sea, a Jersey village brief as a trick of light on the rearing coast. It had been hers. She knew its history, the lure
and flight that had brought families from Gaspésie or the
nearby Isle of Anticosti, the first settlements when a

certain Capitaine Fortin discovered a school of cod out past Rigge-Point in the 1860s. The name, Rivière-au-Tonnerre, she loved to clarify, came not from the first waterfall where the houses ended but another, three miles in, two hundred feet high and with the spring debacle loud enough to merit its thunder.

Her first years she lived for those gulf breaths of salt and mountain air. Tall and broad shouldered, she favoured dark dresses that set off hands as big as her father's. As a girl she'd learned that all callings were inferior to sacrifice. Her mother had died in childbirth and her father depended on her to manage the house and oversee her younger sister. She took pleasure in pumping water at dawn, in the smell of matches when she lit the stove, in sewing her sister's clothes. She worked tirelessly, expanding the garden, turning the rot of last year's husks. She wore her father's old boots, and each afternoon, coming in to prepare dinner, she kicked the perfect print of sandy mud from one sole, then the other. The next day, when they'd dried, she swept them from the porch. Born in 1900, she was sure she would outlive the century and she called it her puny twin. She'd been told by her father, even by her younger sister, had even a faint memory of her mother telling her, that she should take care, cover up better. She knew the holy books called for meekness, modesty, and at church it was her pride she confessed, that she was stronger, that certain concerns need not apply.

When she was eighteen, the influenza arrived, believed to have bred in the trenches of the war, now working its way around the world, hundreds of thousands dying up the east coast, shortages of coffins in Boston and Washington. Not worried for herself, she didn't think to worry for others. She watched as black-draped wagons rolled in, as first individuals, then families were carted into town, the Gendrons, father and wife and all five children, half the Levesques, a Lapierre and Bourque and God knows how many others. Her father had decided the family would stay at home, let it pass. One evening they heard someone climb the porch. She went to the door and saw that it was a neighbour, Jérôme Marceau. Her father had been reading aloud the funny bits in the back of the paper, though they'd heard them before. Her sister stopped brushing her hair and the oil lamp shone a silver band along it as if it were one continuous surface. The first snow of the year was falling, and Jérôme leaned against the door and knocked loudly though she was just inside. His breath misted and his face looked rucked and deflated, and he knocked again. His hand held a necklace with a dangling crucifix that tapped the glass.

We can't just leave him out there, her father said.

That night became the winter, the yellow wings of dusk in a distant cloud-break, the lit billows of fine snow blown in from the gulf and the door opening with a sound like a seal on a jar being broken, flooding them with cold air. Jérôme's lips were blue, and as he told them everyone was dead, his wife and daughters and sons, Georgianne's sister watched her with dark, scared eyes. Later, when everyone had gone to sleep, Georgianne left her bed and lay with her face in her sister's hair and lifted it and let the heavy strands fall on her cheeks.

Two weeks afterwards, morning sunlight roiled in clouds and struck her eyelids and she woke, breath misting, still no fever. The stove was open and wind through the flue had spread a half-circle of ash on the floor. She lit the first fire in a week and began eating again. Men from the village came and took the bodies away, and in May she saw her father and sister put in the ground with hundreds of others. June was unreal. She walked out past the house through the yarrow and burdock that grew up around the garden. All night she stepped past boreal fir and poplar, through twinflower and wood sorrel and nettles that she tore up with her hands and rubbed on her arms. Village dogs barked at the silent pulse of lightning over the gulf, magnesium flares from cloud to cloud. She came down out of the brush and the dogs raced towards her and set about in a circle, and she shooed them violently with a stick.

That Sunday, after church, the gossip was that a man named Hervé Hervé had come into town looking for a wife, that he had children at home under the care of his eldest, then twelve. He stood in a tan shirt rolled at the elbows and a captain's hat, which he wore at an angle. He had an eye patch like a pirate and was a head taller than any other man and looked at them as if they couldn't look back. Through his breast pocket showed the outlines of dark cigarettes.

She caught up with him on the rocky slope above the docks. Clouds blew past so that shadows moved along the coast like those of passing giants. I'll be your wife, she told him. He looked at the clean hem of her dress and up along her, at her throat and finally into her face and stood there, smoking. She watched the muscles beneath his rolled sleeve. He nodded and motioned her along, and they returned to the church, where he spoke with the priest, not knowing her name yet though the three of them were alone and he could point. The next day, when the formalities were finished, they went to the house. Afterwards she helped him load everything into his boat. Then she stepped in and they sailed south across the St. Lawrence, to a town that looked held together by strung-up fishing nets, to a farm that made her think, upon seeing it, of mud.

195

Thirty-eight years she gave herself to work, weaned children and husband from the bottle, the former easily, the latter not so and never for the last time. She learned this family's myths and curses, didn't let herself fade to what else might have been and watched with her husband's same static ken while children grew old too soon and feeble ones died. For him pride was a strong family; for her it was a holy one. In this their contest began. He was ashamed when villagers commented on the runts just as she was furious when the others skipped Mass and abandoned themselves to depravity.

There had been no way to have imagined that such a clan might exist. With time she ceased to think of her sons as sons but rather as the brothers. Runts excepted, they hung about with the demeanour of a street gang, harassed passing children and at night stole cigarettes and bottles from drunks. They were the biggest men any had seen up the coast. On the rare occasion that they spoke it was to brag. She'd heard them talk of bumping up against sailors to start fights, of taking out a man's eye with a broken bottle, of catching a hotel maid on her way home. Otherwise the house remained silent and she was relieved at the deeper silence of winter when they departed for the logging camps up north.

One afternoon she came upon her second son, Jean, kneeling in the sitting room, on the rug, praying for the family's salvation. She joined him, and when he finished she reminded him that the meek would inherit the world, though from that point on it wasn't with meekness that she defended him. He was a quick study and soon a favourite of the curé, and from then on it was generally assumed that he would join the clergy.

At first, with so many mouths to feed, she'd understood why Hervé Hervé had given a few runts away, one to a childless couple and another to an obese baker who was happy with what he could get. She'd been angry but had known the runts would be better off elsewhere. But the day Jean didn't return from school and the others told her that Hervé Hervé had given him to the innkeeper, she went and got him back. Three times she had to find him, and once she walked forty miles to a shop where she discovered him in a neat apron, stencilling rosettes on the borders of mirrors. From then on she took him everywhere. Evenings they went to the church, and while she scrubbed the floors, he did his homework in the pews. Every word of worship that she spoke, he repeated, and even once he insisted on helping her. That night, she found him in the bathroom picking at his hands. When she asked him what it was, he hid them behind his back, then cried when she brought them out and saw the raised blisters from scrubbing. After that he no longer repeated her words or helped though he stayed and studied and listened.   197

When the war began, she was surprised not so much to learn that a few of the older brothers had enlisted but that Jean had. The first letter they got back said that he had a job as a typist, and the second brought condolences from her majesty for the death of another son. Four years later, when Jean returned, he was a small, pallid man with shadowed eyes and he wouldn't look at anyone. His hands never stayed still unless he was smoking, and he tucked his elbow and held the cigarette guardedly next to his cheek like a femme fatale. Georgianne spoke of how he would go into the seminary now that the war was over. When she'd finished, he said only, Oh boy, the way the tourists did. The next day he was gone.

Later Hervé Hervé told her that Jean had been the only one who hadn't sent a portion of his army pay, and she said nothing because she knew. Over the next month she received two postcards, one with a picture of Montréal that bore the inscription *Pas loin!* and the other of the Canadian Rockies, snow-capped and immense, and which read, *Loin mais bien content.* A week later her fourteen-year-old daughter ran away, leaving her with twins.

That evening, after cleaning the church, she sat in the detergent-smelling dark. A few candles burned low in the glass and threw broken shadows against the stone. Once, in Rivière-au-Tonnerre, whales had come near the coast, rolling and blowing mist, and she'd taken her sister to see them. Those gathered had stopped watching the whales and turned to gaze at her sister, who'd reached for Georgianne's hand to go. You have the same eyelashes as me, she'd told Georgianne that night. Yes, but just that, Georgianne had said. It surprised her to remember. She touched her face. Age had made her cheeks and fingers numb as if with cold. Her joints ached. She wanted to cry but it was easier to forget.

Those years she found comfort only in church and the sewing of clothes. She dressed the family, though garments came home torn from fights, smeared with dirt and indeterminable blood. Listening to the curé she was caught by the Bible's repetition, the earth and dust and stones in which men laboured, and she knew now that sickness and child-bearing, the hard days in high wind-struck fields had been retribution. She'd been too prideful, too confident of her strength. But now, as the needle dipped and pulled, she let herself dream, flashes of youths lifted from toil by a perfect shirt, like a picture in the Eaton's catalogue. It was age, she thought, shaking it off.

That spring was sudden after a relentless winter, hot days, warm nights with uncommon southern winds broken by torrential rains. Ice floes split loudly as they descended towards the gulf. Plants grew and bloomed before the ground had dried, wet earth with minute flowers sprouting over it. Late one afternoon she left her daughters preparing dinner. She climbed the stairs and went into her room and eased the door closed, and guiltily lay down so as not to muss the bed. Outside, the sun shone like a yellow flare in thin cloud banks. There was the steady chopping of shovels in wet earth and the slapping of thrown mud and the wind with a sound like a sail being blown. It seemed she had dozed. She had a sensation of falling, of rushing air and a rising shape as if the wind had billowed the curtain though the sash was down, and when she opened her eyes, the figure stood not so much in stillness as suspended upon it, like dust motes in light. He looked older in that way of schoolchildren with flour on their faces for Christmas plays, though he wore a blue-and-white-striped shirt, each bar distinct, almost brilliant. He stood stiffly and his expression recalled that of a man she'd once seen frozen in river ice, cut out and carried to the village in a crystalline coffin. It was dead and blissful all at once and it held her. Then maybe she blinked—she couldn't mark the moment—and she sat up kicking.

Evening had made clefts of shadow along the mountain's incline, and she stood awhile, caught in residual stillness before she knelt on the rug. There wasn't the faintest impression of footprints. She could think of nothing else. Jean, she finally said, *reviens*, then added a brief, uncertain prayer. If the apparition had been Jean as a boy in his beaver-lined jacket and overalls, the leather cap he'd wanted for his eleventh birthday and that she'd secretly made, she'd have known she was tired and thinking him up, but why this, her son dressed like a tourist?

In the days that followed she mentioned the apparition only to the young curé with the pale eyes, asking him if it was a message. She'd heard him speak on the subject of miracles, the bishop in Montréal who'd healed the crippled black child, true charity. The curé listened, then visited the next day to inspect the house, to speak with Hervé Hervé.

That evening she took the postcards from an apple crate that had, almost forty years before, been converted into something of a hope chest. She didn't doubt she was getting soft but senile, crazy? For ten years she'd prayed for Jean regularly. In ten years he would have had children. What else was there for her here? Her sons and daughters were disappearing, fleeing. She'd tried too long to preserve this family, but the conditions that had once made the country inhospitable had lived on with Hervé Hervé. She'd been too strong to see and now her blindness had ended.

She went downstairs. Jude had come in, hours after the others. He removed boots caked with mud. At ten he looked like a cavern dweller with his flat, inexpressive face, the layer of dirt, muscles on every part of him. He glanced at her indifferently. He had her eyelashes, her sister's, and she couldn't help considering how in another time or place they might all have been different.

When she left, despite everything she'd lived, she

knew only two villages. She took what money she'd secreted and a bag of hand-me-downs. She walked out along the coast, spring moon, high tides ravaging below the road, darker pines like rents in a dark sky. Villagers had believed those who went south or west were different, and if they returned it was to suspicion. Hervé Hervé had called them *traitres*. The Ouellets' daughter had moved to Boston with a tourist and later brought back her own daughter to visit. A girl named Mava Rattledge. Such an ugly name. And in one generation. So perhaps the stories held some truth. Before Georgianne's father's time, priests were rumoured to have wandered throughout the States in search of French-Canadians gone astray or the Acadians deported long ago by the British.

201

Over the years, listening to talk of French places, Louisiana or St. Boniface, she came to think they were close, a few days' journey, but week after week she travelled west, past billowing and laddered city sky, fields stepped between forest and Laurentide rock. She spoke of a lost son and the children he would have left behind. Months later, in the prairies, the French families who invited her in asked of the Québec where they'd been born. She repeated the hearsay she'd long ignored, herself never speculative, not a gossip: the pollution from the U.S., or the factory trawlers, *les bateaux-usines* that dragged the cod from the gulf.

But alone, walking, she asked herself what had become of the young men with their dreams of swimming pools and barbecues. Had this immensity simply absorbed Jean? Québec had improved after the Second War. There had been work, possibility. Yes, winters were unforgiving, snow until April, lakes thawing in May, but when the earth breathed and the landscape bloomed, it was a soft country. Not this world without tide. She wouldn't have continued had she not known what awaited her at home. Once, a few years after marrying Hervé Hervé, as she'd been returning from Saturday Mass, she'd paused on the village road. From other houses, not from a few but from many, came music, children and parents playing together on the violins and piano and guitar, all recreating the steady, pleasant songs of the country. She'd had to ask why God had given her silence.

Winter caught her unprepared. She stayed in cheap rooms. Winnipeg. Regina. Saskatoon. Moose Jaw and Portage la Prairie. She worked where she could, ironing in factories with hundreds of coughing women, fingers gnarled with cold. Her entire life, all beyond her farm and shore had been no more than the quilted colours of a map, but now she doubted God's presence within this landscape. She'd sensed primitive religions, in storms and prairie fires, in the stillness of winter so far from the sea. It frightened her that she could think this.

The first days of spring, she set off again. Now, when invited in, she told stories she'd once considered silly, of fights and feats of strength. The world she'd struggled against lived on within her like a kind of love, Hervé Hervé who'd been there when she'd needed a new life.

But in the end, it was Jean she spoke of, because she knew that hope and love were not the same.

Each year more and more cars and trucks raced past, clothing her in dust. She saw machines as big as houses cutting swaths through the prairies, pounding highways onto the earth. She paused at every church and prayed. Summer nights she slept in ditches. She dreamed of heaven, of passing Jean in his striped shirt and him not knowing her. After an autumn rain she stopped to dry the hand-me-downs that she still carried, mildewed scraps that recalled lost children or herself, lean in fields, strong in maternity. Garments that had fit no one, like dreams, a stillborn's first outfit never worn, bad luck, the hollow recognition she'd once been. On that leafless roadside oak, on the Manitoba plains, wind shook the antique rags, terrifying travellers with the loneliness of their flapping.

Then, in a church, half lame and clutching herself, she was shocked to feel the weight of her own hands. She recalled her sister's hair falling on her cheeks. The blue and white shirt reappeared. The jeans walked past. She limped after. The ghost was the same as seven years before, on that afternoon soft as a bonnet.

Back another road without perspective, a few unkempt houses against planted fields, a weedy yard and a doorway with a cowering boy who saw not a servant of God, eyes bright with prophecy, dust of saints on her shoes, but a stooped woman with a wide jaw and a head as squat as a bullfrog's. She didn't speak, just inspected the house as he retreated backwards. She

203

went into the kitchen. Dishes filled the sink. The bedroom was musty, the shades drawn. A woman was in
bed, turned in her sheets.

Mama? the woman called.

204   *Oui, ma chère,* Georgianne told her, taking her thin,
dry hand. I'm here. *Chus là, chus là.*

Manitoba–Montréal
1963–1974

Only when Georgianne had
gone into the bedroom and shut the door did François
come out from behind the couch. He stood, breathing as
if testing the air, his curls mussed about his head like a
large, dark brain. Day had grown faint in the windows.
He went outside and crossed the yard and stepped
through the weeds where the fence had fallen, and into
the cornfield. Thick stalks ran on against the gathering
dark and he walked between them until the world
remained only as a sense of wind falling on dry husks. He

lay down. Sometime in the night he heard the sounds of truck engines, voices, doors closing. In the morning he woke to bars of sunlight. He saw tiny blue flowers grown in the furrows, and farther off, the black high-laced shoes, the swollen black-stockinged ankles and the patched dress of his grandmother.

From that day on the world seemed an old place, growing older in those weeks that he learned to live in a presence whose severity was the only he'd known. As long as he could recall, he'd roamed. He'd befriended dogs and walked with them and given them names from picture books, Cabot or Cartier. Now he learned of commandments and deadly sins, of his father's goodness and his family's strength. He felt tiny compared to this God who was surely waiting to get into the world, the house, to break the windows and overturn the tables and piss on the floor with the self-righteousness of a stallion. When the sky burst with lightning and flooded the ditches, he thought, Here's God again, messing things up. Then he ran home, terrified that God would let fall something heavy, a well cover or a refrigerator.

In the kitchen, a Bible now sat on the drop-leaf table, a piece of quilted fabric below, thicker than a pot holder, as if the book contained something hot. Under his grandmother's supervision he read the family tree inside the cover, two centuries of ancestors with mean, historical-sounding names. She told him that he must learn to be like his father, and when she wrote his name—Hervé-François Hervé—he recognized only the middle one. She said if he wanted to be a priest, he must protect his soul, though when he closed his eyes to find it, he saw only swirling, stellar darkness made by the sunlight on his eyelids.

To Georgianne it was clear that François was one of the runts though she saw no reason to plant this seed of doom. She edited the Hervé story. She decided the best education would be to convince him of his own goodness. Man was born in sin, she knew, and the teachings saved few from their own savageness. Jean was his model, strong when there was need, gentle in his heart, clever at school and bestowed with clarity of purpose, which was bringing François into the world so that he could be a priest.

When in doubt, François had only to ask, and together he and his grandmother would add to the missing father until she lost track and rambled about others, burly uncles, a boy born with a fighter's face, and Hervé Hervé, for whom there wasn't a thing not pulled down or knocked over or soundly beaten. Sometimes her murmuring sounded like coffee percolating.

But my father, he asked, he was gentle?

Doux, très doux, she said. Very gentle and good. Like you. You are a good person.

And wanted to be a priest?

Would have, she said and lifted her hands, but wasn't. So he could have you. A good person.

François found it odd that his mother had never mentioned any of this. But she'd been sick. The father he worked to recall had seemed more like those other men his grandmother mentioned, strong, with a burlap hug and a lead soldier gifted from a big palm, a smell of plowed fields. One night François had been carried from bed, wrapped in sheets, to the porch. Mosquitoes nudged at his ear as he dipped in and out of sleep. The east turned blue. His father's hand was in a bandage. He spoke and the only word François would recall was *Alaska*, pronounced with intensity, like Georgianne's Amen. Alaska, his father repeated, each syllable even. In the morning he was gone. A-las-ka, François sang, walking the fields, swinging a stick at dandelion heads with a feeling of joy.

Most upsetting, though, was the disappearance of his mother. That first morning, when Georgianne had brought him in from the cornfield, she'd held his wrist in a hand whose calluses were as hard as the bone beneath. Inside she sat him down.

Ta mère est morte, she told him sternly. Then she explained that because his father was also dead, she, his grandmother, would raise him, but that it wouldn't be easy—that it was never easy to raise a priest. They are so quickly spoiled, she said.

That evening, after being fed bowls of potatoes and more stuffed than he'd ever been, he pushed his mother's door open. The shade had always been drawn in the single window, but now a brilliant sky hung above the swollen darks of sunset and that immense earth. The room seemed too small. He touched the cool fabric of the naked mattress and began to shiver. He ran outside, through the fields. In the distance the lights of a farm showed on the plain like those of a vessel at sea. Cicadas whirred in the windbreaks. He vomited. He came to an electric fence and grabbed it and hung on as the ground bucked. When he opened his eyes, stars glittered above. He lay in the grass, his voice crying all around him.

Those first months, when his grandmother dozed, he put down the Bible and snuck outside, now off limits, as if nature were a bad neighbourhood. Late summer brought rainless clouds, and he went out through the rattling corn. He'd always been here, humming songs from his mother's radio or picking flowers for her. He paused to hear the movement of the stalks. He crumbled starchy tassels in his fingers, then peeled an ear without breaking it off. The corn was luminous in the shadow, like exposed skin. He counted the kernels, opened and tasted them with his thumbnail. He lay on the tamped furrows and curled his fingers through the dry earth to where it was cool and moist.

On the first crisp autumn day, his grandmother took his hand and led him from the house, along the road, past fields of nodding wheat to the bus station. East, the signs said as they left town, and he wondered if the first children of creation had travelled those same highways.

Montréal was his new home, buttressed sky, rooftops climbing like ziggurats, and a shabby apartment twenty minutes from the downtown, on Lionais near De Bullion. He walked to school, returned for lunch, and each night, a half-hour before bed, was allowed to read from a stack of yellowed comics that his grandmother had discovered in a cupboard and that dated back twenty years. She received charity from the church and other

institutions, boxes with dried goods and castoffs. What little money she earned was from knitting with three
elderly neighbours, and together they sat in the crammed
living room, talking in vivid bursts. Sometimes they listened to a radio station that played classics, the folk songs
of *la Bolduc* or *le Quatuor Alouette,* during which they
became silent but for mild exclamations of *Oh, le temps*
and *Mon Dieu.* Often they asked François to read from
the Bible and interrupted with their praises.

His room was the pantry, emptied of shelves, its only
decorations a crucifix and a metallic print of the Virgin.
A tablecloth hung in the doorway, checkered red and
white and so threadbare that, winter mornings, when the
harsh, low sun shone through, he could see the yellowed
walls of the kitchen. Unable to sleep, he lay his head on
the windowsill and gazed up at the prairie moon. He listened for each hoot in the street, for the discordant note
from a distant guitar or a girl's laugh.

His grandmother arranged for him to be an altar
boy, and he was sent home with a dollar for her after
every Mass. He helped Père Wilbrod, an ancient priest
who reeked of cigarette smoke. Though François
wanted to please his grandmother, he struggled in his
studies and in catechism. He was shy and dreamy, tiny
for his age and often picked on. His grandmother sewed
his outfits, his underwear even, cloth so coarse that on
humid days the seams crawled like ants along his
thighs. His hair was cropped, nearly a tonsure, she having perceived evil in curls. He believed her decree that
he was good and that the other children his age had

been corrupted. He concluded that he would someday be a priest, though he felt little in the pews, nothing like standing among the corn, tassels swaying above as he closed his eyes to the sun and turned, eager to be lost, to wander those fields forever.

When François's mother had died, Georgianne had gone through every drawer and closet but found no trace of Jean, only the mother's birth certificate, a list of debts and a stack of letters in English, which she could not read but kept just in case. The rest she burned with the sheets from the death bed. She had no doubts. The ghost had brought her, and so she gave herself to raising François, afraid only that he might die like a runt or that the septic drone outside her window take him away. She'd have preferred a village, the quiet to meditate on salvation, but unknown origins would be noticed and gossip could hurt prospects.

Her years of wandering had not been kind. Her knees and ankles were gnarled, feet as twisted as roots. Soon she could no longer go out. François ran errands, and she sat by the radio, dipped into sleep and woke to the puffing of an accordion. Sometimes he pretended to have questions about his father just so he could hear those other, much better stories, Hervé Hervé who'd wrestled champions from miles away, *le Suède, le Géant, le Russe Noir*, or that of the brawny boy and his frail sister. He thrilled at this incredible love.

Only when he was almost sixteen did François begin to doubt. He tallied the years. His grandmother had searched for him seven, a saintly number hence suspect, and he'd been six. He learned from the encyclopedia that gestation lasted about 280 days, a little more than nine months. He tried a computation, discovering that if his father had appeared to her as a ghost, it must have been within weeks of conception. But François vaguely recalled that even in the last months of his mother's life she'd still been waiting. A few warm evenings she'd believed his father would return, and because of the unsteadiness of her hands, she'd taught François to do her makeup. Together they'd stared at her reflection, her jet hair seeming alive against her skin. With unnecessary slowness he'd drawn in her lips and eyes and cheeks, each minute stroke tugging at her skin so that she'd made sounds in her breathing as if with pleasure. Afterwards they'd waited on the porch as mosquitoes swarmed up from the fields like smoke against the low sun.

On the first day of Christmas break, he began to search. A cold snap had covered the windows in frost, and his grandmother had surrendered to a soporific stupor next to the radiator. The site for the Stade Olympique had been planned not far from their block, and with the thundering of cranes and cement trucks and jackhammers she wouldn't hear him. At the bottom of her sewing kit, next to her spare rosaries, he found a bundle of letters.

At school he'd learned a rudimentary English, just enough to make sense of what was written. Dear Madeleine, each one began and went on to mention a mining town or a new construction project in the Yukon or Alaska. They spoke of money and said that he would be home in the winter if all went well, and each, at one point, asked about little Frank. How is little Frank? Is he growing up well? In some dim, distant place François could recall his father calling his mother Madeleine. Each letter was signed Frank and almost every one had a different return address, in the Yukon or Saskatchewan or British Columbia, two in Alberta, one in Alaska. A few mentioned her illness and asked if she'd been taking her medicine. The last in the pile read, Tell little Frank I said hello, or do you still insist on calling him François?

A snowplow dragged its blade along the street. It was a merciless early-winter afternoon, the sun glaring on snowbanks, the radiator clanking and hissing. Jackhammers worked in the distance. His grandmother snored with her mouth open, showing brown molars.

He took out his English grammar. More meticulous than he'd been in all his years of schooling, he wrote a simple letter explaining who he was, that his mother had died and that he was seeking his father. He copied it eleven times, once for each of the various addresses, pausing to rub the cramps out of his hand. Then he filched money from the can beneath the sink. He bundled against the cold and mailed them in the few minutes he had free before Mass.

By that summer François still had no response. Being small for his age he'd kept on as an altar boy, and Père Wilbrod, who took sips, as cross-eyed by litany as a trucker by the shear of highway, hardly paid him any mind. But he'd stopped sending money home and François's grandmother had become too blind to knit, could barely pay the rent and feed them both with the welfare cheque. She was no longer the woman whose jaw distilled the wrath of God.

Will you be a priest soon? she asked and spoke of how priests received a stipend for life.

François considered getting a job but hardly knew where to begin he looked so young. Money offered possibilities, freedom, normal clothes, a ticket back to the prairies. Did he need a reason to want it? The solution came a few days before school let out. After Mass, Philippe, another altar boy, showed him an ad in the paper: two hundred dollars for young men willing to go through sleep deprivation in a room without light.

There are better ones, Philippe told him, and reading the ads, François agreed that taking medicine didn't sound bad. After all, medicine is good for you, they agreed.

Those first weeks of summer vacation, as the sun dried out alleys and girls wore clothes they kept only for those months, he and Philippe applied to several of these positions but were turned away for being too young. Otherwise they walked, seeing hippies kissing on the greens or shimmying to frenzied tam-tams on the Mont Royal. In a ten-cent theatre they watched a lurid film about time travellers.

At the fifth job they applied to, a survey of nasal sprays, the lounge was filled with students and homeless people. While Philippe was getting applications, a prostitute—François was almost certain—came in and sat

214

next to him. A few times he'd seen them lounging in the street in vinyl suits, but even for a *guidoune* this one looked odd—a halter that read New Jersey in peeling letters, white boots, cowgirl style with silver studs and tassels. She was clearly pigeon-chested, shoulders hung back as if with elegance. Lipstick marked her buck-teeth. Her hair was black and ratty and cut just above her eyes. She wasn't wearing a bra, and through the last *e* in *Jersey* he could see the imprint of her nipple. He moved a seat away.

I don't bite, she said with an accent from up north somewhere. She tugged at her skirt. Her voice was nasal, and François considered that the spray she was about to get might change that. He joined Philippe at the counter, where he learned that it was a no go. They left, and a few days later, when François showed him a flyer he'd found on a telephone pole, Preference Test—All Men, All Ages, Philippe said that he was getting a real job. You'll probably drink juice, he concluded after reading the flyer.

The address was in the downtown, in a skyscraper as strange as a spaceship, made of concrete and curved glass and with indentations like streamlines. He went inside and up an elevator to the fourteenth floor. The office he was looking for was crammed with buzzing consoles, wires criss-crossed under tables, monitors flickering and walls hung with graphs. Half the fluorescent tubes in the ceiling had burned out, and a man was scanning words and numbers on a stack of accordion printouts that he flipped through without detaching the sheets. On the desk next to him was an ashtray so crammed with upright cigarette butts it looked like a sea urchin.

Can I help you? he asked, still reading. The room smelled of smoke and paint fumes.

I am here for test, François managed in his poor English.

Yes, of course. The man spoke evenly, his movements brusque and mechanical. He had an equine face, impassive and without wrinkles. He picked up an application form. You are, what, fourteen, fifteen?

Eighteen, François said.

The man's eyes flickered up from the paper and back. He wrote down fifteen, then slid François the questionnaire.

There's no legal requirement, he told him. Just try to tell the truth. It's confidential.

François checked boxes and scribbled answers: religion, schooling, colour, food preferences, employment goals. Other goals. Are you a virgin? Homosexual?

When he'd finished, the man told him to follow. He opened a door.

At first glance the darkness was absolute. No light from outside penetrated. François took a few testing steps before he began to discern walls that had been painted black.

A moment later the man wheeled in a slide projector. He crossed the room and reached up to emptiness and pulled down a screen.

This is a preference test, he said. Since it's your first time, I'll give you the first one. If you come back in a few days, I'll give you the second as well. Twenty dollars each time.

Okay, François said. Okay.

The man brought in a cardboard box and what looked like a starkly futuristic vacuum cleaner. He flicked a switch and several red lights came on. He hooked a cord into the back. It ran into a hole in the wall.

The vacuum hose wasn't making a sucking noise but seemed to be humming. From the box the man took a pair of bulky rubber underwear that could be tightened with a strap. There was a circular plug-in on the front that he hooked the hose into. All right, he said, you can drop your pants. François reluctantly undid the button and pushed them down. The air caressed his thighs and gave him gooseflesh. *Vingt dollars*, he told himself.

Your underwear, too, the man said. It won't hurt.

The room was dark. François lowered his underwear. His scrotum tightened. The man knelt and fitted him, the rubber smooth and elastic. François flinched as the hose took hold gently as a mouth sucking a thumb. A green light flickered on the vacuum. The man wiggled the underwear. The tiny light stayed on. The contraption emitted a low, almost comforting beep.

I want you to count from zero to one hundred and thirty-two by increments of twelve, then back to zero and up again and so on. Don't think about anything but counting. Just look at the pictures that come up.

He went out and closed the door. The way the light cut away from the darkness reminded François of the sci-fi film, the hero about to be teleported into a future populated by beautiful, lonely women. The projector clicked, a blinding square on the screen, then again. The image of a tree appeared, branches laden with red apples. François lost count at seventy-two and had to close his eyes for a second to get to eighty-four. The projector hummed and clicked. A billy goat stood in a churned-up barnyard, its legs slightly splayed, as if it had come to a sudden stop. It tilted its black-striped face to the camera. It had long, curved horns.

François continued counting and each click brought a new image: a half-eaten apple, a bowl of glistening cherries, a man's hairy foot with yellow, ingrown toenails, the Notre Dame Cathedral, mountains, ballerina toe shoes, an aerial view of New York, a crumpled cassock, a soapbox house, a rose, a block of melting ice. Then the projector shut off and François was left to stew in the dark before the underwear was removed.

What was de . . . eh . . . de reason for dat? he asked, blinking in the office that before had seemed quite dim. His scrotum and thighs felt breezy.

The purpose, the man said, is to study subliminal reactions.

What is subliminal? François asked, but the man waved his hand and said in sloppy French, just as mysteriously, that the machine measured changes in tumescence.

While François pondered this, the man took twenty dollars from a cashbox. Don't forget to return in three days, he said. The second test is a lulu.

What is a lulu?

You'll see, the man said and gave him the money.

During the cold, slow months of January and February
François's letters had crossed the country to non-existent
boarding houses, to post offices in quiet towns, their dams
and power plants long since built. Letters with no return
addresses were kept a month or two, thrown in the trash.
For years a man had visited these places, retracing his life.
He rattled doors of boarded-up houses. He asked for girls
by name decades after brothels had been burned down.

Almost forty years he'd followed jobs from Ontario to
Alaska, mining, logging, building dams and pipelines.
He'd kept a half-Inuit girl near Fairbanks who had two
boys, an Irish woman in Vancouver kept by others as well
and who'd birthed a colourful race of children, and the
French girl in Manitoba, whom he'd liked best, the boy,
too, his, no doubt. On one visit the Inuit woman was
gone, the house occupied by another family. The Irish
woman died of pneumonia and the children, he'd later
heard, were scattered to orphanages. She'd had a daughter by him, she'd claimed, and it had been this girl he'd
recalled while he was lying in a prostitute's bed. The
young woman had gotten up and had gone to the mirror.
She put on a summer hat and took a long ribbon and tied
it above the brim so that the ends hung against her naked
shoulders. Gradually he realized he'd seen this before,
the daughter who'd supposedly been his and who'd followed him about whenever he visited. She'd once stood
in the doorway and put on a hat and tied a ribbon to it.
Though by now she might be the age of the girl at the

mirror, she'd been a redhead and this one had dusky colouring. He got up and dressed and drove through the day to Vancouver. He visited every orphanage, but he'd lost track of the years and she might have grown or died or been adopted. Then he made the arduous drive to Manitoba. The house was rented by another family, the woman and his son gone.

Work had kept him sober, but over the months that he searched there was more time to drink and more reason until he was hardly searching, just wandering. As a boy, he'd been the smallest in the family, and there had been a bad winter when his joints had begun to ache and swell until he had the knuckles of an old man, bulbous elbows and knees. On the day the doctor told him he would be a cripple, he crawled outside to where the firewood was stacked. He took the biggest piece he could handle and lifted it repeatedly. Each day he worked his gnarled hands around the wood. Despite the pain he was eventually able to pull up a rotten stump and crumble it. Muscle had given shape to warped bones, and he moved awkwardly, but with strength, like a man wearing armour. The pain of this simple achievement, he believed, had hardened him. But seeing the girl tie the ribbon, something gave. Now the buildings he'd built were old and each place he returned to no one remembered him. He sold what he owned to keep drinking. He crossed the prairies on boxcars. The last of the spring rains churned ploughed earth until it reflected the glowering sky. He woke occasionally to anonymous empty plains. A bit of light came through the clouds, but he'd had no taste for religion. He recognized the next town. At the boarding house the man knew him. He fished through a stack of letters until he found one, quite recent—that's why he remembered. Frank, he said. Right. You stayed here in '62. Frank nodded and took the envelope. There were men like this, who never forgot a thing.

The day after the preference test François wandered the city, asking himself what he might desire that he didn't know. He passed a blind man with a guide dog, stores with draped bins of dates and olives. Did the body long for things he could not fathom? And what of the soul?

As he neared home he noticed that a squat man was sitting on the metal stairs. He had his elbows on his knees, his gnarled hands clasped together.

Boy, he said in English, his voice slurred. Is there a young man named François or Frank who lives up here?

François smelled alcohol. The man had on a new button-up shirt but his jacket was dirty.

Frank . . . ? François repeated.

I've tried the apartment up there, but the old lady won't get up to open the door.

Dat apartment, François managed to say. His throat ached. Dat boy, he said, he move out long time a-go.

He looked carefully at the man's swollen features, the food stains on his jacket, the cheap shirt, the veiny nose. Maybe 'e die, François added. 'It by car or someting.

The man stood. He worked his lips. His coarse cheeks bunched beneath his eyes. He pounded down the stairs with short, bulky steps and limped away.

François went in, past his grandmother, who sat with her eyes half-closed. He fell onto his bed and pushed his sleeve into his mouth to stop the sound of his weeping until he no longer could or cared if she heard. Then he got up and ran outside, down the steps and along the street, but the man was gone.

Each day that week he started at the rumbling foundations of the Stade Olympique and walked, to St. Laurent, to Outremont, where Jewish women strolled with their prams and headwraps and wigs. He saw Italians loading trucks and shouting. He saw the Chinese in their stinky butcher shops. He explored Ste. Catherine's from the rundown walk-ups of Hochelaga to the wide, manicured lawns of the west and the English girls with their yellow hair. He skipped Mass.

It was on one of these walks that he saw the prostitute from the clinic. She'd noticed him first and told him he looked lost—*T'as l'air perdu.* Are you the boy I met last week?

Oui, he said. When she asked what he was doing, he told her, Walking. She offered to go along. She introduced herself as Ernestine. At first she talked about medical experiments, that there was a market for contraceptive tests and she'd gotten a couple jobs because of her situation. She stopped and looked at him seriously. He nodded. After a moment she smiled and asked where he was from. He found himself telling everything, the prairies, his mother, the father, the twenty dollars he'd kept, that he was supposed to be good but wasn't and desired things he didn't even know he could. He felt the words would never stop coming.

Do you want to eat something? he asked, and she said, Okay, in a squeaky, surprised voice. The first restaurant they came to was Italian and they ordered plates of spaghetti and worked their forks in circles and took turns talking while the other chewed.

Everyone hates my profession, she said, even though Jesus was always hanging out—*comme il se tenait*—with people like me. It's not that I like what I do. I don't have a choice. But I'm taking classes. She looked at him significantly. I'm good inside, she said, tapping the deformed sternum visible through her tight blouse.

She described how she'd run away from home. She'd been in love and had come to Montréal, but the guy had left her, and her parents wouldn't take her back. As she spoke, her eyes crowded with emotion. She told François that Catholics were mean, that her mother was too Catholic and had named her Ernestine after her aunt who was a nun who was also named after her aunt who was a nun. François imagined generation after generation of pigeon-chested nuns named Ernestine like clipped snowflakes unfolded from paper.

But I'd never run away from anyone, she said. You know what I mean?

Oui, he said. *Absolument. Oui.*

She narrowed her eyes. I believe in things. You don't have to be Catholic to believe.

I know, he said.

I think we're a lot alike, she told him. They'd finished eating. Anyway, I have to go. It's getting late. She wrote her address on the napkin. You know, if you want to visit—not like that. *Pas comme ça.* But just to talk or something, if you're lonely. It happens. But don't come too late. She smiled, seeming to see beyond him. I like you. See you later. *Bonne nuit.* As she kissed his cheek, he looked at her painted eyelids and trumpet nose. *Bonne nuit,* she repeated. He glanced at the address written in looping cursive. Not until she was walking away did he notice how skinny her legs were.

When he arrived for the Lulu, the man was still alone, inscrutable and deliberate, scanning printouts as if not a day had passed.

Come in, he said and made François wait. The same process followed though without the slide projector. François dropped his pants for the rubber underwear. The vacuum hose took hold. The green light flickered and stayed lit, and the man covered it with a piece of electrical tape. This time he brought out padded earphones.

Put these on and begin counting.

He closed the door.

The darkness dizzied François. He blinked but his eyes refused to adjust. Then through the earphones came the hurried breathing of a girl, so near she might have been in the room. Just from the high catch of terror in her throat, he could picture her.

He kept bolting his eyes to see the running feet, the mouth forming each frantic breath. Another pair of footsteps interrupted the continuity, these heavier, faster. Then she cried out, and there was the low, almost inaudible thud of bodies.

Come on, a man's voice said. Bitch. Then just sounds: cloth tearing up what seemed the length of her body, her suppressed squeals as if she was being gagged. A span of near-silence followed, rustling and scraping. Then the breaths returned. His gasps were human only in that they almost formed words, hers shrill. François was painfully erect. The grunts came faster in the man, her breath now a rapid pulse of intermittent, involuntary sound. The rasp of cloth on concrete was briefly lost to the distant honking of a car. Somewhere a window slid in its frame and slammed. Everything ended with the man's panting as he ran into a silence that came too soon. The footsteps simply disappeared.

Eyes shut, François listened for her chattering teeth, her last whimpers and sobs.

After a suitable pause, the man came in and freed him.

In the street François stood with his money. Traffic rushed by. Slanting sunlight lit graffiti and bricked-up windows, pigeons on sills and white smears of shit from storey to storey. A gas station was on the corner. He went in and asked the cashier for the bathroom key. The light hummed. The floor tiles were filthy. Toilet paper hung from the rim of the bowl.

He took off his shirt and lay it on the sink and looked in the mirror. He pushed down his pants and underwear.

He listened for the sound of the girl, but the reek of the bathroom was stifling. He leaned close to the mirror. His chest showed his ribs, the silky patter of his heart.

Outside the sky refused to grow dark. He walked along Ste. Catherine's, past the plywood on abandoned shops, the dusty entrances and cracked windows webbed together with masking tape. The downtown was crowded, raucous, cars blaring horns.

At the church the evening Mass had yet to begin and a few people still waited for confession. He stood in the pews and looked at the saints carved in the wall. For them faith seemed a terrible thing, painful and isolating, and he wondered if they had chosen or if God was simply within them, like an affliction.

He went to the confessional and sat. The wood on the other side of the partition creaked. Wilbrod spoke the usual words. Stale cigarette smoke and the scent of varnish was suddenly nauseating. Wilbrod began to repeat himself, and François threw back the curtain. He ran outside the church and stood, trembling, slugging breaths in the cool air. He found Ernestine's address and the money in his pocket. The sun had set. Wind blew up from the distant river and rustled the leaves of sidewalk trees. Old people were out for the last walk of the day.

Québec–Ontario–Manitoba–
Saskatchewan–Alberta–British Columbia
1977–1981

By twenty François was still small, with the sparse whiskers of a Chinese and the unrelenting hair of a Greek. He'd long ago given up being an altar boy, and when he'd told his grandmother, she hadn't replied. The petrification that eventually reached her heart had already done in her brain. On occasion her eyes blazed and she ranted that the Church was no longer vigilant. *Les jeunes curés d'aujourd'hui,* she said bitterly as if he were one. But this was the habit of anger. She didn't notice his absences, and he had no way of mentioning an amorous interest four years in the making, his first love, that pigeon-chested prostitute named Ernestine. Then his grandmother succumbed, and the century raced past with him on its back. He sold the family Bible to an antique store for two dollars.

His first night with Ernestine he'd explained that nothing was as he'd believed—there'd never been a great family, a shining father—the body was more powerful than any flimsy soul. He spoke of a profound confusion, a force within him. In no great act of genius she, being more intuitive than verbal, let drop her chintzy bathrobe. Her nipples were large for her breasts, and her underwear sagged, taken off and put on a little too often. In this way the years passed.

After his grandmother's death he began living with Ernestine. By then he knew the good life of a guinea pig and was bored perhaps only of nighttime walks, evenings alone. Was it wrong that men took cheap pleasure, Ernestine nothing to advertise, neither ardent Asian nor buxom black nor svelte Russian import, but homegrown, *la pute générique?* Should it bother him that he was a lab rat though it was an easy life? At best he sipped pop, commented on tanginess and effervescence, took a guess at popular brands. But the money was in the at-worst category, washing down pills with beer, headaches and belching, horrible howling gas that had Ernestine out of bed lighting candles. He ate protein mixes and rode exercise bikes while men in lab coats took muscle samples from his anaesthetized thigh. Once, because of a side effect, he stopped urinating for a week. He would have the urge but would stand above the toilet unavailed. When he asked the scientist running the project, Where does it go? the man shrugged and said, The miracles of the human body, the miracles of science, and almost seemed happy.

Back in the street, bleary eyed, François treated him-   229
self to a hot dog. The sun was casting shadows, his home now a place of business.

Those years Ernestine warned François that she was a broken article, that he was made for better, to which he disagreed. He'd never gone back to church. Now it was the other stories that he recalled, the ones that hadn't jived with his grandmother's religion—fighters and soldiers. Was there any of that heroic Hervé blood in him after all? Was the name his even if it hadn't been for those first six muddled but prismatic years? He recalled prairie wind, sunlight that opened outward from the clouds with the power of geologic upheaval. Montréal wanted to inject him with the questions of the age. He and Ernestine would be of value only so long as their bodies held up. When the Olympics had come into town, business had boomed, and since then the stadium provided rich hunting grounds, always a lonely drunk staggering out with the crowds. When François could finally go home, Ernestine was asleep, chaffed thighs to the air, smelling of antiseptic.

They managed to live in the afternoon, picnics at the park, telling the same stories, her memories of up north, his of out west, as if they were children. He welcomed his medication-induced fevers so she'd have to take a night off and coddle him. *Dorloter*, she said, *j'va dorloter mon tit bébé*. She tidied up, burned cheap incense, read from trashy romances and sometimes, sick even, his blood ran hot and she made the only sounds of love her neighbours would hear.

Eventually he started wondering about her clients. He didn't know why. It ate him up. He'd be with a nurse after taking a pill, and she'd say, Well, I don't know if it's you or the medication, but you've got blood pressure through the roof. He'd lie, *Non, pas moi*. He'd return home at five in the morning and, with trembling hands, take Ernestine's shoulders. Smelling like a gym though fresh from the shower, she would let him repossess her until she gave in, bucking and pulling at his hair. She wept like a little girl, retroussé nose puffy. *Je t'aime*, she told him, stroking his neck. He wanted to tear down the black drapes, spill the apartment into the street. Traffic carried past, horns and air brakes and the rumble of cargo. Exhausted after a night watching the emptying street from the plastic counter of a hamburger shack, he listened to the day begin. That was it. The world expanding its sound and light without them.

Finally he told her everything had to change. No more clients, no more experiments. They'd go out west before it was too late. He described the prairie sunsets. But when he returned the next morning it had all been done. The drapes torn and heaped, the puny furnishings kicked into piles, and a note: *François, tu es trop bon. Je ne t'aime pas. Au revoir.*

He cleaned and rehung the drapes and set the tin tea set back on the paisley bandana. He returned the romance novels to a shelf as rickety as a spice rack. He slept now in what he'd hated. He couldn't look at it enough, couldn't turn in the bed too many times. Her hand mirror pooled what light slipped past the curtains. From upstairs the sound of people rising for work came through the vents. The city, as he'd seen it so often, suspended in morning light, held millions of rooms like this one, sleeping, dreaming bodies oblivious to each other, so numerous that perhaps God couldn't touch them all, like the prairie sun at dusk on the reaching grass, each blade lost in the shadow of another.

He left before the rent was due. He hitchhiked, and with each mile he felt himself expanding, taking in rivers and mountains. On his nightly walks he'd talked to hippies and understood how they wanted it, sleeping, eating and making love, smoking weed. Their confidence awed him, a power assumed, an astral alignment that permitted casual living. He imagined that out there, on the boundless Canadian earth, there was a place for him.

His longest ride was with a trucker who shared coffee and sandwiches and who confessed, during the hourless night, that he liked to dress up as a woman and hang around at rest stops. Abba was on the radio, the pleasure at the world's kindness streaking like headlights within them.

By Toronto, François was low on money. He took a damp room in a boarding house and worked all winter

and through the next summer washing dishes and sub-
sisting on leftovers and practising his English on the line
cooks. He was miserable, lonely. He shovelled snow on
the side, saving every penny. He tried not to think of
Ernestine and kept his spirits up by dreaming.

232

After a year and a half, he had enough to buy an old
green Ford. It came with a wooden camper, and just seeing it he thought of how the tortoise must feel with its
home on its back. Spring had finally arrived, and he was
off again, west, rains blowing up into the electrical system, making the truck sputter, though the heaving
engine dried within its own heat. Crossing into
Manitoba, he thought of his grandmother on foot. He
imagined her ghost within the landscape, the strength of
her wandering a slow motion against eternity.

Those next weeks he travelled with a sense of inten-
tion. Every day seemed a revelation. Slight bumps in the
highway radiated through the seat in a gentle coasting
motion. The western sky sopped and drained in an endless dye bath beyond the edge of the earth. The smell of
fields and grass, the wind and rattle of the pickup had an
old-fashioned feeling, like a hayride. Evenings, he
parked on overgrown farm roads, mullein sprouting
hugely from the dry husks of the previous year. The truck
tires crushed wild chamomile, and he sat in the dark,
breathing the perfumed air.

At times, as he meandered west, he stopped on the side
of the highway and walked into the budding fields and
stood, squinting in the flashing sunlight. He tried to sense
that absence of consequence before his grandmother had

arrived with her primitive head. In nature, he'd thought he would always be back where he'd started, but money was running low and he was realizing that there was nothing to return to. It seemed obvious now, but the emotion of finding what he'd lost had been so strong for so long that he'd never considered what he would do here. How long could he wander the prairies? The world seemed to be asking what he was, the farmers with their lead gazes, the squinting cowhands. A few hippies were hitchhiking west, going to B.C. They talked of paradise, El Dorado. They grinned and asked where he was heading.

But three weeks later, though it felt sudden, he wandered too far and reached the mountains. He camped on the shores of lakes and rivers. Sitting alone, he felt erased, the truth of this measureless earth and stone pouring like light into his eyes until there was no room left in his head for himself. He searched for another truth, for one that might include him, but in the end, the only other that he found was money. His truck engine stopped with the thundering of hot steel. Smoke issued from every panel. He lingered awhile, then set off for help. Walking a mountain road, he looked up from the kicking, battered cuffs of his jeans. He saw the vantage of himself from the sky, a diminishing speck between rocks and cliffs and trees. He hardly had a penny to his name.

The next week he slept in a few odd places, tried to make deals with mechanics in towns occasioned by two roads slipping past each other. A man took pity and gave François a lift. But either one lonely valley lane was identical to a thousand others or his truck had vanished. The scenery came in wave upon wave until the sound of shifting gears emanated from their bones. At last, François thanked the man. He opened the door and put his boots on the broken asphalt. He started walking in a direction that turned out to be west.

234

The first job he found was in a valley near Mission, an hour from Vancouver. An elderly Polish couple needed help bucking hay and clearing drainage ditches. They gave him twenty dollars for a day's work and let him live in a damp cabin on the back of their farm. Summer had ripened the sun to golden, and it seemed he'd found paradise at last. But at night he came awake, heart thudding, sweat dampening his chest though he couldn't recall any dream or sound.

He pulled on his jeans and walked from the cabin into the dew-soaked grass. He entered the woods overhanging the stream. Tree frogs croaked in the darkness. Something harmless rattled across last year's leaves, a muskrat or groundhog, sounding enormous. The sky deepened and revolved as he stared upward and swayed and breathed the cold air that poured off the stream, hardly existing, trees cast up against stars. He felt numb, detached, alone, without purpose. He told himself that he should just let things be, that he should work and find peace in nature.

The next afternoon the old Polish man came over. We got troubles, he said.

What?

Troubles, the old man said. A sod company from out in the city is buying up the valley.

What's dat? François asked.

Sod? It's grass. Roll-up grass. Bright green. Sells for a bundle. It's this alluvial soil they want. Moist. It's good for sod. Perfect conditions. They want to strip this all down to nothing and put in sod just far as the eye can see. If I'd of known when I was younger, I'd of done it myself.

What's de trouble den?

Oh, the old man said, mortgage and foreclosure and that company bought us up and wants us off the land. Like as you'd about expect.

But François couldn't take seriously goons who wanted to make rolled-up grass. The old man told him some neighbours were being bullied into selling, that men were going around and to be careful. That night François saw what looked like a shed burning across the valley. The next he heard a few intermittent gunshots.

One afternoon, as he was walking to the gas station to renew his supply of oatmeal and withered apples, he saw a Buick coming down the road and he remembered that it was Wednesday though he couldn't possibly think why that might be important. The Buick glided silently through the shadows of occasional trees, its grille flashing like teeth. It stopped across the ditch from where he stood. The window slid down, warping the reflection of mountains. The driver had a nose long ago broken into two distinct steps and thick, brooding lips.

235

François, he said as if they knew each other. I'm supposed to be telling you you got to vacate. It's not owned by the old folks no more. Time to clear out.

I don boder no one, François said.

What's that? the man asked.

Don bother no one.

He tapped the ash off his cigarette against the sideview mirror and paused as if considering his reflection. You fucking with me, François?

I don 'ave nowhere to go. What I suppose to do, *hein?*

Look. I don't know about all that. I'm just here to tell you to get lost. Otherwise I'm supposed to break your fucking legs. You got it?

He crushed his cigarette and rolled the filter against his thumb. He stared until François looked away, then he drove off.

Two days later, François woke in the cabin from an overlong afternoon nap. He hadn't seen the Polish couple around and so had no work to keep him busy. The fading sun was in the window, and he was sure he'd heard something. He stood and listened. He had to pee and maybe it was just that. As he neared the doorway, he saw someone outside. He tiptoed. It was the man from the Buick, much bigger than he'd appeared sitting down. He wore a suit and was staring into a piece of mirror François had put above the washbasin. The man looked bored and tired and had clearly been waiting. He dipped his fingers in the water and touched his hair, then glanced up.

Jesus, he said, man, you almost gave me a heart attack.

He thumped his chest and took a breath and belched. Goddam, it's like an instant case of heartburn.

He looked around as if someone might be watching. Then he drew himself up. Come on, he said in a different tone. We gotta talk.

Having witnessed the display of vanity, François wasn't too worried. He followed down the grassy ruts towards the road.

Look, the man told him, you got to get off this land. Nothing more complicated. You're a little guy, and I don't want to hurt you. In fact, you got a likeable mug, but I have my reputation at stake. Can't you appreciate that?

Oh, you know, François said, I t'ink I like to stay. It's nice here.

The man stopped and inhaled and glanced off as if trying to get into character. He took a boxy pistol from inside his jacket. He poked François in the chest with it.

Turn around. They told me nobody gives a shit if I kill you.

As François was prodded through the shrubby pines, his legs began to jerk so that he pranced forward like a jester. I need, *eh tabernac*, I need, he repeated though he had no idea what. Every part of him shook until he felt his bladder let go. The barrel pushed into his back, and his leg worked as if at a sewing machine, slapping the wet denim of his pants. Then he gave into full spasm and leapt forward, fumbling and kicking and crying.

You got to leave, the man said. You get the point.

When François made it back to the cabin, he felt as if every inch of him was being chewed on by a different insect. He plunged into the stream and wrung out his pants. He sat on the steps, short-circuiting all over. The kerosene lamp inside was off. The sun was setting and something with a hoarse voice called from below the mountain. He tried to imagine what his parents had felt when he was born, a tiny, happy boy probably. But maybe they'd felt nothing, too caught up in their own lives. He could almost understand that. He wished he had one certainty, that he'd been the son of a smarter, stronger man than himself. If he'd been shot that day, if he were to die now, what difference would it make? The world would go on. No one would miss him. He was nothing. He'd chosen nothing, not his language or scrawny body.

He watched the garden earth darken as if absorbing the blue air. The forest was hushed, the road, the entire valley. Not a single houselight dimmed the stars.

He was still there at dawn and again the next evening. His body cramped with fatigue, and hunger gave way to numbness. It spread through him. His head lolled. For periods it seemed he'd gone blind. Or was it night? He never lost consciousness, but there was no desire to stand, no impulse to care or preserve the self that he was seeing now for what it was, incidental, petty, unremarkable. The dull sun propped itself on his head, and he was no longer sure how many days he'd sat. Rain fell, and he couldn't move from the doorway.

Imperceptibly, a sense of hatred filled him. A flame began to twist inside his silenced body. Mountains reeled up into night, trees and stones and the backward reaching line of a lit stream. Moonlight rippled as if it were water and lifted him. Veins stretched like cables. He drew himself into that point of heat. There had been stories of strength and violence, but the only person to kill was himself.

Then he began to run. Stiff at first, he stumbled through underbrush. But the rage of each fall propelled him and he was soon racing against the gauntlet of branches, striking at trees, leaping stones. He came into clearings where animals stood in patches of moonlight as if on coins. Beavers, moose, bears. Watching, tense with fear. From a ridge he howled until his voice pressed back on him from the valley in wave upon wave of over-lapped echo, a purity of sound, an animal fury. Houselights came on in a ragged string across the dark distance below.

Some time before dawn his hunger possessed him. It was more real than pain. He ran, leapt fences, kicked a farm dog until it yelped and fled. He raided fields of cow corn, blueberry farms, groped like a demon in silos. He knew the ravaging of hoed earth. He ate dog food from the can or bag. Night after night carport freezers went empty, gardens pawed of tubers, vines stripped. Each day, more and more men sat on stumps with rifles or studied tracks, bowels loose with terror of the Sasquatch. Fanatics drove out, measured prints plowed through speed, not the full-grown variety, they determined. Then it all stopped. The beast had moved on, its final crime unre-ported, men's business suits taken from a widow's closet, a bar of soap and some razors.

When the Buick pulled up, its window sliding down on the air-conditioned interior, the man was doing a routine check. His work here was almost finished, and he'd seen no one in weeks. He drove towards the cabin, shocks complaining on the rutted, grassy trail. He was lighting a cigarette, watching himself in the rearview mirror when the figure emerged from shabby pines. He groped on the seat for his pistol but he'd put it underneath. There was a moment of nauseating stillness as François loomed in the man's terror-dilated pupils, his reflection that of a businessman bending at a bright surface to adjust his tie.

British Columbia
1981–1986

François had finished with nature. Let them paint the valley with fluorescent sod. The man in the Buick had complimented him on his suit and offered to drive him into the city, though he'd had one nearby foreclosure to rough up, to which François had lent a hand. On the highway, the man complained about wanting a job working for the real bad guys instead of being a ruffian for a sod company. Downtown, after saying goodbye, François went to a newsstand, and for the first time he bought a paper. He studied job listings, trying to hear each title: manager, clerk, longshoreman. He took a room in a boarding house and washed dishes for fast cash. Alone he read aloud, attempting for the first time to improve his pronunciation. He paused often to do push-ups. In the end he had to give credence to what he'd been, an offer in Miscellaneous. A scientific firm was looking for a person who'd let his big toe be cut off and sewed back on with only local anaesthesia. Compensation: three thousand dollars. Not much but fast, easy in a sense, and enough for a little business capital. At the hospital there were forms and interviews, close inspection of his feet, a makeup artist and a pedicurist.

That's the problem with finding someone, the head clinician told him. Not a lot of people are willing to do this. Mostly bums want the job, but they don't have photogenic feet. We see everything from fungus to missing toes to whitlow and spoon nails and anonychia.

Ano-what? François asked.

The congenital absence of nails. But you, your feet are okay.

François was kept a few days under observation. There was hesitation on the part of a sponsor who thought a Québecer would be bad publicity, but that passed. François's toes were X-rayed and washed. The operating room had the energy of a modelling session. Blond and Asian interns with stylish glasses lined the walls, cameras beneath lighting umbrellas. He was hooked up, strapped in and injected with a new anaesthesia. His heart blipped. After the cold steel of incision, a man approached with a miniature circular saw. François set his teeth. A fiery jet pinged into a metal dish. The clinician nodded. He's a tough little guy, someone whispered.

The laser mending, a specialty technique also on trial, didn't feel great either though some gland in François's pulsing body had poured heroin into his veins. It had happened when he'd seen his toe on the tray, red as a pork hock. Then it had been reattached. It swelled, ached, but, they admitted, practically healed overnight, leaving only a line like that on a soldered pipe. Laser therapy was continued for two weeks, and they credited this with the quick return of sensation.

Every moment left to himself François read, *Time*, *Newsweek*, anything up-to-date, and, of course, the paper. He saw his grandmother's outmoded beliefs now for what they were. He read business and politics. Watching TV, he learned expressions. You're trying to fleece me, he muttered alone, imagining gritty business deals. Weakness angered him. Newspapers predicted a decade of innovation. In the Travel section he came across snippets of history. The Holy Roman Empire, he thought, this is it, business now, corporations, the future, not some hippie dream but another kind of paradise. He was ready for the normal life.

During his convalescence they fed him well. They weighed each entree, classified its nutritional contents and watched it disappear. By the time he left, he was more than when he'd arrived, not limping either. The head clinician showed him his picture in the paper, the headline: *Human Body Mere Mechanics*. François was interviewed. Speaking well, he decided, was the product

243

of deep breaths, a guard-dog propensity for looking in the eye. He made people squirm on pauses and over-articulated words that were hardest to say. When he left the hospital, there was even, waiting on the steps, that sudden Western phenomenon, a fan club. He accepted numbers from pretty girls, though he had no time for this, not yet.

He hitched a ride downtown. He looked in the paper for a cheap room. The only one that wasn't a dive was in the home of Dr. Eduardo Wee, a Peruvian-born Chinese man who'd been raised in Illinois and immigrated to Vancouver in his teens and who, with his Midwestern accent, sounded exactly like Reagan. He even had the Reagan coif, a modest pompadour. He told a little about his history, that he'd never fit in with the local Chinese. He spoke their language poorly, but he'd chosen not to abandon his parents or, later, his wife, who'd become his link to the community and who would never leave. When they all passed away, she too young, his parents too old, he found himself alone, a doctor with a dwindling following. He spoke of a passion for inventing, could manage a few words of sympathetic French though François asked that he speak English — the future world language, he'd read. The house looked somewhat like an English manor and was just out from the downtown, on a scenic stretch. Eduardo lived in the basement. It had low ceilings and cottage-like windows, and he rented it from the woman upstairs, who herself took on boarders. All that François heard of them were their constant comings and goings drumming on the floorboards.

The only problem, Eduardo informed him, and the reason this place is so cheap, is that there's no bathroom down here. She has the only one. He indicated the upstairs with a lift of his eyes. From the back door he showed François where a trail led through the grass to a clump of trees on a rise. There, an outhouse of ancient though sturdy timbers remained from some other era. François didn't like it, and Eduardo admitted he didn't either, especially not in winter. Being an amateur inventor, he'd tried to make an incinerator that would work like a toilet but had almost burned the house down.

If only bodily waste could be eliminated, he said as though facing the critical dilemma of the age.

Those weeks François set to work. He wore a sports jacket with suede patches at the elbows, jeans and polos and tennis shoes. Girls noticed. He honed his projection with daily visits to the fitness club, where women in striped tights, ankle warmers and headbands did aerobics behind a glass wall. Weights gave the Sasquatch a modern allure, though he'd signed up as much for the showers as for the gym. Once he'd walked in on Eduardo standing naked in a ceramic bowl and pouring water over his head.

François planned the practical aspects of earning a fortune. He went to a printer and had seven hundred bumper stickers made. He came up with them on the spot. He'd had a hunch. It was the right time for weirdness. He set up on the street that evening, in Gastown, couples out dining, musicians playing blues and sit-com themes on corners. Within two days he had a thousand more made. They said things such as I Brake for Ice, Love My Dove, A Flower for My Power, any good mix of sounds he could come up with and often their opposite. People laughed at lines that wouldn't have drawn a smirk from him. Often he took newspaper headlines word for word, and passersby bought them up, seeming to find in them some hint or expression of the ineffable. His picture appeared in the paper again. Stickers were flying around town. Young people and married couples forked it out. He upped prices and bought himself a used van. Only when the rage lulled did he hire students. He gave each one a post, had them on commission and told them, square in the eyes, You run on me, I'll break your knees.

Still, for all his effort he had capital for neither house nor commercial space. Those crisp evenings when he crossed the yard, a new roll of toilet paper held close to his sleeve, the life he'd renounced didn't seem so far. As he sat in the outhouse, on the wooded rise above the bay, there were no ambitions, just land and the steep water the Indians had long ago mediated, the mountains massive and invisible above the night.

All that winter and through the next four years he learned. He had a modest library and studied tax and zoning loopholes. He read books on business, bought magazines on money. He played at anything reasonably legal with low overhead. He made friends and financed a buying trip to Guatemala for gaudy cotton. He had people selling fireworks from booths, fresh-pressed juice and exotic smoothies in the downtown, avocado and banana. He backed a clever young man who'd found a way to buy designer clothing labels, and now sold them on the street, lucrative, since many a generic garment could become stylish. François even hired high-school kids to sell No Soliciting signs and stickers in residential neighbourhoods. People appreciated the irony. He had a network for distribution and collection.

But on bad days, he feared that he would never be good at this. Loneliness crept into him and settled so deep that he smelled the staleness of his lungs when he exhaled. The meaning and happiness he'd envisioned seemed too far, and he recalled that old gentle nature, or a picnic with Ernestine near the river, the skyscrapers lit like petals in a refracted sundown and the way she'd looked at the sky, her smile in her front teeth. But he didn't want to suffer over an ugly prostitute. Instead he cut hard deals just to see if he could. He worked his body lifting weights. He even bought a wide girdle fitted with electrical nodes that gave mild shocks that repeatedly flexed the muscles of the belly, resulting in an amazing washboard. As a test of will he wore it day and night, practising holding himself steady. One evening Eduardo noticed François's vibrating midsection. I wouldn't use that if I were you, he said. The body has its own electricity, rather fragile, too.

January brought fog and wet squalls, days of cold rain that never quite became snow. Street business was bad, and on his way back from a collection François again felt his heart go out of it a little. Wanting to get warm and dry off, he stepped in for a drink, but he misjudged the front. Inside was starkly elegant, glass tables and tabourets, a sombre bar, servers in jackets and a woman turned to take him in, alone, a martini in her fingers.

You look cold, she said. Sit down. I'll buy you one.

It was the kind of place where he could imagine himself in some detached future when success verged on bored decadence. Right now it made him a little shy. He'd been avoiding dating, had Prioritized, as his business books said, and didn't want anyone to see his transition. But this woman, though petite and busty, drew on her cigarette as if she'd been resurrected from the shadowy streets of some imagined Paris. It was an act, no doubt, but he had great respect for acts.

Are you expecting someone? she asked.

No, he said, grinding out his accent.

Then let's get out of this dive and go someplace good.

They caught a taxi to a restaurant priced by the table, where she said, Don't worry, I'm paying. Only later she introduced herself as Elaine, in her penthouse suite overlooking the bay, at a better bar than any he'd paid to sit at, where he found himself many of the nights that followed. She had perfection too lasting for youth, the angle of her jaw and tireless blade of cheekbones, the mandarin slant of her eyes. The taut edges of her lips made her appear to smile. There was something fragile about her sensuality, her slow strides. She listed as she walked, as if drawn by desire, always to the left.

Finally, a man my size, she said as she slid off her shoulder straps. But please, be gentle.

Her nipples were small and dark and hard. Don't grab, she whispered when he got heated. Keep it slow.

Those next months, he saw her once or twice a week. He toyed with the idea of getting her to finance a venture, though this would betray the self-reliant man he'd put forth. She hardly talked about her means. She preferred silence, wore him best on her arm in places where sound accompanied the meal like an appetizer, jazz clubs mostly. He knew she was widowed, a Jewess married young to an old man and freed young. Her age he guessed in the late thirties.

She'd said she'd come to Vancouver from New York to escape a high society where everyone knows you and judges. Idiots, she'd added casually. Anything beyond this didn't interest her. Oh, she said with a sigh, after a thin intake through a long cigarette, let the past be.

Only once, when the music took too-extended a pause, was the need for conversation first clear, then crucial, finally polite. The knowing left her eyes. Fear flickered there. Heat touched her cheeks. She pursed her lips as if to spit but swallowed.

Have you thought about taking an investment? she asked.

Because I love you, she added later that night, in that way of hers that made him feel she could continue a conversation one word an hour, two sentences a day. Yes, because I love you, there will be no strings attached. How much do you want?

From the wall she removed a painting of a geisha undoing the front of her dress. In the safe were stacks of big bills.

François's only regret was that his plan wasn't as elegant as the jazz clubs with potted palms, dais and piano and floor-to-ceiling fish tanks. He bought an abandoned garage of red brick at the edge of Gastown and converted it into a car museum/burger joint where clients ate out of chrome hubcaps and sat in booths alongside the polished, rebuilt bodies of roadsters. It had shelves of vintage paraphernalia, good swinging music and long-legged waitresses. Businessmen poured in with colleagues and came back with sons. The ambiance was nostalgic, the food good and plentiful and cheap. The decor suggested that heyday America was the place to be and drew that middle class of Canadians who mostly felt the same way.

On the first clear day of spring François's restaurant received a write-up in the *Vancouver Sun*. He hurried to Elaine's. He'd rented his own apartment, kept a closet of stylish clothes, finally more than a street huckster. The last time he'd seen Elaine, when he'd told her what a hit the restaurant was, she'd been slow to show interest. Now, with a fist of flowers, he wondered if she cared. No matter. In the elevator he hummed the latest rage and found, in the penthouse, a woman who bore remarkable resemblance to Elaine.

Oy, she said. Not another one, and so young.

Another what?

She gave him a steady look. Her eyebrows and piercing gaze were too familiar.

Well, there's time to tell, she said. Sit, sit. Mother's napping. It seems she's been neglecting her medication. Feeling young again, no doubt.

Your mother? Where's Elaine?

Oh, she said as if pained. Sit. Please sit.

And so François learned all—saw, in fact, Elaine stretched on the bed, features peaceful, breathing somewhat shallow. The woman, Margaret Meir, was Elaine's daughter. François sat. Margaret gesticulated as she spoke, then held her hands in her lap self-consciously. The story began with an inheritance, the bit about married young and elderly husband true, though when he conceded to die, Elaine was fifty—Though, Margaret clarified, she was still beautiful. She was uncannily young for her age and didn't need to do all of . . . Well, I'll explain . . .

Still, we always had a theory that she'd never lived her youth and so had never grown old. Anyway. Like I said. I'll explain.

At the age of fifty-five—

Fifty-five, François repeated.

She's now sixty-eight, Margaret said, then went on to tell how, at that respectable age, Elaine began studying means of growing young. She fasted, did heliotherapy, went to cures and mud baths, fraternized with nudists and liberals, submitted herself to fruit regimens and lived in an ashram in the Himalayas where she consumed unheard-of proportions of Asian drugs touted for regeneration and practised deep breathing on glacial slopes until she finally decided that, young as she might become, such a life was a bore. Then, on the verge of giving up—and closing in on sixty—she heard about a group of avant-garde doctors who claimed that the industry of the future was rejuvenation. The incipient techniques of facelift and liposuction and boob job were taking shape in privately financed labs. Techniques used in the world wars for maimed soldiers were perfected for the elderly or the ugly rich. Elaine was a cross between guinea pig (François saw their connection now) and patron of the sciences. The doctors stretched her face, incised her eyes and lips, padded and tucked her breasts, sucked out varicose veins and removed folds of unwanted skin. They cleaned her jaw of canescence and reset her teeth with drills. The result was stunning. She could make grandsons blush and lust, until, of course, they found out this had taken much of their inheritance and that the rest was going to dressing and lavishing this immaculate body.

It isn't natural, Margaret said. She shouldn't have done it. Then she left her family and came out here because . . . and get this . . . because some doctor said cold firms the flesh and this place is as cold as she can tolerate. Of course, it's clear that she just wants to live where nobody knows her. Now she's throwing our fortune to the winds, la-di-da. Don't think we haven't tried to stop her. But imagine having a bombshell committed. She'd sleep with the judge.

As François listened, Margaret explained her trips out, how last year Elaine fell and broke her hip, which shed light on her fragile motions.

252

Left hip? he asked.

Left indeed, she said. Can you imagine what the scar from that operation took to cover? But they did a good job, right? You should be the one telling me.

François tried to excuse himself. Margaret was now practically ranting, Body-sculpting, the future, hah! Well, I'll say. And my sons in college with only me and Herbert to pay tuition and get their careers going. And she has it all. But don't think for a minute I'm jealous.

She told him about her mother's bouts of premature dementia, the great irony of her life that had her spending silly, gaga over the phone late at night and now oblivious, drugged on the bed.

Oh no, Margaret told him. You can't fix a brain.

He stood and left. The elevator blipping down the spine of the building seemed a fine place for loneliness. He couldn't say he had any regrets. He looked at himself in the elevator mirrors. The doors binged. He went outside. It was still early. Couples strolled towards the beach. Two Chinese girls on rollerskates sped along a bike path. A brick cottage stood near the park, not seeming to belong to the city, climbing roses on a trellis. A woman pushed a stroller, the baby asleep in its shade. He went to his car and started home.

He was on the Trans-Canada. The Eurythmics were singing *Sweet Dreams*, and he considered this age of change and its magic. If a second-rate John Wayne with a monkey could run the world's most powerful country then didn't others have a right to their own more humble dreams? A young woman was hitchhiking, and seeing her, he felt that old wheel turning, wind, the scent of ploughed Manitoba plains or the cool shadow the first time he'd walked with Ernestine on the shady side of a Montréal street. The woman was pleasantly short, wore jeans and a halter top, held a bulging plastic bag, a long-sleeve shirt tied at her waist. Traffic wind whipped her hair about her shoulders and sunny arms.

Only when he pulled over did he notice her distress. She had an American accent. Her name was Margaret. What a coincidence, he told her, but this girl's accent was Southern, not Margaret with all of its letters pronounced, but Magret. Call me Peggy, she said, then added, You know—she hesitated—you know, I mean, I'll—and hesitated again. François felt the offer coming. She broke off to say her stuff had been stolen. I was with this guy and I mean . . . Her chin furrowed. She was lovely, thin nose, sunstreaked hair. She bit her bottom lip. Shi-it, she said, quietly, dragging it out. I thought this was the place to be.

I don't have far to go, François told her.

She looked at him across that tiny space as if across a room. I'll give you a blowjob for forty dollars. I'll give it for twenty, she said too fast, her voice absent of emotion. I'll give you a blowjob for something to eat, shit, even a hamburger.

He'd missed his exit and considered that he could continue past the city, up to Squamish or Whistler or just turn around and drive for hours. But he'd never been that way.

I'll take you to get something to eat, he told her. It's on me.

He pulled off at the next exit and found a restaurant. He watched as she scarfed. She bit her tongue. Her lips were swollen. She cried. An American girl, he thought.

I keep on biting my tongue, she said. Jesus, what's wrong with me?

He told her it was all right, don't rush. He was sad, too. And if you need a place to stay until you get organized . . .

Afterwards he took her to his new home. Cool air through the screens, a long, shallow wind of night smells, flowerbeds and barbecue. It all felt new, a different speed and rhythm. But he was wrong. The wheel is always the same when it's turning.

British Columbia
1986–1987

Though scared and lonely and lost, Peggy was not submissive. She drawled, her accent not Southern belle but low and rolling, a man's sound and suitable for congregation. François expected her to drag him to the bathroom and baptize him, but she preferred puffing away in the kitchen, kneading whole-grain bread, soaking seeds and nuts and beans, hacking greens thick enough to make a cow wish for a fifth stomach. She told him about her family, growing up in Alabama before the big move in the seventies, to

Virginia, for the money. After high school she began to travel and eventually decided on Canada, the unexplored north, natural and free. But there were things he glimpsed only in her silences, the way she disappeared into thought and breathed hard, or when she said, Be 257 rough with me, and he was, and she cried like he'd never seen. He wouldn't do it again, not even when she asked.

As for his apartment, she told him she'd dreamed of a country home. He broke his lease. Alone in the car he practised talking to realtors with a voice like those he'd heard watching court TV with Eduardo. You trying to fleece me? he said. In Maple Ridge he found a cheap split-level in a rustic residential neighbourhood, sensible linoleum, shag rugs to curls his toes in, rucked plaster ceiling and wallpaper with subtle yellow-brown flowers. Poker-faced, he worked the realtor, a young man who nervously spruced his buzz cut, square at the ears and neck, lots of pink scalp. François didn't ask Peggy's opinion. He settled. Good taste, he told her that night, keys already in hand, a fast mover, had collateral. Every room smelled like freshly unrolled carpet, new paint on particleboard. In the yard, there were only two trees to clean up after. The neighbouring lawns were separated by picket fences, neatly mowed.

I guess it'll do, she said, though I'd rather not have neighbours.

To his surprise she didn't want a washing machine. She bought an antique washboard and did clothes by hand. She bathed in an oak tub for some holistic property of wood. Soon she learned to make cheese, strained curdled milk through cloth and stunk up the house. We can buy that, you know, he told her. She planted a garden, made grains, steamy jars on every sill. Her last name, he discovered, she'd changed a few years back to Blossom.

François saw himself as a saintly character. When the homeless begged, he offered jobs sweeping and was vindicated when they refused. Peggy had asked for a meal and had gotten a life, had a man who could pick her up, take care of her, do the right thing. He knew he'd wanted more than a business. He wanted a family and children and a plan for a stable future. But Peggy worried him. Some days she wouldn't get up until the afternoon and lazed about in dirty clothes and told him to leave her alone when he asked what was wrong. Sometimes she got up at five a.m. and appeared to be praying to the rising sun. Sometimes he'd come home and she'd be red-in-the-face angry and would hector him. Am I the only girl you picked up? A first, huh? Just picked me up and took me in? Maybe you have houses like this all over the place. Cheap little dumps with bimbos off the highway.

The next day she would be fine, rinsing sprouts, unwrapping rank slabs of cheese. He tolerated her obsessions, bought what she wanted, books depicting four-armed blue beings, naked women with suns bursting at their groins. She insisted he take her to fairs where she saw spiritual masters, all indistinguishable from homeless people but for their robes and harmonious gestures, and their followers huddled patiently by.

After announcing her pregnancy, Peggy coddled herself, careful in the first trimester, eating bowls of sprouting

integuments that, on the tongue, felt like fingernail clippings. François held himself as if he were a fighter wary of
overconfidence. With Peggy just as with Elaine he sensed
his old softness, the possibility of weakness, that there
were things he wasn't wise enough to see. So much had
come to him on the highway, his grandmother and now a
wife. Perhaps he'd had no time for aphorism in his solitary
roving—no Hebrew crossing forty years of wilderness with
his nation. Recalling his past, he feared the innocence of
the small, happy self that he'd abolished.

But work and being a father, he decided, would be
enough. He would set everything straight, buy a bigger
house, own more businesses. He'd already opened a
bumper-sticker boutique. That first night with Peggy he'd
known things would never be the same. A son was coming. He read it in the stars, the generosity of flashing
late-summer leaves, even in the celestial spread below
the turning observation deck at the Harbour Centre
where he took her to eat. For him stars were just a manner of speaking.

During manic hours in the city, he made mental lists
to tell his son: conquests, struggles, how he became self-
made. He would be a hero for that boy, the manly
businessman who divides his time scrupulously between
work and play. The larger Peggy's belly became, the
more he pushed himself. He knew that this was his
chance to have a family and do it right, to be a better
father than his own. Just thinking this gave him a sense
of justice, as if he were a great man. He imagined his son
reading about interstellar travel, going to a big university,

double scholarship, sports and science, or better yet, business. Perhaps there was nothing wrong with François's grandmother's stories after all, the strength, the sense of belonging to a powerful lineage, a true Hervé. François would name the boy Harvey in hopes of that family magic, though he wasn't sure the anglicization would retain the name's power. But he wouldn't even speak to his son in French, and though he was decided about this, oddly, imagining how he would be as a father, he caught himself naming things as if teaching the words. *Une toile d'araignée*, he said of a spider web freshly strung across the backroom of his store and already loaded with dust. Or at night, *la lune*, the pale body glittering like an ice crystal in the winter sky as he turned in his sheets, unable to sleep, but staying there anyway.

part two

Vancouver–Virginia
1987–2003

That Christmas Eve Peggy, wanting a child born on a holy day, began huffing through the house to induce labour. Dressed in sweats, she climbed the stairs, looped into rooms, sat on the bed and bounced, stepped in and out of the dry bathtub and ventured into the mouldy cold of the cellar as if nearing the earth might bring her closer to the coercion of gravity. She sped Lamaze breaths double time, took to the street, nostrils flaring, her body as mechanical as a speed walker's so that as François returned home in the dark he thought he saw a Soviet soldier marching with vigorous arm swings, in a light snow that, just then, the radio announcer said would bring the first white Christmas in years. A Christmas birth François couldn't have cared less about, though before New Year would be nice. He could claim the child on his taxes and so left Peggy to her methods.

That day the front page of the newspaper had carried the story of a life-sized nativity scene carved in ice. François, on an errand downtown, had stopped at the outdoor skating rink to see it. The artifice had not charmed him. Rather, he'd felt disdain for this otherworldly family, poised beatifically, the Virgin with her opening hands, the baby whittled to spare, alien detail, too perfect for life. It called up memories of his churchly youth, the coloured Bible plates of a Christ his grandmother had dreamed he would emulate. He liked to think of himself as the kind of man who kept up, who read the paper and checked things out, had a word or two on the subject, which he did. Still, he regretted having taken the time to come here. He had no place for the divine, and the season he liked was holiday expenditures. But the image stayed, imprinted on a ghostly inner eye, cold like the beginning of a headache, a vitreous baby, too small, too keenly expressive of its perfection. When, that night, he saw his son in this same way, pale, tiny, as neatly fashioned as an idol, his pangs were of a guilt medieval.

The pearly child filled him with a sense of doom — Peggy's hubris, his greed — the simple primitive belief in accountability, that by scorning a baby Christ cast in ice

he'd brought it into his life. Holding this polished creature in his palms, François tried to believe Eduardo,
who'd said, He'll grow—they all do. But years did not
fade the changeling's air. And though minute he was no
midget and did not have the sturdy bearing of a dwarf. If   263
he grew at all, it was incrementally in relation to his
nearly absent appetite. He remained carved and luminous and cold.

So perhaps he would be a genius, François concluded, though with the years, Harvey seemed intent on
nothing more than watching and became quickly bored
of books. François, reading the paper, would hear the
patter of feet and glance over his shoulder to see, peering
from the shadow behind his easy chair, two large, moist
eyes. He recognized the pattern, Peggy hellbent on making a holy man, bringing home pop-up books of the
Buddha and Hindu saints, teaching Harvey to meditate
or to say Shanti, Shanti, Shanti over each meal. Had
François, by forfeiting the divine calling envisioned by
his grandmother, passed the burden on to his son? He
tried to make Harvey eat mussels, oysters, men's food.
Harvey gagged. In restaurants François ordered steaks,
but Harvey peeled and nibbled a few brown fibres before
turning his attention to the lettuce garnish. Though neither François nor Peggy did, Harvey ate in the European
fashion, fork in his left hand, dainty from birth. When he
got his fingers dirty, he shook them like a puppy that had
put a paw in the water bowl.

Those years Peggy immersed herself in the New Age:
crystals, meditation, flower essences, earth-breathing to

balance planetary currents. She took Harvey to visit a fat swami whose picture now hung above his bed, the spitting image of a Greek restaurateur François knew, a man with a bad thyroid and buck-teeth like a mule's, his face saddled in black glasses. Peggy had even joined a congregation where visitors lectured on food combining and past life regression and the sex cults of Jesus. Because of Harvey's tendency to get sick, she began boiling his toys, so that he grew up with a leprous collection of half-melted figurines and hot rods with flat wheels.

Over the years she shooed François's concerns, and it wasn't until Harvey was eight that François realized how far things had gone. That week a business acquaintance from Washington invited François for a drink. After a few, François shared his predicament. The American was heavy-set, with thick hands that didn't move as he spoke, a tanned collar and pale forehead. Earlier, he'd suggested a few ideas for bumper stickers, all based on fishing. Now he sat back, hands limp on the nicked wood as he described what he called Playboy Therapy. His own son had been a twerp, he said, and his solution had been to bribe the boy with *Playboys*. He'd showed him a centrefold now and then and promised that for every month of twenty push-ups a day, the boy would get that issue.

The man let this sink in, hands like dead birds on the table, not even reaching for his beer.

Well, he did it, he said. He's an All-Star linebacker.

When François got home, Peggy was in bed reading a manual on curing common ailments with dandelions. He went into Harvey's room. He sat on the bed and said,

Son, I think you're old enough. Harvey noted this new voice, bigger than his father's. He looked at the magazine, the stockinged legs and lipped delight. He sensed the secret power of revealed bodies, the loneliness in the way the girls looked out, as if trapped. For François the talk went well. Harvey was receptive, even curious. He promised to do the push-ups and not to tell Peggy, though when François came home the following evening, she was stuffing grocery bags with clothes, the skin of her face and arms mottled with rage.

265

For Harvey the years before his parents' separation remained clear. He dreamed of being a psychic, of levitating sheets of paper or blowing out candles with his mind. He'd been taught that God was one soul who was everyone and who, unconstrained by time, lived all their lives. His mother had told him that this divine energy was like the sun, and that he should imagine himself as its light, which he fancied. She said he was destined to be a holy man, and to help him along, she transformed his room into a New Age reading centre, its walls a gallery of saintly images. Together they drew pictures of him meditating on mountaintops, in temples. You'll be a holy man of your own kind, totally original, she wrote in his birthday cards, along with various bits of wisdom remarkably similar to the twelve steps she'd heard nightly at the dinner table from her father when she was growing up.

But for all his dreaminess, aversions obsessed him: mud, rain, the smell of turned compost, of homemade cheese and jars of souring yogurt unwrapped from towels, or the crumbling bread and radish sprouts his mother sent him to school with, for which he was teased. A dollop of mustard on his shirt brought him to the verge of tears. Bird shit on his shoulder or turds in the treads of his shoes froze him in a catatonic rage. He even hated his name. It sounded sloppy. He hated sports and bugs, the girl next door who collected spiders in jars. He avoided his mother when she was gardening or when she farted and swatted her hand and said, Lordy, pardon me. When boys at school gleeked or hawked up mucus to let it dangle from their lips or blew bubbles in it like chewing gum, he gagged. Just beyond the playground fence was a walking path, and during recess old people stopped and waved. He was afraid of their walkers and ugly clothes, their wrinkled heads like brown nuts.

Despite his mother's love somewhere encoded in earliest memory was the knowledge that he made his father sad. Over the years this impression found words, a sense of fault. His father's distracted gazes simmered on him. He was forced to go to tae kwon do, where kids swung their legs like staffs, to a boxing club where East Indians listened to pounding rap and wore Raiders jackets. They looked at him as if he'd floated downstream in a basket. He skinned his knuckles on the punching bag and cried.

Finally his father bought him a Lab mix. Harvey was skeptical, seeing in the dog's tilted gaze a hell of ransacked rooms, dog prints on pants, shit to be scraped off shoes. A little white mouse would be better than the dog, pawing and trampling, jerking its head at sudden unperceived interests, Totally ADD, his mother said. François then, after researching more manly activities, took Harvey salmon fishing, but he misjudged the dates, the runs almost over, rotting salmon on gravel banks, 267 purple with humped backs and hooked jaws and reeking with the pent fury of brief lives. They caught nothing, fishing in gusting stench, the current tugging at their waders. The dog gorged itself on rancid meat and, in the dark cab of the truck, panted into their faces as they drove the long roads home.

The separation, when it came, was a release from inadequacy, especially now that he'd betrayed his father. Long ago he'd learned that everything François said was of interest to his mother. She'd shared various bits of wisdom over time, and Harvey had composed a list beginning with the badness of men and ending in his father's being a man like any other. They just can't evolve, she'd often told him. By the time François came to say goodbye, Peggy was already waiting in the taxi that would take them to the airport. Harvey wanted only to leave, to be as far as possible from all that he'd failed.

You'll visit me, François said, and I'll send money. If she buys you things, it will be with my money, so just know I'm there paying for everything, okay. And remember the push-ups. We'll figure this out. When you visit, I'll buy you those magazines, but don't you tell her again.

In the cab, Harvey asked if they were leaving because of the magazines.

She laughed dryly. No, she said.

———

Harvey's initial impression of the country south of the border was disappointing. When, years later, he wondered if Canada had been any different, he could not properly judge. Whereas Canada was open and windy, the States, the South at least, seemed closed, muggy, full of secret dangers, a slouching fat man wiggling his belt as he came out from an alley, spitting tobacco then saying, Hey, bud, or a spruce black boy surveying a quiet downtown street like a warlord and telling Harvey for no apparent reason, Go'n, get outa here.

Those first days they lived with his grandparents, great bellied and hipped things that hugged and patted him and gave him rock candy then felt they'd done their duty. After a week they lent Peggy enough to buy a used car and to rent a home in the trailer park, and said Bye now, each time Harvey took a bag to load into the trunk.

His mother worked various jobs and made friends at a New Age bookshop and began to work the spiritual dating circuit. In her weeks of being single she got a perfectly round perm with a fringe of bangs, joined aerobics to keep her figure and talked on the phone, often in her yellow and blue leotard.

Jacqueline, she said, I knew it was you calling. I just knew before I picked up.

She talked about her chakras, the energy stagnation she was experiencing in her navel and went on, spurred by something said over the phone, to discuss how what had made Hitler such a bad man was the energy caught in his throat chakra. All that trapped energy, she said. It must have driven him crazy. You can see it when he talks, all jerky, you know, in the movies.

Harvey sat, feeling his throat for heat or static, wondering what his energy was doing and clearing it with gentle coughs to see if that made any difference.

269

He'd read about alchemy, transmutation of the self into god-being, the gold of perfection. In New Age novels people entered dream worlds or became pure energy, and he could imagine this, his quiet size phased into light, now floating away. It was a pleasant thought. But how? In religious fables, the holy men illuminated only criminals. Feeling restless, he walked through the trailer park. He gazed out from a rise, bright embers in the dusk where kids smoked as they wove lazily down the streets on bikes.

Those years Peggy and Harvey moved from one subdivision to the next, always looking for a cheaper place. She graduated him from saintly picture books to the hard autobiographies of holy men. He read how Gandhi's fasts had stopped riots and liberated India, and of his march to the sea for salt. He learned about the Buddha's determination to end suffering, the years he spent alone and looked down upon by those he'd hoped to teach. Even Jesus had hard times and did some good work. But the Buddha had had the best deal, his father having secluded him from the pain of existence, old age and death, until he left one day and witnessed the manifold suffering of the world.

While adolescence sprouted around Harvey like weeds, he remained his same neat self though was loved no better. He mitigated loneliness by reading or practising esoteric breaths from pamphlets his mother brought home. She believed in him and told him this often. She'd gained weight, big in the chest and hips, and even when he was in his early teens, she still lifted him onto her lap and said, Tell me all about those brilliant ideas of yours. He'd speak, perched like a ventriloquist's puppet, but he never voiced his loneliness, his feeling of being stranded.

One day, he read in a science book that domestication resulted in more delicate bone structure, that dogs, cats, horses, even birds became smaller when tamed. That night he held his hand over the flashlight and considered the transparency of his skin, his fine avian bones. Perhaps he was the culmination, the fully evolved human. Alone he could almost believe this. He had a natural attraction to purity. He'd grown up surrounded by pictures of bliss and enlightenment, a karma of learning. But where was the reality? He wished he'd been raised Jewish, could fall back on a rock-hard core of tradition that would give him the courage to dress like a weirdo and pray in public.

He stood at the window. He might search endlessly, might end up chewing a cola nut, all wrinkled and bony, in a breechclout, at the side of a dusty road. What was to guarantee that he'd be loved, that he'd attain some goal? The suburban lane reflected nothing, just trimmed lawns, unused sidewalks. Stop signs cast stretched octagons as the sun descended somewhere far away. In the near dark he could see it all, row upon row of houses like cattle cars that might pull away in the night, occupy another field without the sleepers ever knowing, a field one stop closer to their destruction.

At fifteen he made his first friend, a hulking, mohawked delinquent brought from D.C. to a foster home. The boy had asked to cheat off him, and when Harvey had reluctantly agreed, knowing that his own answers were no doubt flawed, the two had become allies. It was thrilling, to be sought out and admired, the delinquent now pulling in Cs instead of Fs. But a few weeks later, both were given detention, and when the delinquent decided he was going to run away, Harvey couldn't imagine the loss of his friend and so went with him. Unsure of where to go, the boy asked his advice and they ended up stowing away in Peggy's garden shed.

During the next two days, the boy confessed his crimes—thefts, violence, sexual assault. Harvey forgave him. They snoozed, seeing each other by wands of light through the tin walls. Day faded. They heard hysterical voices outside. The delinquent soon wanted to give in. He hadn't spent lifetimes seeking nirvana and living in solitude, meditating in caves. For Harvey it was easy. He wanted to impress this youth who fit in no more than he did, whose purple rages had had him throttling peers, flicking off teachers, tearing textbooks in half. Harvey had been terrified, but friendship had melted all barriers to his heart. At the delinquent's insistence he snuck to the house for food.

What're we going to do? the delinquent asked.

I'm going to live with my father, Harvey told him, in Canada.

In Kansas? the delinquent blurted.

No, in Canada.

Where's that? You sure you don't mean Kansas? There ain't nothing in Kansas.

Canada, Harvey repeated, bitterly conscious of having to explain his lie.

Might be another way of saying Kansas, the delinquent told him, quietly, not willing to give up his position, his only real sense of the place from the Technicolor *Wizard of Oz* he'd seen in the detention ward, to which he would soon return. Enlightenment wasn't for everyone. They sat in darkness, lawn mower between them, rakes and pruning shears and garden tools on the walls. It all smelled of dirt and mouldy grass. And still they waited, for something, for anything to happen.

Virginia–New Mexico
2005–2006

At the age of seventeen, several months before he was to graduate, Harvey began his first fast. He'd been reading about contamination and the modern diet, colonic toxicity and its many effects, among them stunted development. He was five-one, ninety-six pounds, and hoped for a last growth spurt. Five-two would make all the difference, a world away from five-one with its questionable numerological significance. When Peggy came home and found him crosslegged on his bedspread and learned of his plans, she blurted, But you don't eat anything in the first place.

Harvey wasn't dissuaded. He'd also read that fasting could restore an appetite stymied by toxins. It was spring break, and while his peers yanked the canvas off jeeps and raced for the coast or threw parties at which they groped girls they'd known since kindergarten and vomited in sinks, Harvey grew lighter. He liked the sense of airiness, of purity. He'd been a vegan for more than a year, but this was of another order. He lost the need to sleep yet never quite felt awake. His pee turned bright orange. Day three he began to feel feverish. Then it passed.

I'll never get sick again, he told his mother when he'd finished.

Minutes after his first glass of cold apple juice he rushed to the bathroom. Later a tofu sandwich gave him horrible abdominal pain until he brought it up. Two days back to school he had swollen tonsils, a rash on the backs of his thighs from sitting in the heat. He took his books home to recover, perhaps to stay forever, and his mother, after wandering the supermarket uncertainly, brought him a dozen jars of Gerbers.

Apricot's good, he told her.

You just needed to start slow, she said.

Perhaps it was the fast that broke his faith. Years he'd watched his mother pass from fad to fad, listening to cassettes about growing younger through positive thinking, checking her angel cards or standing at the mirror and screaming as if at an intruder, Wrinkles go away! She did the same with bone spurs and menstrual cramps. But nothing stuck. He'd been raised in an aura of glib talk about enlightenment but felt no closer. It was time to check out Christianity.

That same week, Harvey became a born-again. Each evening after school, he climbed into an extra-long white van and rode to prayer meetings, to potlucks and political rallies. He edged into the groups, but when he joined the conversations about sports, prospective colleges or the influence of Satan in the Middle East, the others grew quiet and stared at his glossy face, flinched at his piping voice. He was the closest thing to a minority the congregation had had, this boy with a strangely doubled name and dimensions of Eastern deprivation. These youths were handsome, outfitted and sensibly styled. That first week he'd hauled his substantial collection of occult to the used bookstore and liberated the pagan elements of his altar back to nature. He'd taken to reading the Bible, but he couldn't decide what to make of a book loaded with so much sex and mud and violence. He was still drifting, still without an anchor. The tears that stung his eyes as he prayed were not of fervour. Confused longings merged: a confidante, a girl, love or a glimpse of God. The church smelled of varnish and glue. The pastor tied biblical allusions to jokes about superhero underwear. The singers had acoustic guitars and synthesizers and sang carols in perpetuity.

When the van dropped him off, he walked into the backyard. He and Peggy had recently moved again, this time to a subdivision of identical houses newly built over a defunct farm so that lawn mowers occasionally sucked up rusted strands of barbed wire, and a gigantic cattle syringe with its needle still intact was peeled from the sod by a three-year-old girl. Not far beyond Harvey's back porch manicured green gave onto the shag of unmown pasture, and farther still the skeleton of a barn stood like Gomorrah upon a rise. There was no fence, no ditch or row of ribboned stakes to set off the field, just tufted, uneven earth. He dropped his study Bible as he walked, then lay down in a coffin of tall, cow-smelling grass, the sky above framed raggedly to his shape. With the wind, a loose board on the barn clapped at a post, bringing on the rattling of chains, dogs howling up and down the street. Crickets sawed all around him, so close he felt they would devour him in his sleep like piranhas. The cold pressed into his back and filled his lungs.

Shortly after missing graduation ceremonies because of pneumonia, Harvey departed for his yearly visit to his father. He took the redeye. François was waiting at the airport, looking too healthy, dressed for the times, a leather jacket with a synthetic wool collar.

The sky was barely blue, and tired, they talked quietly over breakfast. Harvey had recently considered Québec, that as a Catholic he might be like one of those consoling New York–Italian priests in the movies. It occurred to him that perhaps he had a family somewhere, a place where he would feel at home, where there were others like himself. He asked about his name, about whether François missed speaking French.

François paused and looked at Harvey as if he'd just noticed he was there. Well, he said and took a deep breath. The sudden enthusiasm in his gaze was frightening.

He started in on stories that Harvey had heard snippets of before and never cared for, though this time he forced himself to listen. François described the Hervé men who were the strongest of any around, who worked and fought and infested the countryside with proud illegitimates. He described the endurance of their lineage that had been among the first to colonize North America, and how his grandmother, in her search for him, had wandered the continent seven years, driven by love and faith. He repeated the stories she'd told him time and time again, of family and history and her visions, embellishing them himself, giving the Hervés a knack for business and a penchant for the sciences.

I seem to remember her saying that one of our ancestors invented a certain kind of sail, François said, scratching his head. Anyway, they were seafarers.

Where are they now? Harvey asked, perched on the edge of his seat, thinking that perhaps there was someplace he could visit after all, a few cousins who, being tiny, hadn't been mentioned.

All gone, I suppose, François replied, then seemed to catch himself. But, you know, I've lived my life that way, too. He went on to describe road trips, adventures crosscountry that he never quite completed so that in the space where he might have told something more, might have finished, a wistful look came into his eye, a sadness that Harvey wanted to understand, to find comfort in.

François appeared unable to draw loose ends together. He backtracked, talking about how the Hervé men loved women and were restless and passionate. In a hushed voice, he told Harvey he'd lived with a prostitute. He conjured visions of buxom flesh, of a woman whose body moved with cold, indifferent perfection. Suddenly, Harvey realized that this family would hate him, that they would be ashamed of a sixty-one-inch descendant who would surely faint in the presence of a prostitute or out on the open sea for that matter.

François noticed his reticence. What's up?

Oh, I was just thinking about how meaningless all that stuff is. Harvey tried to call to mind what mattered. He described his own interests, the importance of good posture and recent discoveries in nutritional healing. He hesitated, suddenly ashamed to hear himself.

François probed his cheek with his tongue and looked away.

A few weeks later, when it was time for Harvey's departure, he'd seen his father's disappointment too often. François sighed as they were saying goodbye. On the plane, after takeoff, Harvey took down the tray on the seatback. He put his head on his crossed arms. He'd read that in some ancient traditions each searcher believed he was completing the journey his ancestors had begun, carrying on a desire that had been cut short by death. But who, dead in the longing for light, for peace and a modest bliss, could he dream back to?

278

As the plane bumped through the uneven sky, he wept. The hostess passed, then backed up and hovered over him. Sweetie, she said, are you flying without your parents?

She held out a heart-shaped lollipop.

College proved a poor substitute for the initiation of a prophet. That fall he attended classes nearby and lived at home. His mother didn't ask him to work but gave him a credit card, which she paid. She bought him a second-hand Toyota that he drove sitting on a cushion. He was humiliated by her willingness to provide, her assumption that he couldn't do it himself. She was now having an email relationship with an Englishman she'd met on the vegidate website. Occasionally, when she'd chattered too long about her mystic friends and the beauty of the New Age, Harvey skulked away and hid himself, afraid to admit that she might be foolish, that so much of him was her. And what did he know? Perhaps the world was simply more than he could handle. His grades were poor. The only assignment he'd found the least bit interesting was to research his name, and though a genealogy had been hopeless, he'd read about the Welsh and Breton saint Harvey, or Hervé, a blind man loved by animals and led by a wolf and whose presence made frogs sing. But this, too, finished in a big So what? He wasn't blind and didn't care much for frogs, which lived in mud, or for animals, especially dogs. Interesting, his professor had written with his red pen: ☺ C+.

Once, after class, Harvey asked his slouching history teacher about Québec. The man was a collector of J.F.K. memorabilia. He had every documentary on the subject, the exact model camera that had filmed the assassination, and the same kind of rifle Oswald had used, which he occasionally brought to class, though he'd been obliged to remove the firing pin to do so.

Québec, he said and nodded, hands in his pockets to accentuate his slouch. Basically, they all speak English but just pretend not to in order to be mean to tourists. You'd be better off going to France if you want to learn the language the way it really is.

Late that December afternoon, when Harvey got home, a letter from the college was in the mailbox. It explained that he was to be put on academic probation. He read it twice, then walked into the withered field and stared at the exposed frame of the barn. Single flakes fell from the dimming sky, too solitary to be flurries, too conscious to be snow. The cold made his eyes stream. Harvey Hervé was no more than a random name, Vancouver or Virginia random places. If he stayed, he would never match up to the lives of holy men. No one would accept if he changed, not even his mother. He didn't want to be part of this world.

He went to his room and threw everything on his bedsheet then folded in the corners and hauled it to his car. His mind quieter than any meditation, he drove through the night. This was his first choice. Somewhere on the road he recalled his father's stories. He felt bright, courageous, that François might finally be proud. He sat primly at the wheel, the rearview mirror casting into his eyes the dawn as it rushed up over the plains behind him.

Bravery was a new thing. The indifferent earth seemed ancient, primitive, far from man's disfigurements, bypasses and industrial parks. Tears welled up at the emptiness before him.

In a spell of uncertain sleet he stopped at a budget motel. Sprawling parking lots rumbled with the bogged idle of semis, and distantly a Budweiser sign glowed in a bar window. He imagined creased dollar bills in the bathroom, truckers undoing flat buckles, waitresses with brown teeth, eyelashes like fishhooks. Perhaps the man at the desk had told them he was here. He got up often to pull back his curtain, to peer out at the terrifying asphalt.

At the Wal-Mart in Amarillo he stocked up on provisions. Women with cumbersome hips moved with the staggered lower-body motion of TV dinosaurs. He called his mother. When her hysterics had passed, her only comment, which she repeated was, You don't need to go so far away to be holy. Afterwards he found a list of ashrams in one of his books. Many were in New Mexico. He continued towards the sunset, atomic over desolate plains.

The interstate rose into rugged desert basins. Silence hummed within him as if he were enlightened already, though he knew it to be fear, the poised listening of an animal. He gained altitude, the engine of his car sounding weedy, like a lawn mower. The big blue sky emptied of light. He slept at a rest stop. He thought of names he'd heard that he might someday put to the thing itself: saguaro and sagebrush, paloverde, piñon. Clouds blew past, a few swollen raindrops on the car roof.

282

In the morning he called the ashram. It was just two hours away but had no vacancies. The woman gave him a number for a man who rented rooms in the nearby trailer park. Harvey dialled, talked a bit, thought the price okay. After the Oklahoma sleet, the Texan wind, he was pleased to end his journey in the high, cold sunlight of New Mexico.

The sign at the entrance read Dry Branch Trailer Park. Originally a commingling of religious misfits, he soon learned, it was built up near a sandy arroyo in the middle of a Martian landscape of dune-like hills and scarps. It had been there since the 1970s, and more than forty families as well as countless singles now swelled its ranks. Windows indicated plurality with Buddhas and dream catchers, blue Shivas, beaded gurus and prayer flags. Organic gardens gave lushness to a few patches between trailers though dust devils passed like spirits along the main road.

His landlord, Brendan Howard, taught religion at the community college. He was a skinny white man with steel-frame glasses, a cardigan often over his shoulders, as if this were not the blazing high desert but a yacht club. He always introduced himself with his full name so that it sounded like a title, the effect being rather cultish. He lived in what appeared to be the library of

Alexandria crammed into a trailer, no walls but shelves, books on tantrism and herbalism and voodoo. Nonetheless, he told Harvey that first day, it is the body that holds all truths.

There were more than twenty-five ashrams, temples, monasteries and retreats within an hour's drive, and those first months Harvey meditated, fasted, did pre-dawn yoga and saw the clear emanation of sunrise as he practised deep breathing on manicured temple greens. But soon it became apparent that little had changed. Spirituality was mostly health, no better than his mother's nutritional animism. Devotees discussed how young famous yogis looked. No one paid him any mind. He wished he had the courage to walk out naked, or mostly naked, along the road, disappear into a river and return in song, sleep in the roots of trees.

A few Western Sikh families lived in the Dry Branch but remained involved with an ashram where, for thirty years, white Americans had attempted to live as in the Punjab of Guru Gobind Singh. They invited Harvey to a lecture at which the lugubrious old Sikh master talked of purity to a hundred students in white robes and turbans. Every step taken away from the soul must be taken back, he told them. They did a chant, almost an hour as they held their hands in the air, sweat pouring from their armpits, shaking, crying.

Don't be so impressed, Brendan Howard said after Harvey had described the power of his experience and the security of the community. Brendan Howard's tone was not unlike that of a high-school counsellor going over colleges. He called the ashram a cultish offshoot of Sikhism. And regardless, he continued, religion is linked with anachronistic practices. In fact the Sikh turban has primitive origins and was merely intended to make the holy man resemble the inseminating organ in his approach to the womblike temple.

At the Sikh ashram Harvey heard other arguments, that anything aside from an ancient path was New Age. Even yoga had been cheapened, though the ashram remained a stronghold of traditional practices. Not a few members had pursued higher education, been professors and psychologists but had seen nothing certain or stable in American culture.

At first Harvey thought the ashram was a throwback, but he learned that even when the spiritual trends of the sixties and seventies had passed, the ashram had endured, incorporating, starting businesses, establishing yoga training programs, its membership still growing. The community now centred around several companies that skyrocketed returns by claiming non-profit status and paying devotees a pittance. Experts in everything from health food to surveillance, CEOs, copywriters and secretaries turned out in droves each morning in turbans and robes to occupy the stucco buildings at the edge of the ashram. Their success, they explained, came of their being spiritual householders, dedicated to raising families and living in the world and not seeking the ascetic's path—what they considered sterile. Their clarity was tempting.

After a brief application process Harvey got himself hired to tend the grounds and to clean up after the Chicano youths who performed lawn jobs and left gutted bags of trash. He also called the pound on strays. Members had made an effort to chain their own dogs as they had a tendency to run with packs of wild dogs and rabies was a concern. But though he bent himself to this new life, the ashram girls, buxom with ghee and chapatis, laughed when they saw him. Marriage was stressed, often young. It is the highest yoga, the master said, true purity. Harvey believed that eventually a girl would perceive the devotion in his heart. She would be small and incorporeal and ageless, like an elf.

In his room in Brendan Howard's trailer he worked into more strenuous postures. He practised intense meditations, hours at a time, holding his palms on his head and inhaling through his curved tongue. Soon he found he wasn't so short of breath from the altitude. He read books on yoga and anatomy and learned to speak of his body in scientific terms. Sweating, holding postures, he felt primal, no longer the domesticated thing he'd been. He was proud of the dawns when he got up for selfless service, warming his car at three a.m. Even his suffering gave him pride, and though the master said that only the ascetic, the sadhu, takes pride in suffering and shirks the responsibilities of the world, Harvey worked for the good of the ashram. He loved the ancient practices, the robes and sense of tradition, the authority of the outmoded. Once, impressed by his newfound presence, he braved asking someone out, a diminutive girl slightly beyond his age range, blue flecks of acne scars on her cheeks.

Sorry, she told him, I'm going chanting with friends tonight.

Oh, he said and waited, but there was no invite. Back home he meditated on his breath, blocked one nostril to exhale from the other, the sound that of a punctured tire.

You must resist thinking yourself through the suffering of life, the master told them in his weekly lecture. Spring winds howled over the hills. Everyone talked about ionic charges in the air, how traditional societies judged crimes more compassionately when committed in seasonal winds. The master's dust and juniper allergies were rampant. His frazzled beard lay on his chest, and he blew his nose frequently.

Listen to the wind, he said. Its chaos scares you. Your chaos scares you. Look at the world. Bonds are disintegrating. The future is shapeless. There is nothing to hold us. We have had chaos before, but nothing like this. Only the teachings can carry us through.

Harvey had often heard the master say that history was a burden, that Americans were blessed to be slipping free. Ancient wisdom was timeless and would transform them. But who would they become? A new order—Jedi knights, the white-clad forefathers of Superman whose minds could move crystals? What of Harvey Hervé? Of Hervé-François Hervé? He thought of those stories, the brutal men, the enduring grandmother.

Let go of your past, the master said, his eyes bugged out, his turban sloppy.

The next afternoon Harvey drove into Santa Fe and went to the mall. He needed underwear but ended up walking for an hour, from store to store, pausing to watch music videos in Foot Locker, movies in Radio Shack. A Chicano girl, probably thirteen, passed with a fishnet shirt showing a black bra. He wished this would all burn away. He didn't want to be like his father.

As he started home, a storm was blowing up. Cars rocked at red lights. The wind scoured his windshield with grit, tiny tumbleweeds crossing the highway like terrified cats. Lightning punctuated the mountain horizon to the south.

History, chaos, suffering? Did words mean anything within nature? Maybe even the ashram was too much, the ascetic's life preferable—a cave or a monastery to protect him from judging eyes. But did he have the heart of a solitary? The master said you had to live in the world. The journey began with taking a name, but then what?

When he arrived for the evening lecture, members had gathered outside. A few had on work goggles to keep sand out of their eyes. Siri Ram, a six-year-old whose husky mutt, Snowball, often ran with strays, had gone missing. They thought that the boy had left to look for Snowball. As search parties gathered, Harvey shivered in the high desert night.

They advanced into the hills, blowing whistles, calling out, flashlights weaving in the dark. The wind buffeted them as if they were walking into surf. Junipers and all the cactuses and cholla of the desert waited for them to stumble. Brief and muted moonlight gave ridges shapes like sunken boats.

A dog's yaps came from below a drop-off. It yelped, then barked, as if wanting out to pee. They edged along the rock face until their flashlights found Snowball in the clouding dust. The wind had almost erased whatever struggle there had been. Bloody paw prints showed on the stone. A dry, bent tree in the hillside was broken, and Snowball stood beneath, head lowered, his panting, bloody muzzle to the dust.

Boy Eaten By His Dog

(NM). Last night, in the worst wind storm in decades, a boy was killed by his own dog . . . Authorities believe that the dog ran off with a pack of strays and, when the boy went to find him, joined in chasing him down . . .

Wind rocked trailers and ruined meditation gardens.

Master, he said. Will you give me a spiritual name?

You will be Sat Puja. It is a powerful mantra. An offering to truth, you will be the true offering, a great devotee.

Each dawn he meditated on his name.

Harvey, his mother said over the phone.

It's Sat Puja, mata.

Such a fanatic, she thought, calling me the Indian word for mother, and he, with a mix of pride and worry and curiosity at the odd mechanisms of self, thought the same.

Why are you doing this? she asked.

He wanted to tell her they'd been living an illusion, but would she be willing to change, or would it require her suffering?

They waited quietly on the phone. Finally in a faint voice—I'm proud of you, she said. Whatever you do, I'm proud.

New Mexico
2006

A week after receiving his name, Sat Puja took an indefinite vow of silence. It was too easy just to bide one's time for a set duration, he told others before he began, in the days that he let everyone know he wouldn't be speaking and made a few phone calls so no one would worry in case he chose to cease communicating altogether. Then, one dawn, when he awoke, he took a deep breath and blew through his mouth as if cleansing the palate of all the nonsense it had spoken. He'd read this was a proper beginning.

Every action was now meditation. It was June, the sun fierce. He'd begun bowing to the holy book, did pre-dawn service in the cold kitchen that smelled of onions and garlic and ghee, and had graduated from a light tur-ban, like an Indian puggree, to a towering beehive. In fact he tied his so high that at times he had to support it and looked like a peevish society lady patting her hair. He purchased the robes and knickknacks of religious life and even worked at growing a beard. He had a fringe of blond fuzz like that of a very old woman.

He continued his yoga, staying in excruciating pos-tures, freeing up the anxiety of past lives. He pressed his fingers over his eyes, phosphenes flowering inside his head: the devoured boy, the bright threads of jacket. He wasn't sure how to give up the world and still live within it with any certainty, and it seemed messy to attempt both. Nor did he care much for groundskeeping. Each second stooping to move a sprinkler was enough for the back of his neck to burn. Mostly he just sat, sweating in the shade as the ashram green longed to return to the baked pie crust of desert.

Perhaps the silence would have gone on forever, and he'd have become one of those unobtrusive ashram members who laid foundations while the others played, but two weeks after he began, a young man arrived in a BMW convertible. Though mute, Sat Puja wasn't deaf. Donald was everywhere at once but never in one place long enough to get hitched. Raised by absentee parents in Carmel on a diet of packaged organic foods with a Mexican maid to open them and throw out the wrappings, he was an old study in the art of drawing attention and became the ashram's heartthrob by artifice alone. Evenly tanned, with a patrician nose that none doubted he would come to own and the coarse beginnings of a dark jaw, he had a physique trained by the popular calisthenic yoga that ashram members held in disdain. They all soon learned his story, which he frequently recounted, as if his arrival at an ashram after two years preparing a double major in political science and philosophy at Yale was as astounding as the conquests of Cortés or the journeys of Magellan. Born into a world of euphemistic money—trading, managing, observing—he'd rarely seen his father, who was among the elite to have mastered the prima materia of the capitalist world, and who could do so easily from his home PC. Like Sat Puja, Donald had had a weak spot for biographies and had noted that a worthy life lay in contradictions. With a profile so like a coin's he'd found it hard to turn his back on money, but he knew that youth necessitated rebellion or else would pass soundlessly into spongy middle age. The day he'd arrived at Yale, he'd made a spectacle of pitching bed and desk from his dorm windows, a bit of ostentation that the financial office put on his father's bill. He meditated often, studied crosslegged and slept on a mat he'd bought at the flea market. He received nighttime visits from stoners seeking consolation or God. He was the dorm wise man. Detached, he passed unscathed through campus debauchery and quoted holy texts on the subject of craving, all the while breezing his academics.

Not long after his arrival at the ashram he beseeched the master for a name. Each time someone arrived, the community waited to learn what name and hence what destiny the master would divine. When Harvey had taken his, he'd heard the assistants discussing Puja, whether it meant worship or reverence and that, really, it better suited a girl. Donald, with all the pleasure the ashram youth expressed at his arrival, was expecting something prophetic. The master grumbled, spat into a tissue and said, Jamgoti. An assistant wrote it down. Jamgoti was whispered around the room. No one had heard it before.

What does it mean? Donald asked.

The master laughed roughly. Loincloth, he said.

The ashram soon decided that this reflected an unworthiness that only the master could perceive. Insincerity most likely, many agreed, so that when Donald applied for jobs, he was refused all but the most transient and ended up at Sat Puja's side. Those who'd resented his popularity, quick wit and expansive learning assumed he'd never use the name. The girls told him that he'd be renamed once he'd proven his devotion. But with a politician's sense of humour, he began introducing himself as Jamgoti. Means loincloth, he clarified even to those who knew—Can't leave home without it.

His first day tending the grounds he took up his rake, thumped himself on the chest in mockery of Sat Puja's silence, then proceeded to talk until well past noon. He was smoothly analytical of what he called the ashram's pedestrian approach to spirituality. With so much emphasis on being a householder, he said, there isn't much time for enlightenment, is there?

Sat Puja tried to appear absorbed in meditative silence, but after Jamgoti had discoursed on his precocious mysticism, a youth of Internet surfing for arcana, meditation with a penny on his third eye and on-line spoon-bending societies that had tried to teach him to shift the molecules of cutlery with his mind, Sat Puja cleared his throat, introduced himself and spoke of his own attempts, his fears and yearnings and pain, on and on and often returning to the essential theme of how similar they were, and on, until it was well past quitting time. Those last weeks he'd reconsidered his projection. He spoke with the deepest voice he could manage, from the navel as he'd learned in his college theatre class. There was nothing he didn't tell and he was somewhat taken aback that he could fit his entire life into an afternoon.

Besides, he said, this job gets you dirty.

They were now sitting under a cottonwood, in its splotch of shadow. Jamgoti chewed a blade of obscenely green grass that probably tasted like hairspray after all they'd done to make it grow. He scratched his calf with a big toe and declared that they needed to take action or drift forever in mediocrity. We must plan, he said. There's no reason to wait.

Far off, ranchera had begun to play from a hotel terrace in the hills above the ashram as it often did this time of year with all the local weddings. After a while, Sat Puja invited Jamgoti to his trailer and couldn't believe his offer was accepted.

Jamgoti insisted they take his convertible. They drove in the warm evening, roof down, wind attempting to unfurl Sat Puja's turban. Jamgoti began explaining the groundwork for a more intensive approach to understanding the divine. But Sat Puja was mute, an invisible touch flourishing in his chest, an emotion that he couldn't name, like a strange bloom in a vast desert.

Despite his questionable name, Jamgoti maintained a celebrity entourage. He'd fashioned a stylish light turban, though for yoga he preferred shorts and tank tops to robes, his legs being as sculpted as a porn star's. But little by little he began to refuse invitations, even when they said he could bring Sat Puja.

I'd have stayed at Yale if I wanted parties. Besides, you're the only one here crazy enough to keep up with me, he said, at once assuaging Sat Puja's jealousy and arousing a sense of worry.

Jamgoti's lectures were numerous. He explained how masters used to leave their students in the middle of nowhere with absolutely nothing and would tell them that they had to find their way back. A medicine man left his student in the middle of Las Vegas, he said. Without a penny.

Sat Puja felt himself being primed.

It's failure till the end that's real, Jamgoti told him. Or almost until the end. It's the love that keeps you from enlightenment that brings you to the true meaning in this world.

But it was on a day that Jamgoti didn't show up until well past noon that he announced his solution.

Sat Puja balanced his turban and looked up.

Sadhus, Jamgoti said. We'll become sadhus.

296   If there was one taboo on an ashram of householders, it was this, and Sat Puja told him so. That the master had lectured severely against those who chose to renounce the world. The sadhu was supposed to near God through deprivation and suffering, but the master set them straight. The sadhu, he'd said, doesn't marry. He called them tourists in life's pain.

And I'm sure people say the opposite somewhere else, Jamgoti told Sat Puja. I'm sure others would accuse householders of clinging to worldly security. Just imagine, he said, the power of committing to nothing but enlightenment.

But Sat Puja wasn't convinced.

I don't think you really believe in all this, Jamgoti told him, narrowing his eyes with consideration and making Sat Puja feel not only that he was worth close scrutiny but that he was being dared. You know, I think that most young people who come here are trying to spice up their middle-class existence. Maybe you're just running away.

Sat Puja had considered this argument a thousand times. Inwardly he chastised himself for spiritual motives that weren't pure. At community meals, turbaned company directors discussed corporate imaging. Though the possibility that he might someday belong tempted him, he could see all this through Jamgoti's eyes—that the

Sikhs could but tie him to a system, to rules that were, quite simply, worldly. He'd read the work of a Buddhist who said that cruelty came when one's rule for life failed and that all worldly love or desire for love ended in hatred and pain.

Sat Puja put down his rake and listened. The sprinklers clucked and chuckled. Distance blurred. The sky wavered. What was this place? he wondered. This desert? These weirdos in the American landscape searching for tradition? Would they disappear like the gunslingers and saloons? This was too in the middle of nowhere. The sun seemed to be approaching the earth, the ashram itself. Would it bounce off like a rubber ball, leaving a faint burnt splat, this artificial green desert again?

Their preparation consisted of improvised ceremonies, cutting up credit cards, leaving uneven stacks of books about the trailer park like primitive stone piles. Harvey took his Toyota to a used-car lot. Three hundred, the fat man said, his speckled belly visible between the taut buttons of his shirt. Sat Puja tried to insist on its relative worth, but Jamgoti laid a hand on his shoulder.

As for the BMW, Jamgoti admitted that it was his mother's and couldn't legally be sold. Sat Puja imagined running it off a hill or parking it in a bad neighbourhood or selling it for pennies to a Mexican chopshop. Instead Jamgoti called a drive-away service to take it home.

A hip pouch, a blanket, turbans and a pair of baggy yoga clothes were all they agreed on as well as whatever they had in cash, less for themselves, Jamgoti pointed out, than to regale the needy they might encounter. They took a few minor cosmetic objects, a nail clipper, tooth-brushes, floss, a needle and thread to stitch rags into cloaks like itinerant Buddhists. Sat Puja was tempted to sneak a credit card or even to withdraw a substantial amount of cash and hide it. He did, however, secrete his driver's licence and passport, surprised at the power of his instinct for survival.

298

They set out at the hour of the pre-dawn meditation. This was when mystics went deepest, in the chill, living air. Wrapped in blankets they followed the arroyo on a trail used by dirt bikes. Aren't we near Los Alamos, Jamgoti asked, where they made the first atom bomb? The moon had set. The stars were a molten path along the sky.

After a while they stopped on a hill to meditate, their breaths controlled like those of divers, their eyes closed as if they were falling back into water. Their blankets and robes had turned red from the dust. Sat Puja felt a tightness in his chest and tried to calm his rushing mind. Jamgoti's words returned to him—the love that keeps you from enlightenment. He pictured himself gone off to surrender attachments, embittered by the world. What love, what willowy figure, would save him from cold immortality?

Later, when they tried to rest, both were too excited. They headed randomly downhill, surprised to find a path of sorts. By early morning the sun had muscled back the shadows. Surveying the distance from an

outcropping, Jamgoti not only resembled Lawrence of
Arabia but looked as if he felt like him, too. Finally
unable to bear the heat they sat under an overhanging
rock, bandits at wait.

I'm thirsty, Sat Puja said. He was thinking about the
299
money in his hip pouch and where they might buy
something. Jamgoti suggested this was just nervousness
and that it would pass. Dust and heat conspired to make
Sat Puja's eyes water. He felt a shortness of breath, regret
that they hadn't brought drinks. He stared at the fissured
earth, an intricate puzzle that stretched infinitely before
them. He'd imagined begging for rice at huts, meditating beneath trees, crossing uninhabited distances. The
ascetic life was supposed to be purified of all things, but
this was the world and then some. He worried that they
looked like homeless people.

Near dark they were unsteady on their feet. They'd
meditated and napped. A few times, when a breeze had
passed over the baking earth, its hot, thin air drying the
sweat beneath his clothes, Sat Puja had felt his spirit lift,
but only briefly—these were earthly sensations, con-
flicted and fleeting, not what he'd hoped. When the day
had cooled enough, they set out again. Cresting a rise,
they saw the highway and the beacon of a Chevron. They
started down in a giddy, shuffling run. The man behind
the counter watched them, phone ready, finger on the
hook. They bought Gatorade and chocolate bars.
Moderation, moderation, Jamgoti repeated as they tore
through the wrappers with their teeth. The man rang up
their purchases with one hand.

Outside again they ate and belched. Sat Puja immediately felt nauseous but too happy to let it show. They
headed back out from the gas station across a colourless,
lunar plain, occasionally picking their way over forgotten
strands of barbed wire. Soon there was only the strange
silence of the desert night, disturbed by a distant baseline
or the downshifting of a tractor-trailer.

They'd walked long enough to lose all notion of time
and had come into view of a mesa's single turret when,
across a range of juniper, a flare rose as if from the earth.
It dipped, briefly disappeared, rose again and separated
into headlights. A pickup slowed on a dirt road they
wouldn't otherwise have noticed.

You boys lost? a man asked with a faintly lilting
Chicano accent. From the shape of the headlights and
the grille, the smoothness of the idle, the truck was
clearly new. This calmed Sat Puja. The cab light came
on. The man had a dark, round face and high cheekbones. He leaned heavily over the door.

Hop in back. I'll give you a ride over to my place and
you can use the phone.

Sat Puja was about to refuse politely when Jamgoti
thanked the man and climbed over the tailgate. He
hauled Sat Puja up like a child and whispered,
Adventure. As they began moving, he explained that they
had to let the world take them where it would.

They rode through the still air, now heavy and cool on
their bodies. Not far from where they'd been picked up,
the landscape descended. They passed the occasional
tree, patchy tall grass, and to the side, farther down,

undergrowth and a narrow river. The truck pulled into what had once been a farm, sheds and a sagging barn, a house stacked back in ever more rickety additions.

The man driving was at most thirty, and his size would have been imposing if it weren't for the jean jacket that made him look pinched at the shoulders, his cowboy boots dainty as high heels beneath his big frame. He introduced himself as Danny. He was returning home with a half-dozen new PlayStation rentals.

Another man, slightly younger, met them at the door, and Danny did no more than introduce them as guests. This is my brother, Andy, he said.

You guys prophets or something? Andy asked, tugging at his sparse moustache. If either brother was surprised by the two filthy young men wearing turbans, they hardly let it show.

Jamgoti led them into uncertain laughter by abbreviating their adventure, saying they'd dared themselves to live like holy men.

The sound of coughing came from the backroom, and when Sat Puja glanced in that direction, Danny explained that his *abuelo*—his grandfather—was sick. Don't worry, our sister takes care of anything if he needs it.

Danny then told them that they could spend the night on the couches, which they accepted after a few rounds at the PlayStation, at which Jamgoti appeared quite skilled.

Morning came too soon with a yellow, intersecting light. Sat Puja's lungs felt furry, his eyes pinched and sore. He looked for the bathroom so he could blow his nose.

Danny came into the kitchen with a rifle. Coffee's on, he said, then went out. Sat Puja watched him go up the driveway, past outbuildings half-lost in a flame of wild grass. The night before Danny had explained that for the past seven months he'd been visiting the neighbours, whose cousin from Mexico had gotten his sister, Juanita, pregnant then disappeared. Though Danny confessed to being a softy, he remained volatile in regards to his sister, explaining that their father had abandoned them and that she, not yet born, had been sent along years later. After a few questions from Jamgoti, Danny had told the story, explaining that his *abuelo*, a hard man in his youth, had been the town constable for more than three decades and had hated drifters and criminals. One day, the grandfather heard that Danny and Andy's father was dealing drugs, and he drove to the trailer where the young man lived with his girlfriend and boys. The aging constable showed up holding an old leather harness and repeatedly tossed his son to the ground with one hand as he struck. He left him on the trailer's cinderblock steps that the next owner would have to paint black, and a week later woke in the night to find Danny and Andy, aged three and one, in the kitchen with a garbage bag of clothes and a half-empty box of diapers. Nine years afterwards a stranger arrived in a truck and brought a baby girl into the house. She'd been stuffed naked into the cut-off leg of a woman's jeans, insulated with cotton balls, a napkin pinned to the denim reading Juanita. The stranger spoke with the grandfather, described the man with the scarred face and

so confirmed that this was Danny and Andy's father. He
had breakfast, tried his hand at a few bouts of *Space
Invaders* with the boys, then put on his hat and left. Why
the girl had received a Mexican name remained a mystery unless it was meant as a jab at Juan, the grandfather.
Danny and Andy had been the first in the family with
gringo names, their mother being uppity. Also, the napkin
it was printed on came from Denny's, which Danny had
seen as something of an omen, the closest God could
come in worldly terms to an edict.

And now she's pregnant, Danny had told them. The
guy who did it was real little, like you. He gestured to Sat
Puja. I don't know what I'm going to do if I catch him.
But no one's going to want her now but us, and he
should pay.

Jamgoti was still asleep on the couch, an arm flung
against the sunlight. The grandfather hollered toothlessly,
and Sat Puja went to the door. He eased it back. Danny
had told him that one day his *abuelo* had woken with
numb fingertips and that this had by degrees spread
throughout his body. The old man lay stiff on the mattress, his head twisted against the pillow. His eyes were
wide. Sat Puja had retied his turban that morning, revers-
ing the cloth to hide the dirt, and the old man stared as if
this were indeed the end, a half-pint Eastern angel sent to
collect his soul. A glass of water sat on a rickety night
table, and he'd manoeuvred a skeletal arm towards it, the
hand suspended in a rictus of bone. The girl lay in the
bed across the room, curled halfway. She had faint dark
hairs on her upper lip and sweat along the side of her

nose. Her face glistened, her hair pushed up in a nest away from her neck. Both stared, the old man with cartoon eyes, the girl with a prisoner's veiled look of curiosity.

It wasn't until Sat Puja closed the door that the moment struck him. He couldn't recall how long they'd paused, watching each other in the dim, hospital-smelling room with its drawn blinds and undertones of earth and decaying floor joists. Danny's words returned to him, that she'd loved a little guy like him and that no one would want her now.

To calm this sudden emotion, Sat Puja meditated in the living room while he waited for Jamgoti to get up. It was the first time he'd missed his pre-dawn meditations since he'd joined the ashram.

When Jamgoti was finally awake, Juanita was sitting in the kitchen, spooning corn flakes from a bowl of milk. She perched forward on her chair and wore a ballooning white dress, her legs thatched with hair. The arches of her feet hugged the rungs, and she smiled shyly, her cheeks swollen with sleep.

Jamgoti sat across from her. We haven't met, he said and introduced himself. Do you mind if I join you for cereal?

No, she murmured and blushed. Danny and Andy were in the other room, and Jamgoti kept up a patter of light questions. You go to school? Ah, no—finished? Have you given college any thought? Of course, it's not for everyone.

I know, Juanita told him, that I'll be perfectly happy raising my child.

Sat Puja considered that she said it as if it was the sort of thing she'd often thought about saying, as if she expected the kinds of questions Jamgoti was asking.

I have a guidance counsellor, she told him, who keeps calling. I had good grades, but it's true—it wasn't for me.

Do you know, Jamgoti said and smiled, that was my experience, too? We can't all hope to be happy with the same things that others are.

Sat Puja cleared his throat. He'd been standing at the door. He had the impression that Jamgoti had said everything he himself might have liked to say in an introductory conversation. He was certain that there would never be another original introductory conversation again, if not on earth, then at least not here. His innards felt like a sponge being violently wrung.

Afterwards, as they walked out through the brittle grass, Jamgoti told him that they could sleep there again that night. Danny had said so.

None of this was what Sat Puja had wanted. Crossing the shallow river on stones, he considered what their journey should have been: a brief, clear fantasy of bathing in crisp water, of washing robes and laying them out to dry. But perhaps someone like the grandfather would have taken them for vagrants and run them out of town, or jailed them, tied them to fence posts and whipped them with jumper cables. Oddly, the tradition of being lost in America seemed right. It was old, venerable even, and made him proud when he thought of his family history. Perhaps his father wouldn't appreciate the specifics, but Sat Puja was of another time. And perhaps he might actually stumble upon some truth out here. He considered Juanita.

Jamgoti now appeared tired as they picked through sharp weeds. Sat Puja sensed something in Jamgoti he hadn't noticed until then—what seemed like laziness or a lack of genuine yearning for anything beyond admiration. For the first time he saw a spark of authenticity in his own desperation. His gut calmed. Are you tired? he asked, picking up the pace. Jamgoti licked his lips and rubbed the back of his neck. Sun's hot, he said.

They meditated in the shadow of a steep hill. Though their shelter was not as good as that of the previous day, they could see over the dry land to the river, even to the brothers' farm and farther still to mountains like immense fins. A shadow occasionally fell past them, made by the ragged wings of a circling vulture. Jamgoti stretched his back and rolled his head. He sighed. Sat Puja gazed beneath his slitted eyes. He slowed his breathing, mind mirrored within stillness. Pinned by the sun, the landscape revolved, crags and mesas like eroding temples. A faroff tin roof flapped silver wings in a mirage of heat. Jamgoti had gone to sleep. Sat Puja was at peace.

Towards evening, as they returned, Jamgoti said they should be careful of dehydration. At the edge of the river, a farmer had built a bonfire of brush and trash, the breeze sweet with burning plastic. A rust-coloured bulldozer was parked on the rise, treadmarks bandaging the earth and heaps of torn-up trees near the water.

Jamgoti had become watchful, tossing questions at Sat Puja to test his mood, asking how his meditations were or whether he wanted to give up. Jamgoti seemed to consider, then began laying the groundwork for an argument against turbans. He stopped so that Sat Puja had to give up his steady clip and come back. Sadhus don't wear turbans, Jamgoti said. He pulled his off, then waxed on what must be done with the hair, shaving or matting, and finally decided that he felt closer to the Rastafarians than to the skinheads.

I'm keeping the turban, Sat Puja said.

It's a crutch, you know.

With the smell of plastic came the suffocating odour of disturbed earth carried by the wind. Sat Puja had to slow his breath.

Weltschmerz, Jamgoti exclaimed. It's why we're doing this? Because we can't make the world match our ideals. We're afraid of our portion of life. Our world suffering. Our *weltschmerz*.

Sat Puja decided then that no matter how eloquent and philosophical Jamgoti became, he would not be convinced.

Weltschmerz, Jamgoti repeated and gestured to the land beyond the river, the bulldozer and the man swatting dusty gloves against his jeans. None of this is what we dream. In fact, the idea can be sentimental, the bitter sweetness of staying here. You know, the scriptures call our lives on earth the mud of time, but maybe the people who wrote them were also fleeing. I mean, to me at least the world doesn't seem so bad.

Sat Puja no longer knew where the argument had begun or how turbans related to sadhus and to their pie portion of suffering. He wasn't sure whether he was being told to return to the world or to give up his turban and be a proper sadhu. The former it seemed until Jamgoti reached over and pulled off his turban and unfurled it into the dirt with the precision of a hoodlum sending toilet paper into trees. The material flapped a few times, grew heavy with dust and lay still. Then Jamgoti set out into the brush alongside the river, and Sat Puja hurried behind, branches whipping back into his face.

Long after everyone had fallen asleep, Sat Puja lay awake, furious. His guts felt hot and loose and gurgled frequently. Heat flashed along his skin, and though his lips and mouth were dry, he didn't want to add water to the chaos within. Each time he calmed his mind enough to drift off, a mosquito homed in on his ear and he ended up thinking back to Danny's story of his *abuelo*. He disliked that savage past, its brutal love and laws. He had no notion of violence or intensity, of where it might reside. He quieted his breathing and listened to the silence of his body, the empty spaces like dark matter around the amphibious patter of his heart. The mosquito neared again and he swatted.

The sound of radio static and a faint melody came from the far end of the house. He got up from the couch. Light showed through a crack in a door. The announcers' voices had a sober quality as in old wartime reels, the music exotic. Static buzzed between channels. He knocked.

Come in, Andy said. Sit down. He was fiddling with a boxy, military-looking radio. Sat Puja sat and watched the dial move along the lit face. A computer hummed in the corner, fractals unfolding on its screen. A workbench extended the length of the wall, covered in phials and pipettes, the various beaked and gourd-shaped glassware of an alchemist.

Andy plucked at his moustache. It's a shortwave, he explained, saying that when he'd been sixteen, Danny had joined the army and returned four months later with an injured knee, a discharge and the radio he'd bought in a pawnshop as a gift. Andy said that he liked listening to it at night because it sounded different then. Sat Puja sensed this, the way the music swelled, tuned sharply—the voices, even the static, fuller, charged with the high, lonely distances. Shyly, Andy explained that it gave him hope somehow. He searched the channels, the talk in unknown languages, the English and Spanish news from around the world. Wind blew in along the dark, sand rattling the windows, and Sat Puja found that the faint static was as soothing as the voices, ice storms and floods and fires, new novels, illegal poppy crops, dance troupes.

It makes me feel like I'm at war, Andy said. Like I'm part of something important.

Why didn't you join the army?

No way. After I saw Danny with his knee tore up and all skinny, I never wanted to go in.

309

Something about Andy's observations touched Sat Puja. He thought of Jamgoti's glibness, the way he uncovered the hearts of others as if they were nothing new. Was Sat Puja just the sidekick, the necessary element in every adventure? The occasion for Jamgoti to hear his own wisdom and be impressed? Andy found a broadcast of Asian music, a warbling stringed instrument with a sound like a woman's mournful voice. Sat Puja felt tired. He wanted to absolve himself of all this, to be good and pure and make a few peaceful hand gestures, shoulders relaxed, face sunny. This had never been about adventure.

If you're seeking God, Andy said, you should try some of that. He pointed to a corked beaker filled with fluid.

Sat Puja considered his readings on alchemy years ago, encoded instructions to make gold but that were in fact to transform the base soul into the essence of immortality. And now, here he was, in a drug shop in a blistered, alien world.

He sat with Andy until late, listening to the rhythms of other languages, the foreign laughter. The moment might have become simply another dose of that world pain, his *weltschmerz*, his desire for things to be a little better, sweet longing—wind at the windows, the cool summer night of the desert. But he was thinking now, listening no less, no less conscious of Andy's quiet perceptions.

Do you think there's anything in all that? Sat Puja asked Jamgoti the next day, meaning the drugs, the LSD—the potential for mystical experience. He loaded his voice with insecurity, with perfunctory disdain and the longing to hear his wise friend speak.

In fact, Sat Puja, Jamgoti said, in fact I think there might be something to be learned.

A little later Andy told them, It's on the house, boys. He took a Q-tip from a carton and dipped it in the fluid. Suck on that. There's enough to take you through tomorrow.

Jamgoti did. Sat Puja, he said and smacked his lips. Your turn.

But the nervousness had gone out of Sat Puja. With his grime and matted hair and fuzzy chin, he looked like an old-world thief, cunning, weasel eyed, never quite more than a child.

Sorry, he said in a voice he didn't recognize. You're in this one on your own.

Vancouver–New Mexico
2006

There was the way life had become a list. François had tried to make sense of it. He'd attempted to see it as headlines, as a miniseries or a how-to guide. He was just forty-nine but felt old. Whereas work had once been the only necessity, it now seemed an indulgence. Years collapsed to the form of an average day. Age came in hints, the softening of his features, the unfamiliar talk on dates. Exhausted, he slipped into old mispronunciations. An accent, he'd learned for all his tired will, could never truly be erased.

Whereas he'd once sought to forget, he now found himself trying to remember, to understand how he'd come to this place. He ate his meals alone, in hubcaps in his mostly empty restaurant, staring at posters of James Dean and Marilyn Monroe.

He began having night sweats. He came awake suffocating, hot, dizzy, a faint white powder on his lips, perhaps from gritting his teeth. He went to the doctor. He discovered that at different walk-in clinics they gave different prescriptions, all of which he took. He woke one night and stood at the window. Snow covered the rooftop and yard. Winter had been so much more intense in the prairies, a vanishing point of pale fields, flurries falling along distance. Then he realized he could make out weeds through the snow. It was June. This was moonlight. He had to go outside to get his bearings, to feel the warm air.

Soon after, he submitted himself to tests and X-rays. The doctor looked him in the eye. François listened, but the words didn't come together to have meaning.

You're otherwise healthy, the doctor said at one point, but this is all over the place.

François took the X-rays from the screen and left. In his car he almost reconsidered and went back, thinking he'd missed something, that there was a possibility the doctor had forgotten. Instead he visited Eduardo.

An X-ray held to the kitchen light, Eduardo studied it and said, True enough.

On the way home François had to swerve off the street for a bathroom. It was filthy, the light dead, the handle punched from the metal door. A syringe cracked under his shoe. Whatever had burned through him, fear or cancer, was burning through him now. He'd seen the grapevine of his intestines as if his strength was boiling, bubbling up. Was dying now worth all those years of perfect abs? No doubt it had been that damned electric belt, as dangerous as Eduardo had warned. It could have even been his time as a guinea pig. Perhaps he was decaying from the inside. Just that morning he'd felt a cavity in his molar. He was sure his breath stank. He was still young. He felt power in his bones like the hot metal of an oven. He'd earned money, had watched friends drift away and become grandparents. His son was off seeking a life of bland perfection. Peggy had told him that Harvey had gone mad, joined a cult in the Southwest—cult even by her standards, mad indeed.

What would be a last meaningful action? A few days before, reading the paper at the bar, he'd run across an article on cryogenics. It had given a few round-figure prices, and in the realm of such things he'd earned nothing at all, was a small fry. But now, considering a future that wouldn't include him, he understood the desire to be preserved, Walt Disney and Ted Williams in their cryogenic suspension, and many others, heads cut off and frozen, sealed in arctic air until new bodies could be grown from lurid slime and grafted on. He wanted to trust civilization's most absurd dreams, but he wasn't wealthy enough. His tear ducts felt tight, his eyes itched and just thinking about this, he felt the breath in his nostrils become brittle with cold. The cancer had spread

throughout his body. Survival was doubtful, and the pro-
longation of life, the doctor had said, though possible at
his age, would be unpleasant. The only means of contin-
uance François could imagine was in finding Harvey and
setting him on a better path. He himself had taken years   315
to discover his strength.

He sat more than an hour in the ammoniac reek of piss.
He raged with disappointment at his body. Layer upon
layer of graffiti showed faintly on the walls, in the darkness
like vines on a trellis. He'd wanted a son in his image, and
perhaps it wasn't too late after all. But when he pictured
himself now, the face was frozen, hard and unforgiving.

Those next weeks he sold everything, even his house and
businesses. He didn't want to risk all that he'd built
becoming worthless in his absence. But his heap of assets
weren't what he'd thought, especially not when sold in a
rush. He wrote up a will, leaving everything to Harvey
with instructions, and he took out forty thousand
American dollars in big bills that he zipped into the compartments of a nylon money belt. Those days, he slept
often. He watched late-night television and saw a martial-
arts film for the first time—the drunken master, the
avenging understudy, the great warrior leaving a
monastery's silence. Discourses on concentration, wisdom and form—dragon, tiger, crane—and the way these
bodies took flight reminded him of how natural it was to
dream. He was suddenly exhausted. He turned off the
television. For the last two days that the house remained

legally his, he stayed in bed. Then it was time. Cars were backing from driveways up and down the street, leaving for work. At a wedge of morning sunlight between two houses, they passed like camera flashes. He was no longer part of all this.

316

He drove that day in silence. Time passed in the way of quick beginnings, crossings and preparations that give on swollen, motionless drift. Numbers and names meant nothing, were no more than indications across an infinite expanse: I-82 to Yakima, through the corner of Oregon, past Eagle Cap and Red Mountain, past La Grande and Baker City and a place called Ontario, then to Boise, the Snake River and into Utah. Not just the vastness, the sky-swept expanses, but the light itself led him to compare Montréal, the lean light of the east, with this one, falling like rain, full as if fattened by the country it had crossed, a grazing light. Day fled, and even the darkness was a sense of open, empty space. In the gusts of passing semis, in sensory lapses of midnight highway, in the shadows swept by headlights at the side of the road, he recalled old journeys. He was overwhelmed by how much he'd given up for the life he'd led, and he mused that he might see that innocent self hitchhiking, who'd loved the fields and longed for them and who'd never been at home in the city. Years ago he'd found his grandmother in her chair, skin grey, veins collapsed in her forearms, death's eyes the faint blue of a blind dog's. Was there a wisdom to all this or was the earth simply what it was, grown and savaged by its own seasons? He gripped the wheel against exhaustion and memories and regret.

He finished the night in a highway motel and started again the next morning and again drove through the day, through the Canyonlands and Rockies, the high slow interstates, dark pauses in windy passes for coffee. Then south to Las Vegas, New Mexico, and finally a fishhook sketched on the map: back west to Santa Fe, north on 84 through the dry, red broken lands.

It was late in the afternoon when he stopped at a casino surrounded by a mostly empty parking lot in a dusty excavated bowl. He got a room in the hotel. Afterwards, he found the pay phones and called Peggy. Over the years, they'd spoken only when it concerned Harvey. He asked for his address but didn't tell her where he was. She said she'd called to see if Harvey was still on a vow of silence, but the man he lived with had said he'd gone. François didn't want to betray his worry, but he'd never heard of a sadhu and judging by Peggy's faltering description of what the man had told her, she hadn't either.

She sighed. I don't know what he's doing, but he isn't even answering his emails.

François got the address and said goodbye. He went to the bar for directions. A doorless entranceway gave onto a conference chamber. Dozens of slinky young women in evening gowns and heels were taking their places at tables while an older woman spoke in a French accent. The bartender told François, when he'd elbowed against the bar and asked, that it was a two-day workshop in etiquette and social graces for the Miss New Mexico contenders.

Out here?

Scenic, the bartender said, and inexpensive.

François didn't want to get distracted, but when he passed the doorway, a cold breathlessness took his chest. Looking at the slender shoulders, the artificial bosoms, 318 he wondered if he'd ever gone beyond wanting this. The girls smiled at nothing apparent, their skin tight with stupid youth. The immensity of the country still buzzed within him like feedback behind his eyes, and it was impossible to believe in dying. How could he put everything right in one lifetime? He had so many images of those he'd loved, of himself when love was such a bright thing, Ernestine or his hopes for Harvey.

In a fumbling sweat he went to the car. The asphalt of the parking lot radiated the day's heat.

The trailer park wasn't far. There, the strange withered man invited him in and served him tea like that he'd once endured with Peggy. But the walls of books impressed him, so much learning and, in a sense, hope. Perhaps there were answers here for even his sickness.

Harvey's gone, Brendan Howard told him. It had grown dark out. The trailer roof ticked as it cooled. Good luck finding him, and by the way, he's called Sat Puja now.

Afterwards, François drove aimlessly. He followed narrow roads with cattle guards, past clusters of trailers or the occasional garage with stripped cars parked bumper to bumper. This was another's land and truth. He'd realized coming here that only the highway was familiar, like a river depended on for sustenance. How far had he come since his first journeys? What could he teach? What if sameness settled about you like dust and you never found the secrets, never grew wise in anything but waiting? Perhaps he'd passed a poverty of spirit on to Harvey. He'd given him no dreams of the land. For years he'd thought he'd lost the family strength in translation. But that or blaming Peggy could go only so far. There had been the tenderness François had tried to abolish within himself, and so perhaps Harvey was living out the cycle. What had François known of his mother anyway? His father? He recalled only landscape. He was impressed that his son had come to such a place. He drove, slowly turning bends, the red earth rising up ahead as if the headlights were splashing the hills in blood.

319

The day after Sat Puja had stayed up until dawn, the night's emotions lingered. Not only the radio but Andy's talk had carried him into another world. A few times Sat Puja had asked about Juanita, and Andy had told stories, sadly hesitant and pausing often to tug at the strands of his moustache. He explained that when she'd found out she was pregnant, she'd set off after her boyfriend.

She thought she could walk down the highway and find him. Maybe she just wanted to get away. I wouldn't blame her.

Andy later explained his plan to go to school for computers, open a computer-repair shop, maybe even become a programmer. He told Sat Puja that he would finance it all by selling LSD. Because the LSD market had fallen off, there was pretty much no competition as far as sales went, heroin having taken the field.

It's like being a small business owner, he said. The money's okay.

320 Sat Puja understood Andy's wisdom, his nobility in wanting to save his family. Andy talked about rebuilding the house so that Juanita could raise her baby somewhere nice. The conversation stirred so many emotions in Sat Puja. He wanted to snap out of his entire life, to wake up and be someone stronger. He considered that Juanita might like the ashram's calm.

The next morning, after Jamgoti had taken the LSD, Juanita was in the kitchen again. She smiled at him but received no attention. He stomped outside, and though Sat Puja wanted to linger and talk, he had a sense that he'd begun something that needed finishing. Juanita looked at him quizzically as he hurried out.

You know, Jamgoti told him once he'd caught up. I didn't really come for God the way others did, but you didn't either. It's true what I said that time. You came to run away. You don't even have the courage for insight, which is what I have, even if it isn't necessarily about God or religion or anything, all of which is rather barbaric.

Sat Puja nodded. He sensed Jamgoti's fury as if by radar and avoided his gaze, all the while trying not to dispel the memory of Juanita's.

Jamgoti explicated his thoughts with furious rationale: the renewed popularity of Eastern philosophies that had more to do with stress than any desire for wisdom. His passions had never implied the daily gruel of the follower's life, therapy raking a garden until the master gave you a word or two. Emotion and desire, he said, those are the source of man's power. Even the master knows that. When was the last time you saw the meek do any inheriting?

He ranted, surefooted, and walked for so long into the desert that Sat Puja doubted anything had been on the Q-tip. They'd travelled far, vaguely aimed away from all landmarks, the river lost to sight, the sounds of the highway gone.

Sat Puja again found himself swept up by Jamgoti's conviction. Everything he believed was suddenly infiltrated by doubt. But what do you do, he asked, when life is . . . is terrible?

Jamgoti chuckled. You ask your old man for cash.

Sat Puja stood against this desert with its old sea dreams and sand winds. He wasn't made for this, didn't want more than a little piece of the world, meek indeed. He knew that no one moment was ever as in the pictures of enlightenment his mother used to give him. Artists and storytellers had made saints and gods by freeing them from time's routine. The master had said something like this. There had been poetry in the way he'd talked. He'd said the ascetic's life was a rose pressed beneath glass, a snapshot of the ocean at its loveliest swell. Sat Puja could picture Jamgoti, Donald again, sitting in one of the future's many backyards, with orange trees and wrought-iron lawn chairs, smoking big cigars and drinking something aged in a medieval cellar and telling, to the sound of hearty big-money laughter, the wily details of his mystic youth.

Jamgoti had begun pacing in a circle, still talking—
something about absolute truth, how seeking it now was
like the first land dwellers heading back for the sea, for a
single element in which to live. But in mid-stride he
322   paused and widened his eyes. He touched tentatively
between his legs.

Jamgoti, Sat Puja said.

Who? Jamgoti asked, startled. He scuffed down awkwardly. Jesus, he said, you got to be where I am. Beads of
sweat ticked along his skin. He touched the dust with his
fingertips as if testing the plush of a bed.

Sat Puja joined him, and neither spoke, both staring
off. On that shield of blasted earth, he sensed the continent beneath them. The distance was crag after crag like
breaking waves, reaching back, he imagined, to the
ocean that had brought his first ancestors. What was
more ancient than raising a family, than living simply
and well? Was this the love that kept you from enlightenment? He wanted to sacrifice something. The sun
had become unbearable, unpleasantly near, their shadows dissolving, and what he felt now was anger so
new and strange he sensed it like a second self sitting
down within him. They weren't far from Los Alamos,
the dreams and intentions of that age. Men had come
here to test their ability to destroy. He could almost
understand that. His memory of that violence in the
hills remained strong, paw prints a shade redder than
the dust.

What's all this talk about returning to the old ways?
Jamgoti said suddenly, appearing to have regained his

composure. People are always talking about how things were better before. But back then the real good times were slaughter. You went to a nearby village and killed and raped and looted, and you remembered those moments as the greatest of your life. Think how far we've come. We'd be afraid of our ancestors. They'd be like animals. Just read the Old Testament. Beasts!

He stood and stumbled down along the hillside, tracing everything, pinching pleasurably his own reddening skin.

Sat Puja knew that Jamgoti was right again. He considered this wisdom, then got up quietly. He crept away in the direction from which they'd come, following along washed-out lines.

By the time Sat Puja had passed through the rugged hills below the ashram, the flesh of his face and neck and arms was bright and hot. He'd pulled his shirt over his head, amazed at how far they'd gone and beginning to understand what would happen to Jamgoti under that sun. He considered going back. He'd never done anything like this or wanted to. The decision seemed as monumental as the one that had brought him so far from home. Instead, he avoided the ashram green, cutting across the arid landscape until he found the sandy arroyo, which he followed to the Dry Branch.

Brendan Howard wasn't home, but Sat Puja knew where a key was hidden under a chunk of amethyst in the garden. He let himself in and went into the bathroom.

His clothes were ruined. He put them in the trash, then showered and combed the knots from his hair. Sunburn outlined the bones of his face. He stared at this new self. It was as if he'd suddenly appeared and stood where he was now standing and stared. This face was stronger than anything he'd known, bright as war paint.

Not long afterwards, Brendan Howard came home. Sat Puja was in one of his bathrobes. Brendan Howard didn't appear surprised. Sat Puja said he would like his room back, which was fine—agreed to with a teacherly nod.

And you should know, Brendan Howard told him, your father stopped by last night.

Sat Puja struggled to take a breath. It made sense—he could see it—his father coming to drag him away. From beneath the kitchen counter Brendan Howard had produced a bag of repudiated possessions. Sat Puja found his extra robes. He dressed quickly, tied a tall turban and tugged at the hairs on his chin.

Where are you going? Brendan Howard asked as Sat Puja opened the door.

To the ashram. To meditate. I have to be ready.

In a rare premonition of his own, Brendan Howard handed him a sheaf of mail forwarded by Sat Puja's mother. In case you don't end up keeping the room after all, he said.

Meditation proved impossible. Sat Puja waited in the gazebo. A breeze stirred and died. Cottonwood leaves blinked against the sky. A few passing members of the ashram saw him and looked twice. He slowed his breath,

attempting to focus away fear, the day's end lit in a flame
of suffocating neurons. He thought of Juanita, and briefly
it seemed that a translucent figure hovered in the sky.
Oddly, his longing no longer felt so desperate. Just sitting
here now, seeing the sunlight disperse, he sensed that   325
something was finishing and being let go. The figure
shimmered and faded. He gazed out at the golden dome
and the desert. What was it? he wondered.

From across the green, François approached. The sun
had become a warm flower setting far below, as if to the
south. Sat Puja was surprised to notice how short his
father actually was.

François sat and took a breath. There was softness in
his gaze. Sat Puja recalled his father's face from long ago,
on a winter day, snowflakes in his hair, on his lashes as he
came in the door tired from a day at work, the disappointment of a home where no one longed for his return. Still,
his eyes had been bright. Had it been love or courage or
hope?

I'm proud of you, François said when the ritual
silence had expired. If I could go back, I'd probably be
right here with you.

From the way he said this, Sat Puja sensed the power
of the land around them as he had the first time he'd
seen it.

A wind strove and faded and picked up again. A few
strands of cranky music sounded from the nearby hotel,
something like overturned trash cans, a live band tonight.

So what are you planning? François asked.

Sat Puja admitted he wasn't sure but did so in that

practised deep, wise-sounding voice, as if this was just a business decision to be made. I'm in love, he added, trying this on. He described Juanita, that she was pregnant and that he wanted to give her a good life.

Pregnant, François said and smiled.

It's not mine.

Oh . . . I see. But she's in agreement.

I haven't talked to her yet.

About this?

No, at all, Sat Puja admitted.

François furrowed his brow but agreed that this was just a detail. I've been through similar situations, he said. It's not easy.

Having shared with his father that he was in love, Sat Puja felt noble.

Listen, François finally told him. I may be dying.

Sat Puja's thoughts fled with his breath. He couldn't see it, his father dressed so young. François explained, and Sat Puja tried to make his lungs work. He wanted to be brave, matter-of-fact, like his father. He thought of everything he'd learned, meditations and prayers, but it all suddenly seemed silly. What his father had told him felt impossibly private. It demanded silence. Sat Puja's eyes filled with tears.

You're sure?

Yes. Actually. There's no doubt about it.

Some unnamed bird called and wheeled in the cooling metal of the sky. Land stretched, folded on distance. Wind, after the heat of day, was as if there had been no wind before. There were the hidden fragrances of night, the cool of a dry summer evening, the quiet of dark divides.

This is a good place, François told him.

The remaining sunlight had turned the world golden.

Within this quiet they heard concerned voices, san- dals slapping tiles as a young woman in white ran along the ashram path. Others had gathered in doors, one man with a warrior's turban holding a cell phone and shaking his head, his hand covering his mouth as he spoke. He was staring at Sat Puja and François.

Sat Puja, the young woman said. Jamgoti's dead. The police just called. They want you to stay here. They're going to want to talk to you.

Already four dark cars were filing into the parking lot. Two men climbed from each. For a moment they stood there, eight big shadows, like pictures of moose in police uniforms Sat Puja had once seen. He expected them to come charging on all fours. He could barely breathe.

When François looked at him, it was with eyes that knew everything. He whipped off his money belt and pushed it into Sat Puja's hands.

Run, he said and grabbed his elbow and hauled him up.

They stumbled down the hills from the ashram, caught in the thrill of fear and complicity and love. François waved his arms to create a diversion, shouting Run! as he split off, parallel to the police, who now stomped along beside him.

Junipers rose from shadow. Footpaths crossed naked stone. François's feet glided on the brittle earth. He knew this decision was perhaps among his worst, but he'd felt too full of love. He whooped with joy. Though his son might be innocent, he was better off guilty.

The police were above him, running fast with choppy strides, when François stopped to dance around in the dirt. He held his arms out like those of a drunken master imitating the crane. There would be no more false dreams, no frozen heads or new confused bodies grown centuries from now.

The police thought they had him, but he raced off with an ancient speed and soon disappeared.

That evening there was yet time for contemplation. The percussive rhythms of ranchera began at the hotel terrace as, at the ashram, a murmuring crowd of men and women in white robes gathered. They came out past the dead fountains and overgrown meditation gardens dating to their settlement's first innocent days. They stood together before that dusty expanse of dissolving slopes and deep gullies. But there was nothing to see, only the dry, unnamed crags at sunset, the light resonating within silence.

François was the first to find the highway. A semi slowed, air hissing in the brakes. He ran to the door. The driver nodded and asked where he was going. North was all François said. He held himself still, jittery, trying to catch his breath. He considered what would be next.

He'd been sitting a while, the radio buzzing with lonesome tunes, when he glanced over. In the light of the dash, he noticed that the trucker was wearing a teddy beneath his T-shirt, the outlines of strained and sweaty lace showing through, frilly on the shoulders but heart-shaped where his belly met the steering wheel.

At first Sat Puja could hardly run. He stumbled, wanted to fall down and curl up, a high-pitched squealing coming involuntarily from his throat. He'd have been caught had François not made the diversion. Finally he'd controlled himself until he was only yipping and panting. Soon his robes turned brown and made for good camouflage. He still hoped to reach Juanita. He recalled how pride had lit his father's face like a crystal. It felt like a shared secret. Though Sat Puja's lungs were drawing into a searing knot, he commanded his body and made it run.

The dark world muscled, branches striking, cactuses at his shins like snakes. He had on the hip pouch with his passport and ID. He'd shoved the mail and money belt deeper into the pockets of his robe and was wheezing. An image came to him of Jamgoti crying beneath a violent sun, his reason having abandoned him at last, destroyed by so much light. Sat Puja had been innocent to think that anyone was strong enough to survive that. Within the knowledge of what he'd done was terrible calm. For the first time he had no choice but to be himself. What else was there? Just this life, to await rebirth, to live and be born again a little better.

In the distance, as if carried on the breeze, was the glow and hum of the highway. He could hardly breathe. He climbed towards it and fell against the steep incline. He scrambled up through the trash and dust until he reached the side of the pavement. His lungs froze. Veins throbbed in his temples. He lay there, unable to move, his body a strobe of adrenaline.

330

A passing truck slowed and stopped. A tarpaulin was tied to the metal posts of the sidewalls, and a few men crawled from underneath. They were small and dark. In Spanish they offered words of muted encouragement to each other. Two climbed off. They paused to tug at their dirty jeans, then bent to examine Sat Puja. They muttered and shrugged, then lifted him. The others came out and carried him back.

The truck started forward, the tarpaulin rippling. They took turns keeping the edges from flapping. Harvey felt his chest easing. The wind seemed a new air. The men watched him silently. Suffocation held him in a timeless lull. Then the first cough broke, and he twisted until his lungs pounded, his mouth open as if to cry. He lay on the uneven planks, aware of rushing, of nothing to hold to, the tarpaulin flapping like giant wings. He breathed, great breaths across those blind ranges, the engine battering beneath, the highway receding to far-off houselights against a dark outer rim, gasping.

epilogue

Louisiana

The hardest years were those when Isabelle was still too young for nursery. Bart had to work the night shift in a drab motel to be with her, half-asleep during the day or later, at the counter with her basket as he napped, chin on his fist and poorly paid. When she was three, the dial of his brain had been set to nights and he got the same shift at the Conoco plant and left her at daycare, regretting every minute of it, relieved only when he discovered that she was the one eating other children's food and snapping toys with the audacity of a carnival strongman. She remained big for her age through elementary, and waiting for her after school he'd seen her knock boys down, freely distributing charley horses and snake burns. He'd feared for her grades, but her leanings had been determined by their time together, lying around reading novel after novel, quietly or to each other or flipping through the library's stock of picture books until she said, Let's do something else, and he asked, Do we have to? Even after-school detention did her no harm because she managed to finish her textbooks and skip a grade.

By junior high she was a jock and a brain, almost expelled for running a pair of stained underwear up the flagpole after having written the principal's name on them, and kept in only because they couldn't win the regional basketball tournament without her. Though Bart had worried that she would turn out lumbering and ugly like himself, she was lean enough, muscular with a pretty tanned face. In high school she was the youngest in her grade by two years, ready, he knew, for the cataclysm of love. She was fifteen, six foot three, the boy she chose six-eight, a cut-up, a quarterback, a grin like a pirate's. Together they'd gone in the night to the high school of their regional contenders and spraypainted its name, Sacred Heart, and a few other words that the local papers declined to print but referred to as symbols of our national decay. Her aura of love wounded Bart so deeply that she saw and sat down with him and asked why he'd chosen to stay single all these years.

By then at the Conoco plant he'd been promoted from clean-up to general maintenance to pipefitting and finally, after a period of training, to foreman. When she'd been five he'd seen a cheap house on a list of foreclosures and had made a down payment. It was set off a quiet road, a stone's throw from a narrow bayou and a marsh. That first day, while he was painting, she'd snuck around back, through the overgrown pasture, past the old barn to the bayou. From yellow water, gars surfaced into sunbeams, big fish with torpedo bodies and eyes like rubber plugs, their duck's bills opening on floating insects. On the other side was a junkyard, the low trampled stretch near the shore heaped with tires and car seats, vacuum hoses and dashboards. Above the trees the sky was the colour of wet cotton. After her father this was her first love. For years, she would leave the house alone, go out past the shed and barn, in along the woods to where the roots were washed clean from years of rain and the dense, dark air smelled of mud.

Bart first tried to deter her, then simply kept the house stocked with insect repellent and bought her a hat with a protective screen like a mourning veil so that mosquitoes wouldn't land on her face, though she never used it. At the bayou she asked her first questions of life. He'd explained that her mother had died in a car accident, and she had a photo of a woman near a lamppost, head tilted, each cheekbone as strong as the heel of a hand. Her hair was copper in the fading light, her lips pale. She'd mused each feature, even the grey street, which, with its few lettered storefronts and an old marquee, seemed grateful. Later, when she'd become interested in genealogy, Bart had hooked up to the Internet for her.

Though she was never able to track down Bart's father, she did manage to place Jude. She sent out photocopies of his driver's licence, and a genealogist told her he thought the White name was false, once commonly used on fake IDs. Bart recalled that her grandfather had been a boxer, and searching the web, she'd found Jude White mentioned on a site that was the work of an aficionado. He'd compiled information on the lost great up-and-comers, boxers with undefeated records and unexplained disappearances. Who was Jude White? he wrote. The man who broke Leon Brown's jaw and his own hand . . . The article mentioned facts from across the continent and that, before his last fight, Jude had filled out his release with Jude Hervé. Isabelle was off and running. The next connection, after extended work, was to a family in Québec, in Gaspésie, the birthdate the same, just three years off. From there she laboured as if rebuilding a lost history, discovering the name Hervé in out-of-the-way places, isolated occurrences like virulent outbreaks. And so she sent more letters. One day Bart gave her a discoloured package from a private investigation agency. It contained information on her grandmother and mentioned Jude White in connection with a child theft not two hours from where they lived. She had just started the search for this woman, sending out letters again, when she fell in love.

That fall and winter she went everywhere with her boyfriend on his motorcycle. They rode for simple pleasure, following the interstate to where it lifted onto pillars above treetops and swamps, to New Orleans or the shacks on back roads where they ate platters of bright red crawfish and cooled their illegal hearts with beer. On the gapped planks of the loft they listened to hooting in the rafters. The highway was loud in the darkness. They went out and lay on the roof's overhang, the tin panels still warm from the sun. After school, when she was a girl, Jehovah's Witnesses and Mormon elders had talked to her of God, their suits soaked through with sweat and humidity right down to their strange undershirts. She imagined God as nothing more than a feeling—what she felt now, her fingertips at the inside of her arm, her hair in her eyes so that she could look at him.

When, one day, he told her of his desire to see the country, she understood and wanted to go too but rather on her own and to meet him somewhere. She imagined hitchhiking, sleeping in strange places, catching rides or taking buses across dusty plains, gradually becoming what she would be. That month had been cool, chill mist, rain thrashing windowpanes, and she walked the bayou often, pleased with sweet winter mud. She followed the path towards the windy rumble of the highway, the heavy turning of engines and wheels. She inhaled diesel exhaust, hot rubber and metal and grease. Rainbow blooms of oil moved in the ebb. She stared at the thin golden surface that made her think she was seeing deep until a gar lifted, barely moving from below, and she realized the murk went down and down.

Low clouds filled the highway sky. Rain found its way along her scalp, her throat and shoulders. Wind rattled the trees. Shoes sopping, she returned, the tall grass of the pasture matted into whorls like eddies on water. The living room looked dark in water-rippled light. She gathered a few things. At the mirror she waited for the storm to pass.

336

Her father had called her a pagan for her love of the bayou and for what she'd named the Burn Season, when the junkyard men heaped trash and car parts—a fifth season like the Chinese New Year, she'd told him, and one that always coincided with her birthday. She saw her father as a good man, simple and unambitious, who lived for her and hid his love in quiet manias, cooking or historical novels or gangster movies. He was heavy-set, with a knobbed chin and a bulbous nose. She'd admired his big smudged hands, had believed there was nothing stronger in the world. When developers on the rise began building closed neighbourhoods with manors and clearing the forest along the bayou, he became an outspoken member of a local conservation group. All that fell within the limits of his little world he cherished. He remodelled frequently, tearing out divisions and letting in sunlight and jacking up the foundation so that doors no longer closed and faults appeared in the drywall, all of which he happily set right. He studied modern architecture and painted one outside wall sky blue and bottom-lit it. He took a course in making furniture and redesigned the interior for their proportions. On a chill February night, he drove her north while she slept and woke her in the mountains of Tennessee so that she could walk in the snow for the first time.

When she'd fallen in love, he'd started exercising, going to a local boxing gym as a last means of fending off madness. He recalled lost vitality, and in the prolonged pauses when he leaned against the punching bag like an old friend, gasping, he thought more than he might otherwise have. His life, he could see, was fabulous: for more than a decade he'd been famous in his daughter's eyes, and nothing, not poverty or the silences and gawking stares at their size when they entered a room, had so much as fazed them. Work and raising her had left little time for his regrets or guilt, and he'd learned to let the dead live, to breathe and come to him when they wished, sudden, violent with anger, or forgiving and filled with love. It was a shared space and none questioned the other. Years of being a father had taught him the true imperatives of love, and when he recalled Isa, so much fell away to this one clear impulse, absolute enough for him. The least sure of all roads, he now knew, was that which took you towards God, and only when he thought of his daughter, her beauty despite the violence of her birth—that she was one of the loved ones—did he look to the stars.

Late one afternoon he came home. He went to the bayou. The forest was as quiet as a guest bedroom but for the distant, low throttle of the interstate. Bright, nameless winter flowers grew from the mud, vivid even in the bluing light. A little gator nosed sadly through the murk. A mullet jumped three times, flashing its pale sides in alarm. Across the marsh indolent men in red shirts and overalls were lighting up tires and seats, slashed ragtops and crushed plastic bumpers on the watery grass. Then he knew. The nearest path to the highway was through the pasture to the new housing development. He caught her there, his gym hours paying off. She had her backpack but had paused with sadness on the rise.

338

He tried to tell her why she couldn't, the dangers, the impossibility, but he met the gaze of that girl who'd overcome fear in oratory contests and spell-outs and lead roles, who'd won her class in wrestling and had thrown firecrackers under the feet of an enemy mascot. Who'd done pull-ups on the bar and measured her biceps daily with a ribbon and told Bart that love could never last because no one had a heart big enough for a girl her size. In whose eyes he'd seen room for the light of it all, the supernova, the crushed beer bottles in gravel, the candle flames in the shards of wineglasses. He'd once warned that her children would be walruses like himself, that the good luck couldn't last forever. The gods would be jealous.

The wind carried to them a sulphurous reek. Oh, they're burning, she said with a voice of breathless regret, one he was familiar with and which had always flabbergasted him. Nearby, at the housing development, young men worked late, unloading sod rolled up like carpets and peeling it over the raked earth. The asphalt leading to the houses was fresh, the bulky structures set in barren spaces, their windows not yet installed so that they looked haunted, plastic flapping in doorways.

Listen, he said, and she, who'd loved him with tenacity and who'd always thought him understated, too good and calm, listened. Far off the wind was carrying away clouds, and at his words she was struck by the brightness of the sky, like the blue of a television screen when the DVD clicks on. Smoke muscled up. They stood and she listened until the fires flickered in the dead grass, until the sunset was a golden mist over swamps, the trees a single brambly presence.

I can't imagine, she said. She thought of everything she could want, hardly able to breathe, of all that she might have and leave, the full fragrance of sweet winter mud, the cool nights reading together, the smell of burning in the wind, sudden and gone.

Wait, he said. Just a little longer. Wait.

Every letter brought home an answer, a mystery, a lost piece of history.

Harvey had been living in St. Louis under the name Juan Elhuésped. He meticulously coloured his moustache and eyebrows with permanent marker, and his home was in a sub-basement apartment in a dilapidated building built at the low end of an old canal and under the overhanging lower levels of an eight-storey parking garage. Only he and his Mexican allies could live comfortably under such low roofs, and with time they developed the large eyes and earthy stoutness of dwarves. He learned to eat tortillas slopped with canned beans, to drink cheap watery beer, to cross himself at the sight of misfortune and to keep his silence while manicuring the lawns of wealthy citizens. He'd picked up a fair Spanish despite the laconic disposition of his friends. Together after work they went downtown and made laser photocopies of his passport.

340   Those months he'd kept the money belt hidden, wearing it always. He became savvy, tough, learned to spit long distances and to lie on the spur of the moment so that the few times the nylon belt was noticed, he said it was for intestinal problems and forced himself to pass gas. He contemplated the uses of his wealth, wondering how he could get out of the country, to Central America, where he was told the women were small and that he might live in sunny courtyards with banana trees of his own. He imagined that he could have himself deported to Mexico easily enough but was worried about having the money taken away by a mean Norteño border guard. The letter he'd received at Brendan Howard's he'd kept only out of consideration that this might provide a possibility, that distant relations might be willing to help repatriate him. But at the moment he saw no reason to change. Being a fugitive had given him a practical edge, a keen sense of appreciation. He liked to pause and stretch and take deep breaths. The fragrances of life finally reached him, cut grass and turned earth, the ripe emanations of his own body. He liked the smell of deserted streets, the music at dusk and the way the black families on their porches paid him no mind. This was the true sadhu, he one day realized, on a neglected sidewalk, eating salty blackberries grown up around a fire hydrant.

One afternoon, when the police raided, he hid himself in an old tire outside. After nightfall he slunk out, gave his limbs a shake, performed a few yogic stretches, then headed south. By now he knew the Mexican underground. In bread, laundry or delivery vans or sitting in compartments with rattling bottles of beer that he drank after popping the caps with his teeth, he made it to Louisiana. A dirt-brown blue-eyed Mexican of indigenous descent, he affected an overbite and a flatfooted step that hugged the earth, and, with his growing belly, looked like an upright squirrel. It was evening when he arrived.

Something was burning. Petals of ash descended over the yard and leaden billows that didn't rise or dissipate drifted, dark clouds in the grass like sleeping hoboes. The house had one blue wall and high windows. The steps required that he lift on his knee in order for his foot to reach. He knocked. No one answered, and after he'd waited a while, the sky almost dark, he pulled on the door. He went inside. A few tall lamps were on. A pair of running shoes were big enough to be flowerpots, and the couch looked as if it were cut from living trees and had mattresses for cushions. Doorways were flush with the ceiling. From where he stood a kitchen stool had a strong soaring quality like that of the Eiffel Tower. With both hands he pulled out a chair and, using the rungs like those of a ladder, he climbed on. He kicked his feet a little, feeling this was a new world, unexpected and good. The final rays of sunset shone golden in the windows. He whistled a sad melody about a crying woman. Then he settled back, tired from his journey, closing his eyes and ready to wait.

Acknowledgements

A novel written over eight years, and a first novel at that, requires the acknowledgement of more people than I can possibly name or recall. I'd like to begin by thanking my early teachers T. Wilson, J. Birjepatil and Laura Stevenson, and especially Bob Butler, for his hard-edged criticism and for a piece of sound advice that I have attempted to follow to its conclusion. A few people have provided facts and various information that I may or may not have used: Denise Beaugrand-Champagne, Colette Chenel, Hector

343

MacNeil, Dennis Headrick of the Lompoc Valley Historical Society, and Terry Jones of Catholic-Forum.com. I'd also like to thank the Vermont Studio Centre for a grant and a peaceful work environment. Friends and critics and family, often all of these simultaneously, have offered invaluable support: my brother and sister, Marc-André and Ré Lise; Korrie Brooks; Tracy Motz; Ritsuko Kakuma for encouragement in the last stages of writing; my grandfather James Ellis for his World War II stories; Mr. Hebert for boxing instruction of a quality far superior to my ambition; J. Musi and the Musi family for generosity and for finding me a place to work in Mexico; Katerina Ring for orchestrating one cheap Italian living situation after another; Francesco, Antonio and Iolanda La Torre for providing accommodation in Calabria and for driving me down the mountain when I ran out of drinking water; Matthieu Verrette and Susie Springer, for the occasional social life when I lost contact and for calling the police when I disappeared for a week; Aaron Leff, for years of midnight conversations and pipedreams that have somehow managed to live on; Joanna Cockerline and George Grinnel for friendship, encouragement and (to Joanna) for peddling and pushing my work and at times believing in it more than I did; Greg Foster, for years of friendship and support and for employing me when I was broke, not to mention letting me quit at extremely short notice (often around noon) when I wanted to be writing; aunts and uncles (Francine, Pâquerette et al.) for stories and friendship; Marie-Eve, Wilbert and Pierre Béchard as well as Ermelle Landry,

344

for bringing me into your family and sharing memories; my aunt Colette for genealogical information and also for making me feel part of the family; my grandmother Yvonne Béchard for stories of a world that I would never otherwise have known; my agent, Denise Bukowski, whose enthusiasm is greatly appreciated; her assistant, Kara Bristow; everyone at Doubleday, those that I know and that I do not know, but whose support has been invaluable, and more specifically Maya Mavjee, Susan Burns, Lara Hinchberger and Christine Innes; my mother, Bonadele Ellis, for decades of encouragement; and to my editor, Martha Kanya-Forstner, for patience and peerless criticism.

About the Author

D.Y. Béchard was born in
the mountains of British Columbia to French-Canadian
and American parents, and has lived throughout Canada
and the United States. *Vandal Love* is his first novel. He
currently resides in Montréal.